WHAT SHE DIDN'T SEE

Angela C Nurse

F & J
Publishing

I

All rights reserved. No part of this book may be reproduced or used in any manner without written permission of the copyright owner except for the use of quotations in a book review. For more information contact:
F and J Publishing,
fandjpublishing.co.uk@gmail.com

First e-book edition August 2022
First paperback edition August 2022

ISBN 978-1-914597-07-7 (paperback)
ISBN 978-1-914597-06-0 (ebook)

www.angelacnurse.com

A Note from the Author

Please note this book is written by a British author and is set in Scotland. All spellings are the British versions

Also by Angela C Nurse

THE ROWAN MCFARLANE DETECTIVE

MYSTERIES

Discarded

Jack In A Box

Sally In The Woods

WHAT SHE DIDN'T SEE

A ROWAN MCFARLANE DETECTIVE

MYSTERY

Chapter One

My phone rang when I was standing in the line for the checkout with a trolley full of food that I hoped would feed everyone at this evening's gathering. I'd refused to call it a dinner party, it wasn't going to be anything like that fancy.

'Hi, is that Rowan McFarlane the private detective?'

'Yes, who is this?' I replied.

'My name's Ellie McIntyre and I need your help, my friend has vanished.'

I was dangerously close to being served now, trying to load my groceries on to the conveyer belt, the cashier giving me a look that let me know she thought I was being rude.

'Okay, I'm in the middle of something but if you give me a couple of hours, I can meet you in the Sunshine Café and you can tell me everything.'

I put the last bottle of prosecco on to the belt from my trolley and gave the woman an apologetic smile as she began ringing my purchases through.

There was a small pause before Ellie replied, 'Okay I'll be there at 12.30.'

'Great, thanks.' I said before hanging up. 'Sorry, work,' I smiled at the unforgiving cashier. 'Self-employed.' I continued shoving the phone in my pocket and rushing to catch up with the bagging. She maintained the flat look of disapproval, I wondered why I'd even tried.

I rushed home and left the majority of the shopping in their reusable bags on the kitchen floor, only taking the time to stick the perishables and the alcohol in the fridge, before heading to my office to sort out some documents I like to give to new clients. Ellie had sounded like she was making the phone call from inside a cupboard, her voice both muffled and echoey. I wondered if speaking to me about her friend's disappearance was going against…against what? I asked myself, who would be against trying to find someone they cared about?

Ideally, I would've wanted until tomorrow to have a new client meeting. I had so much to prepare for this evening, but I'd got the impression it had taken a lot for Ellie to call me and I didn't want to put her off. Besides, it had been a dry couple of months and my bank balance could do with another case.

I took one last look around the kitchen, hoping that I would be back shortly to get ready. I left a note for Alana in case she was home before me.

Had to go meet a client, sorry. Could you start getting things ready if you get in before me. I promise I'll be home as soon as possible.

Mum xxxx

Tonight is Maureen's 75th birthday gathering, it had been Alana's idea to throw her Great Gran a surprise party and I'd agreed that she deserved it. After having us thrust into her life a couple of years ago, she'd welcomed us with open arms, and we were long overdue to do something special for her.

Thank God I'd decided to do the cleaning yesterday I thought before closing the front door and heading to meet Ellie. The Sunshine Café is where I take all new clients for my first meeting where possible. It's an eccentric little place down an old side street serving the most amazing raw carrot cake and other vegan delights made by my friend and owner Star. It was the perfect out of the way neutral location, clients would feel unthreatened by their surroundings and, if anything did go wrong I had the comfort of knowing Billy would be around to help me if need be.

I'd sat at the same table drinking camomile tea a hundred times, the only downside the constant smell of incense burning on the tables. The windchimes above the door tinkled as I entered, Star appeared from the back kitchen. She came round the counter and embraced me.

'Didn't expect to see you in here today,' she said. Star and Billy were on this evening's guest list. 'You coming to make sure I've made the cakes?'

I smiled; I knew that she'd have that under control. 'Last minute client meeting.'

'Aren't you supposed to be taking the day off?'

'You know what it's like, can't turn down business.'

'Grab a seat and I'll bring you a tea in a minute.'

I'd barely sat down when the chimes signalled someone coming in, I looked up to see a short woman with bright pink hair. I was about to look away when I noticed she was looking around and I realised that this might be Ellie. I stood up so she could see me better. She gave a little wave and then bustled her way towards me almost toppling a man's drink as he lifted his cup to his mouth.

'Rowan?' She asked, pink cheeked and out of breath.

3

'Yes, you must be Ellie?'

She took off her bright yellow duffle coat to reveal a purple dress with a fox pattern on it. Underneath she wore bottle green tights with flowery Doc Martins on her feet. She would look at home with Star and her more hippy friends but at the same time there was something smart and business like about the way she behaved.

'Yes, thank you for agreeing to meet me so soon, I didn't know what to do or who to call. It's just it's not like Harmony at all. I'm sorry it took me so long to get here, I was at work you see and anyway my boss, well my boss's boss actually, he's such a dick, I knew he wouldn't just give me the afternoon off so I had to pretend to be sick and even then he wasn't keen to let me go home. Wasn't until I threatened to vomit on him that he finally gave in. So long story short I've now got the afternoon off.'

If that was the short version, I couldn't imagine how long it might take to get all the details out of her, I hoped she wasn't expecting our conversation to take all afternoon. 'Harmony, is that the name of the friend you said is missing?'

'Her name is Harmony Adams; she didn't come in to work yesterday or today and I haven't been able to get hold of her at all. And it's not like her, she's always so conscientious, I don't think she's ever been late for anything,' She paused looking over at me, spotting that I was struggling to follow her chain of thought and said, 'I'm her PA, that's how we met, but we became really good friends,' she paused. 'Actually, I might be her only friend. I'm the only one who cares enough to be worried about her anyway.'

What She Didn't See

I turned my Dictaphone on, a digital model I'd bought last year after realising how much easier it would be if I was able to listen back to the conversations I'd had with people. 'Okay,' I felt like I needed a moment to process everything she'd said, she spoke so quickly. 'Let's try to start at the beginning. When was the last time you saw Harmony?'

'Wednesday evening, I have a part in a play. I'm an actress really, I do the PA stuff to pay the bills till I hit the big time,' she frowned. 'Sorry, that sounded really inappropriate in the circumstances, it's just what I normally say when someone asks me.'

'Wednesday night, did Harmony come and see you perform?'

'Yes. The play is only on for one week, tomorrow's our last showing and she said on Tuesday could I get her a ticket. Well, I was thrilled that she wanted to see me, so I got one for the next day. I met her in the bar after and we had a few drinks.'

'How did she seem?'

'It's hard to describe, you see Harmony isn't like other people. She's had a really tough life, but you'd never know it. Some of the men at work call her an ice queen because she never shows her emotions, she doesn't date and she doesn't really have friends. They think she's a cold fish.'

'A cold fish?' I queried.

'Sorry, I've been reading a lot of Shakespeare lately – standoffish, she didn't get involved in the office banter or gossip.'

'Okay, you know her the best, so compared to how she normally was with you how did she seem on Wednesday night?'

'Fine, I think,' she looked away. 'To be honest I was on such a high from performing there's a chance that I wasn't fully paying attention. I was probably prattling on about the show.'

'No wonder, you'd have been proud, don't give yourself a hard time, there was no way you could've known that you wouldn't see her again after that.'

'Still, I'm not normally so self-centred, honestly…' she trailed off.

'You said you were her PA, what does she do?' I asked trying to get the conversation back on track.

'She's a marketing manager for Hobbs & Brody. Her clients love her, but no one ever wants to be in her team because she expects everyone to work super hard and won't accept anything that doesn't meet her standards or vision.'

'How long have you worked for her?' I was eyeing Ellie wondering how this explosion of colour and non-conformity had come to work in such a corporate environment.

'Two years. Her boss Stephen, he's a colossal dickhead by the way, went absolutely ape shit when she hired me. He said I 'didn't fit the corporate mould'.' Ellie pulled a face and used air quotations around the words. 'Anyway, Harmony said that was the point, she wanted someone different and that I had all the relevant qualifications and experience. Stephen agreed but I was on a six-month probation, after that when he couldn't find anything to criticise with my work, he had no choice but to make me permanent.'

'You got on well with Harmony from the beginning?'

'She's a different person when she's with me. I saw a lightness in her that wasn't there when she spoke to other people. She was in a really unhappy marriage when we first met but she left him soon after.'

I made a mental note to come back to the unhappy marriage, but for now I wanted to concentrate on the last time Ellie had seen her friend. 'Wednesday evening, did you see her before the performance?'

'Yes, she text me to say she was there and I popped out to say hello and tell her I'd meet her afterwards.

'And after the show you met up for drinks?'

'Harmony wasn't a big drinker, but we had a couple of celebratory cocktails.'

'And as far as you were concerned there was nothing out of the ordinary?'

Ellie paused. 'Not on Wednesday, no, but about a month ago she got a package, hand delivered to her door. That in itself freaked her out, she lives in a building with crazy security.'

'What was in the package?' I wanted to know more about Harmony's reason for seeking out security, another thing to come back to.

'It was a sketch book, one of her mums. And a note that said, 'I know who killed Tabitha Adams', that was her mum, you see, she was a really talented artist.'

'When did her mum die?'

'When Harmony was seven, there was a break in. Harmony and her mum were in the studio – I assume Tabitha was painting, I guess they didn't realise there was anyone in the house and when she disturbed them, they shot her, I think. Harmony didn't like talking about it for obvious reasons and I never asked, it just didn't seem appropriate, I always figured she'd let me know if she needed someone to talk to about it.'

'They killed her mum but not her?'

'They didn't know she was in the house. She was hiding.'

'Hiding?'

'From what Harmony told me her mum heard a noise and told her to hide whilst she went and checked it out, so Harmony climbed into one of her mum's supply cupboards.'

'She saw her mum getting murdered?' I shuddered to think of the combination of terror and heartbreak that must have instilled in her.

'She was there, but she has always said she didn't see anything.'

'Where was her father?'

'He was out of town at a business meeting, he's something important in a big finance firm I think.'

'And did they catch the people responsible?'

'They did, both were convicted of murder, but I'm guessing that they're not in prison anymore, at least if they are it will be for something else, this all happened twenty-five years ago.'

'Did Harmony say where someone might have got hold of one of her mum's sketch books?'

'No, and I think that's what freaked her out about it, because she didn't know anything like that still existed.'

'Do you know if she went to the police with the package.'

'I don't think so, she seemed to want to forget all about it.'

'Can you think of any reason that Harmony would need to get away without letting anyone know where she was going? You mentioned she was in an unhappy marriage, could her ex have something to do with her leaving?'

'I don't know. All I know is it isn't like her to disappear like this. She's by the book, she wouldn't just not turn up to work without taking holidays or phoning Stephen.'

'Have you been to the police?'

'Yeah, not that it did me much good. They took me into a room and took some details, and said they'd look into it. But I got the impression they didn't think there was much they could do. I think they thought I was being over the top.'

'Did you tell them about the sketch book and the letter?'

'I was going to, but I'm not sure they would've taken it seriously, anyway that's when I decided that I'd contact you. I read about you in the newspaper last year, you found that woman who'd been missing for twelve years.'

Finding Sally Mitchell alive last year, twelve years after she'd been abducted had certainly made the phones ring. The only trouble was people now seemed to think I was some kind of miracle worker.

'Do you have a spare key to Harmony's home?'

'I've checked, she's not there.'

'I thought you would've, but I'd like to have a look round and see what I can find. Could you meet me there tomorrow?'

'It'll need to be in the morning. It's the last day of the show tomorrow and we've got a matinée and an evening showing with it being a Saturday. Would 9.30 be okay?'

Inwardly I shuddered, it would probably be a late night this evening and I would have relished the chance to lie in. 'That would be great, I'll see you tomorrow and we'll take it from there.' I stood up to leave.

'There's one other thing I think you should know. Harmony shouldn't have been home the night her mum died. She was scheduled to be at her grandparents for the weekend. Her grandfather was taken sick on the Friday and Harmony had to go home unexpectedly.'

Chapter Two

'Surprise!' the chorus of voices filled the house as I led Maureen and Eddie into the kitchen. She'd been deceived into believing she was coming for a family dinner to celebrate her birthday, now faced with a room full of friends and family she began to cry happy tears.

She took my hand and smiled at me, 'you shouldn't have gone to so much trouble.'

'Don't look at me, this was all Alana's idea.'

Maureen embraced her great granddaughter kissing her lovingly on the cheek. 'You're a wonderful girl.'

'You deserve it gran.' Alana said.

I'd been with Ellie longer than I'd intended and then I'd spent a little bit of time trying to find out about Tabitha's murder and by the time I got home I was running late. Thankfully Alana had taken charge and enlisted the help of Mel and her daughter Becky to get everything ready. She'd given me a 'where the hell have you been' look when I'd rushed through the front door. Sometimes it felt like she thought she was the parent.

We'd clubbed together to pay for Maureen and Eddie to take a cruise to the Caribbean, Eddie had helped to get the passports organised, they'd never been further than Cornwall and even then, not since their children had been small.

It was a lovely evening, I stood back by the kitchen sink watching everyone enjoying themselves, wondering if I should put another bottle of prosecco in the fridge and if I'd bought enough for everyone to drink.

'You did really good,' Carol said joining me. I found out that Carol was my birth mother last year. We were working really hard to build a relationship, but there still felt like there was a void between us. I often wondered if it was because Jack, the man I'd believed to be my uncle all my life died trying to help her and it wasn't until after he was gone that I discovered he was my father. I didn't like to accept it but there was some residual resentment that he was dead, and she was alive. Not that I wanted her to be dead of course, she was in fact making a great recovery after kidney transplant surgery and I was glad, it was just that I still missed Jack so much.

'Thanks,' I replied. 'She deserves it.'

'I can't believe how grown-up Alana is,' she smiled. 'Off to uni this year as well.'

Although Carol was technically Alana's grandmother, she called Maureen Gran and their bond was natural and strong. Like me she'd struggled more with Carol, but I was glad that she was in Alana's life.

'I know.' I looked into the glass of orange juice and lemonade that I was holding in my hands. 'It's going to be very weird without her around.' Alana had got into every university she'd applied to and in the end had opted for Dundee to study Forensic Anthropology. Commuting daily would have taken ages and been impractical so we'd agreed that she should live in halls for the first year and then we'd look for a flat near the uni. I hadn't allowed myself to think about how much I was going to miss seeing her face every day.

'She'll be okay you know,' Carol said patting me on the arm.

I looked up, 'it's not her I'm worried about,' I was ashamed to feel tears welling in the corner of my eyes.

'Come on, let's go and join the party.' Carol said looping her arm in mine. For once I let myself relax and enjoy the event. I'd deal with tomorrow, tomorrow.

I'd set my alarm for 8am giving me plenty of time to get ready and meet Ellie at 9.30am. Mel and Becky had stayed over last night, Mel was already up and making breakfast as I came into the kitchen, thankfully not hung over.

Mel, despite having had plenty to drink last night, still looked fresh as a daisy. 'I don't know how you do it,' I said taking a plate of bacon and eggs from her.

'I've told you before, girl. You stick to the rum and you're fine, it's all that stuff with bubbles in it that make your head thump.'

'Breakfast is ready. Get your backsides down here.' Mel called into the hallway

Becky and Alana appeared a couple of moments later, I wasn't surprised, she was a very commanding woman, and I don't think I would disobey her myself.

'What are you two going to do whilst I'm out this morning?' I asked.

'Me and Becky are going to hang out for a while, maybe go into town later.'

Becky had gone to university this academic year and was at Edinburgh University studying pharmacology. She'd decided to live at home, I'd be lying if I said I wasn't envious of Mel for this.

'Okay, have fun,' I said as I got ready to leave. I handed Alana two twenty-pound notes. 'Don't do anything I wouldn't do.' I smiled.

'Doesn't give me much in the way of boundaries,' Alana laughed.

'Fine, do what Mel tells you then. I'll be back for dinner, see you then.' I kissed her on the cheek and left.

I pulled into the car park of Harmony's building, a camera watching the entrance, taking note of every registration number. Ellie was already there; her bright yellow coat was hard to miss.

We made our way in silence up to the third floor flat. It was a huge, modern space, large windows allowing plenty of light to flood into the rooms. It was also the tidiest space I'd ever seen.

'It looks like a show house,' I said.

'It was the show apartment when the place was being built, Harmony bought it furniture and all.'

'Didn't she want to put her own stamp on the place?'

Ellie turned to look at me, 'I'm not sure she knew what that was. She bought this place to get away from Martin, her husband. I helped her move in, she had a suitcase of clothes and one holdall. That was it, she had less than some people take to Spain for two weeks.'

'How long did you say she'd lived here?'

'Nearly two years.'

I walked round the living room randomly opening the drawers in the oak sideboard which by and large were empty. The kitchen was stunning, high gloss sparkling work surfaces and fashionable grey units, a top end coffee machine the only thing not hidden away in a cupboard. Her second bedroom had been transformed into a home gym, Ellie explained that Harmony was an avid runner and a bit of a fitness fanatic.

'This is the only room she decorated herself,' Ellie announced before she opened the door to the master bedroom.

I was taken aback by the bright, beautiful artwork painted directly onto the main wall. 'She did this herself?'

'Yeah, she's a super talented artist. She wanted to go to art college when she was younger, but her dad told her he wouldn't support "such a pointless waste of time". She did marketing in the hopes that it would involve some level of creativity.'

It was hard not to stand and stare at the wall, everywhere my eyes moved I noticed a new detail. 'I thought you said her mother was an artist?'

'She was.'

'I don't understand, if he married an artist why didn't he want his daughter to grow up to be one?'

She shrugged, 'she didn't talk about her family a lot. All I know is that after her mum died, art was pretty much banned.'

'That must've been difficult for her.' I assumed that seeing his daughter follow in her mother's footsteps had been too painful for him.

Despite the burst of colour on the wall Harmony's wardrobe mostly consisted of dark suits and white shirts, although she had workout clothes and a few nice pairs of jeans. Everything was high end and generally lacking in any form of individuality.

'Does it look like any of her stuff is missing?' I asked.

'I don't think so, her travel bags are still here.'

I rummaged around the bottom of the wardrobe, reaching far into the back of the space. My hand touched against something solid. I scrabbled further to get purchase on it enough to drag it far enough forward to be able to take hold of it with both hands. I placed the painted wooden box on the thick pile grey carpet in front of me.

'Have you seen this before?'

'No.' Ellie sat down beside me.

I opened the lid of the box and began lifting items out, everything was neatly organised and arranged. On the top was a stack of Christmas cards held together with an elastic band, then birthday cards contained the same way. Delicately I peeled off the band and began opening the cards. They all seemed to be from one man, Amadeus McInroy. Each card bore a message of support and each one dated annually over the last twenty-five years.

There were a few photographs of what I took to be a young Harmony and her mother, both looked truly happy. Then a stack of business cards with various incarnations of the police logo but all with the name Amadeus McInroy, the most recent showing that he was now a Detective Inspector.

I made a note to ask my friend George Johnston if he knew him, we'd worked alongside each other on a couple of cases in the last year. The most recent of which had seen him being promoted to Detective Chief Inspector.

At the bottom of the box was a small sketch book, the pages felt old and delicate, each page depicting a beautiful pastel scene. Given the age of the book and the level of talent in the art work it was probably Tabitha's.

Ellie was on her feet now looking at the large double bed, probably a super-king size. She pulled back the immaculately smooth duvet and then got to her knees to look underneath.

'What's wrong?' I asked.

'I don't know, but Harmony had this teddy bear, it had been her mother's and she'd had it since she was a baby. When her mum died her dad made her get rid of everything that reminded him of her including the teddy. He put everything in black sacks, but Harmony snuck out to the bins and took the bear out. She had a few things of her mum's that she kept, she told me she'd hidden it under a loose floorboard.'

'Bloody hell that's tough for a little kid,' I said. 'Do you know where she kept it?

'Yeah, it always sat on her bed, I remember when she moved in she said it took months before she felt safe putting him on her bed, there was always some latent part of her mind that thought he would be taken away from her.'

'Do you think she would've taken him with her if she'd gone somewhere.' I asked.

'I don't know, but if he's not in the flat she must've taken him,' she paused kneeling on the floor next to the bed. 'Does that mean she *did* leave of her own free will?'

'I'm not sure, but I don't think it's enough of a reason to assume she went away somewhere on her own. I know the bear must be really important to her, but she sounds like she's incredibly practical and I doubt she would have left home with a bear but not any of her clothes or toiletries.'

I took a final walk around the apartment double checking nothing had been missed before we left.

Ellie walked me to my car. 'What happens now?' She asked.

'Now I start digging into her life and trying to find out what happened to her, hopefully this will be a false alarm and she'll turn up safe and sound before the weekend is over.'

Ellie didn't look convinced, and I couldn't blame her, I didn't hold out any chance of Harmony appearing any time soon.

'What should I do?'

'Whatever it is you normally do. Do you have a key for her office, desk drawers, that sort of thing?'

'Yes.'

'Okay, it would be really helpful if you could look through them and send me photos of everything you find, even if you don't think it's important.'

'No problem.' Ellie looked delighted to have been given a job to do.

'I'll phone you if I find anything out,' I said.

'And I'll phone you if I hear from Harmony.'

I drove out of the car park thinking about Harmony living in that show home. It was possible that after almost three decades of having to suppress her emotions that receiving a package referencing her mother's murder might've been enough to make her snap.

Chapter Three

The library café was one of Sonya's favourite places to meet. It reminded me of the start of our friendship, the moment when she'd decided that she wanted to help me find out who murdered Jack and risked her career to do so. Today though we were two friends meeting for a catch up. I waited as she carried over a tray with coffee and sandwiches, weaving her way through the busy tables.

'I hear you've taken on a new case?' She said as she sat down opposite me.

'You been speaking to Alana?' I smiled, Sonya had taken a shine to my daughter when she'd realised she was keen to enter the world of forensics, since then she'd mentored her and helped her get an internship with an entomologist named Dr Ahura Ormesher.

'Yeah, I was speaking to her this morning. She tells me that's why you were late back to the house yesterday.'

'Well, I can't really afford to turn down the work just now and it sounded interesting. It's a missing person.'

'Are you sure this is just a friendly lunch or am I here in a professional capacity?'

'Friendly lunch,' I smiled. 'The only death in this case happened twenty five years ago so a bit before your time.' Sonya will be forty later this year and unlike many other women in this position, she was looking forward to entering a new decade in her life.

'That didn't stop you last time,' she said taking a bite of her sandwich. It was true, she'd helped me find out who killed Gordon Monteith after his body was discovered thirty years after it had been hidden in a concrete floor.

'That was different,' I paused to eat. 'Gordon's remains had only just been discovered.'

'I know,' she smiled. 'Alana seems keen to get on with her studies,' Sonya said changing the subject.

'She'll be okay at uni, won't she? You don't think I'm crazy letting her move away from home?'

Sonya placed her hand on top of mine. 'I know after everything you two have been through it must be terrifying to let her out of your sight but yes, you're doing the right thing.' She patted my hand and then let it go. 'You know you can't keep her at home forever, that wouldn't be good for either of you. And besides she's a good kid.'

I hoped she was right. I'd been Alana's mother since I was sixteen, I didn't have normal teenage years, go to uni or any of it. I had no personal experience to base my decisions off of. 'I know, I just worry that she'll end up preferring partying to studying.'

Sonya laughed at me, 'you've seen the way she studies at the moment, she'll have had plenty of opportunity to go to parties or whatever and she's chosen to study or work. I don't think you've got anything to worry about.'

I gave her a weak smile.

'I do have an old friend that lectures at Dundee though, I can always ask him to keep an eye on her if it would make you feel better.'

On the one hand spying on Alana seemed like a terrible idea but on the other…'No, it's okay. I know I have to trust her.'

'Good, now tell me about your new case.'

I told her what little I knew about Harmony Adams and what had happened to her mother.

'I can see if the post mortem was uploaded to the digital files if you like.'

I was glad of the extra support and whilst I didn't think it would harbour any secrets, I was curious to understand more about how Tabitha had been murdered. 'I'm going to see if George knows anything about it as well.'

'You think her friend is right to be worried?'

I shrugged, 'it's hard to tell. She seems genuinely concerned and I can only assume that Harmony trusted her, she had a key to her home after all.'

'From everything you've said so far, her leaving appears out of character.' She paused taking a few mouthfuls of food. 'The fact that she wasn't supposed to be home the evening her mum died makes it feel a bit pre-planned, don't you think?'

The same thought had crossed my mind as well. 'They were caught though and apparently no one else was involved.'

'Hmm,' she said doubtfully. 'All feels a bit convenient to me, could they have been hired to kill Tabatha perhaps?

'It's possible, I'll find out more when I start digging.'

'Good luck, let me know if there's anything I can do to help.'

Sonya was one of the few people in my life who didn't regularly tell me to be careful and honestly, I loved her for it. Perhaps it was only because she knew I wouldn't listen anyway, but I liked to think it was because she believed I was capable of looking after myself.

After lunch Sonya and I went our separate ways, her promising to let me know if she found anything I might be interested in. I left another message on George's answer machine. I imagined him listening to it and thinking 'what now' to himself, in the last two years my calls had generally led him to trouble. But without my help he would never have found who killed Louisa Thornton last year and over a dozen other teenage girls in a case that spanned three decades.

Last night, before I'd gone to sleep, I'd searched the internet for information on Tabitha Adams and had come up with very little bar a tribute site and an art gallery featuring her work. I'd made a note to visit them next week. Twenty-five years ago the internet in its modern form didn't exist so I made my way to the research and archive section of the library preparing myself for an afternoon of trawling through archived newspapers, thankfully most of which had been uploaded into digital files.

Home Invasion Killers Caught

There was praise today for Fife Constabulary for apprehending the two men responsible for the murder of local artist Tabitha Lockland (nee Adams). Mrs Lockland was brutally murdered when two men, now identified as Simon Cummings,19, and Patrick O'Brian, 23, forced their way into her home.

DCI Vincent Williams said in a press conference that the two men had been charged after their DNA and fingerprints had been found at the crime scene.

Alistair Lockland thanked the police for their swift work, the couple's seven year old daughter had also been home at the time of the home invasion but mercifully had been spared, her mother having the foresight to make the child hide when she realised someone was in the house.

The Hyde Gallery in Edinburgh said that with the family's blessing they would like to go ahead with the showing of Tabitha's latest work, stating they believed that it is what she would have wanted.

Cummings and O'Brian had been arrested just five days after Tabitha was murdered. They were later found guilty of breaking and entering and murder. Both had continued to maintain that they had been framed for Tabitha's murder although admitted breaking into the property. Tabitha had been shot, one single shot to the head, the pair said they were unarmed when they entered the home, claiming that a third intruder was present at the time.

There had been no physical evidence of anyone else in the house and nothing else to corroborate their story. They had both independently appealed their sentences, Simon's was declined, however Patrick's was upheld, when his lawyer stated proved that there was no evidence tying him to the murder, the advancements in DNA evidence showed that a sample the police had used in the original trial had been cross contaminated. In the end Patrick had served 10 years, he always maintained that he had no idea who killed Tabitha. Simon on the other hand served 15 years. There was one further news story involving him, a drink driving conviction 3 years ago. He was stopped doing 70mph in a 40mph zone, he'd been driving a brand new BMW M4. He was banned for 6 months and fined £1,000.

I wasn't that up on cars, but a quick Google search told me that it wasn't a cheap car, it would've set him back at least £55,000.

George finally returned my call, claiming to have been snowed under with paperwork, reminding me that I had no comprehension of the level of back-office work required to finish up a case the size of the serial kidnapper and killer Alexander Evans, the man that had held Sally Mitchell captive for over a decade and had killed at least twenty teenage girls. It was true, I couldn't imagine the amount of paperwork that went into signing off a case of that magnitude. I was glad my job was done when I discovered what happened to Sally. All the same he agreed to pop by to see me this evening on his way home.

Back at the house Alana and Becky had already begun work on dinner, they were making curry and had Mel on Facetime throughout to make sure they were following the recipe correctly. The kitchen looked a state I left them to it in the knowledge that the price I'd pay for having them cook for me was cleaning up afterwards. I sat in my office filling out the paperwork to request the transcripts of the original trial, I requested to have them within 48 hours, it may end up costing more, but I was impatient. The only thing that had happened out of the ordinary recently was Harmony receiving the package and the note that suggested the wrong people were sent to prison for her mother's murder.

The men had been represented together during the trial but had separate lawyers for the appeals. I decided to start with Simon Cummings, he had chosen a lawyer from a local firm, I hoped I'd have more luck persuading him to speak to me. Graham Bellingham's secretary had not been keen to put me through to her boss and in the end, I'd agreed to make an appointment for the following Monday. She had been most put out when I'd refused to reveal the reason for my wanting to see him.

George arrived just as the girls were retreating to Alana's bedroom and I'd begun the task of loading the dishwasher so I was happy to abandon domesticity to talk to him in the office.

'Is this another one of those times where I regret responding to a telephone call from you?' He said lowering himself into the seat on the other side of the desk.

'You never regret speaking to me,' I smiled.

'If you say so,' he replied. 'To what do I owe the pleasure of this summons?'

'I've got a new case and I'm looking for a Detective Inspector Amadeus McIlroy.'

'Why?' His brow furrowing.

'Because I think there's a link between him and my investigation.'

'You're going to have to give me more than that.'

'I've been asked to look into a missing person, a woman in her thirties. She's been gone since Wednesday night.'

'Has she been reported?' He interrupted.

'Yes, but the uniformed officer wasn't all that interested apparently. Anyway, this woman had birthday and Christmas cards from DI McIlroy, with his business card. And I'm thinking there must be a reason for that, so I'd like to ask him about it.'

George sat up tall in the chair, 'are you suggesting some kind of impropriety by DI McIlroy?'

'No, nothing like that. These are just nice cards letting her know that if she ever needs his help to call. Her mother was murdered, I'm assuming that's how and when he met her. I was hoping I'd be able to talk to him about the case and see what he remembers.'

'I'd swear you're stalking me.' He shook his head. 'I know Amadeus, he was assigned to my team last week.'

'Fantastic, you can do the introductions then.'

'Listen Rowan, our working relationship is unusual to say the least and you know I've always been keen to keep it under the radar but when you start involving other members of my team then I'm worried questions might start getting asked that neither of us want to have to answer.'

'I promise not to give up all your deepest, darkest secrets,' I said. 'But after the Sally Mitchell case our paths crossing is fairly well documented. But I've no intention of telling anyone that we share information the way we do, that wouldn't be good for either of us. I just want to ask him what he remembers and get a sense of why he kept in contact all this time.'

'Fine, leave it with me. I've got to get home.'

I watched as he drove down the street, realising that despite him knowing almost everything about me, I knew very little about him. Was he rushing home to an ever tolerant wife or a friendly poker game with his mates? I made a mental note to find out, some detective I was.

Chapter Four

The Hyde Gallery opened 12 – 4pm on a Sunday, I don't know what I was expecting but whatever that was the Hyde Gallery was not it. It was a bright open space that felt half museum and half art shop. I noted from the posters in the window that there was an artist's community you could apply to join as well providing lessons both in groups and one to one.

The door made a low beep as I entered, the type of device that recorded how many people came and left. I man smiled at me from behind a curved wooden desk. He was handsome in an unconventional way, tattoos covering his arms and neck, a healthy beard which once would have been black now speckled with grey.

'Hi, I'm hoping you can help me. I've heard you have some of Tabitha Adams work on display here?'

He tilted his head to one side. 'We do.' There was a little wrinkle in his forehead as he spoke. 'Did you know her?' I tried to recognise his accent but couldn't place it, north of Scotland, maybe one of the islands.

I shook my head.

'I didn't think so, you look too young.'

I found myself shift uncomfortably in my shoes begging my cheeks not to flush, it had been a long time since someone looking at me had given me a little flip in my stomach. I flicked my eyes away to break the connection and put myself back into cold professional mode.

'Why the interest?' He asked.

'I'm a private detective and I'm looking for her daughter Harmony.' I said, deciding that honesty was the way to go.

'Harmony's missing?' His face clouded as he spoke.

'According to her friend, she's been missing a few days.'

'Ellie?' He asked

'You seem to know a lot about her,' maybe he had a habit of flirting with younger women.

'Tabitha was my friend,' he looked down at the counter. 'Have you got time for a coffee?'

'Yeah okay.'

He lifted the handset of the fake rotary phone from the counter and spoke quietly to someone named Luke. A couple of minutes later another man appeared leaving my host free to give up his position.

'I'm Nathaniel, my friends call me Nate.' He held out his hand.

'Rowan,' I smiled shaking his hand, the skin was soft and the grip firm.

He took me through a door and downstairs into a small basement area that was half kitchen half studio.

He put the coffee machine on, 'so you're a private detective?' He asked.

'Yep.' I waited for the follow up of surprise that a woman had that sort of job or commenting on how dangerous it must be.

'Cool.'

I allowed myself a half smile pleased to be proved wrong for once. 'You?'

'An artist.' He smiled. 'I have my own tattoo shop but that looks after itself these days, it gives me the liberty to just paint.'

'How did you know Tabitha?'

He poured the coffee, 'milk?'

I nodded.

He sat opposite me cradling his mug making it look small in his large, tattooed hands. 'When I was a kid I used to get in a lot of bother, graffiti, running away from foster homes that kind of thing. When I was twelve, I got my big break, I was fostered by Tabitha's parents. They had this big house in the country, both of them artists,' he smiled. 'proper hippies, grew their own food, encouraged me to express myself but at the same time taught me discipline. They were the best people.'

'So, you grew up with Tabitha.'

'Yeah she was a couple of years older. An amazing artist, her murals were all over the walls of her parent's place. I really think she would've gone far if she hadn't married that twat.'

'You didn't approve?' I said trying to give the impression that I knew more than I really did. 'How did she meet Alistair?' I asked glad that I'd taken the time to trawl through newspaper archives yesterday.

'He came to one of her shows and bought about four pieces, and that was a big deal for her. He was sophisticated, he took her out and treated her like a princess, they went to see the orchestra and to fancy restaurants. It was so far from her life I think she got caught up in the difference of it all without ever stopping to consider if it was right, you know?'

'It must've been enjoyable for her.'

'Alistair talked about her having her own studio looking out over the Forth, it was a whirlwind and as it turned out a massive lie'

'Not a happy ending for her then.' I said quietly.

'She was young still and he was impressive, she thought he loved her for who she was.'

'Had they been together long before they got married?'

'I think she'd known him six months tops and then it was down to earth with a colossal bump. Yeah, they lived in a nice house in Dalgety Bay and she did have a view of the Forth but turns out he was less than keen on his wife hanging out with 'hippy arty types' than he had led her to believe,' he used air quotes for the last part. 'He wanted her to look a certain way, make house and all that crap.'

'Why didn't she just leave?' I asked, but I knew in reality leaving wasn't always possible.

'She got pregnant really soon after they were married, she did leave for a little bit, she went home, then Harmony was born. After that he constantly badgered Tabitha to come back to him, he visited her practically every day making out that he was so sorry and loved her so much. But what he was really doing was making sure she couldn't form any sort of routine without him being around, making her feel inadequate. He got in her head so much she wasn't able to imagine not being with him, but I think what really got to her was him making her feel guilty for making Harmony grow up without a father. In the end she caved and went back to him. It was a mistake of course, he got worse, she couldn't leave the house without telling him exactly where she was going, who she was going to see.'

'But she kept painting?'

'Yes, she was already relatively well-known, and I think he knew that if she completely disappeared it would attract more attention. He did everything to try to stop Harmony taking after her mother though.'

'What was Harmony like as a kid.'

Nate smiled, 'A real free spirit, a proper creative soul. Loved life.' He paused and pursed his lips. 'but after, I mean you'd expect it to affect a kid. She saw her mother die and you can't imagine what that must've done to her. But Alistair he did everything to erase Tabitha from their lives. I think he hated that Harmony had bright red curly hair just like Tabby.'

'I guess it was hard to keep in contact after…'

'Alistair cut everyone out, even stopped Harmony from seeing Tabitha's parents, there was a big falling out. It was a bolt out of the blue when Harmony turned up here a month or so ago. To be honest it freaked me out for a second when she came in the gallery, long red hair, jeans, cowboy boots, carrying the tapestry carpet bag her mum took everywhere. For a moment I thought it was Tabby.'

'Harmony was here?'

He frowned, 'yeah I figured that's why you'd come.'

'I was just trying to find out more about Tabitha, maybe speak to someone who knew her. Why was Harmony here?'

'Same as you. I think she'd forgotten about me until she walked through that door, she just froze for a minute and then she said 'Nate?' And I was just so relieved to see her. We had a good chat, and a cry. We looked at Tabitha's art work together. Tabitha left me as the custodian of it and I've been rotating the pictures on display. I think I always hoped they'd be Harmony's.'

'Did she ask you anything about Tabitha's murder?'

'Yes, I said to her it wasn't good to dwell on the past, but she said it was important.'

'What did she want to know?'

'She wanted to know what was going on in her life at the time.'

'What did you tell her?'

'I wasn't seeing much of Tabby by then, she could barely get away from Alistair and even when she had exhibitions he was there always at her side. I saw her as often as I could but other than thinking she was trapped, there didn't seem to be anything that made me think she was at risk.'

'Did she say why she wanted to know?'

'She said that she'd been contacted by a charity representing one of the men who killed Tabby. He was doing some programme where he wanted to talk to families of his victims, say he was sorry.'

'Was she planning on meeting up with him?'

'I think so. She thought it might be good for her.'

'Do you know which of the two it was?'

'She didn't mention a name. She did say something weird though, she asked me if I thought it was possible that her dad murdered her mum.'

'And do you?'

Nate shrugged, 'I told her I honestly didn't know but I wouldn't be shocked if he had.'

'Was Harmony here long?'

'Couple of hours, we were scheduled to meet up for lunch last weekend, but she cancelled on me, said she had a big deadline at work and was working overtime.'

I made a mental note to check with Ellie if that were true. 'Have you heard from her since.'

He swallowed the last of his coffee and placed the mug down gently. 'No, and I didn't want to harass her, she'd just walked back into my life, I didn't want to scare her away again.'

'Thanks for the information and the coffee,' I said smiling. 'I need to get going?'

'You want to see some of Tabitha's work before you leave?'

I nodded. He took me back up to the gallery, through to the back section where eight large paintings hung on the wall. They were stunning, mostly woodland paintings of trees and waterfalls using muted colours. Looking at them made you feel like you were being drawn into their landscape.

'Impressive, right?' Nate said.

'Amazing,' I agreed.

He walked me to the door.

'Thanks,' I said awkwardly knowing that I needed to leave but at the same time sad that I wasn't going to have his company.

'Look tell me to sod off if you think this is off the mark, but you seem great and I'd like to spend some time getting to know you properly, you fancy going to dinner with me?'

This time I knew I was blushing, 'that would be nice but maybe we could wait till this has resolved itself?'

He grinned, 'do you have me pegged as a suspect?'

I didn't but I probably should do, we'd only just met and having a kind face and beautiful eyes were not a guarantee of innocence. 'No,' I said feeling like a bloody school girl. 'Of course not, it's just I'm going to be a bit tied up working for a little bit.'

'Rain check?'

'That would be good.'

As I opened the door to leave Nate said, 'you'll let me know if I can help in any way or when you find her, right?'

'I will.'

Back in my car I typed notes into my phone trying to remember everything Nate had said and wishing that I'd recorded our conversation, but it had been such an organic chat it had felt inappropriate to whip out a Dictaphone. It had taken me by surprise how much I'd learnt. Nate's face with warm smile and blue eyes passed through my mind and I felt the flutter of some butterflies in my stomach. I shook my head, embarrassed by myself, I'm only thirty-three, a bit young to be having a mid-life crisis. It was probably just with Alana going away to uni I had begun to think what life would look like for me. I refused to let myself accept that maybe I felt like this because there had been some kind of genuine spark between us. It wasn't the sort of feeling I was used to having and it felt uncomfortable.

Chapter Five

The waiting area at Olson & Black solicitors was dated and a bit shabby. The Chesterfield sofa was the only thing that had weathered well, the dark red leather still intact, the rest of the room looked like a reconstruction for a living museum and I wondered why they hadn't thought to modernise the space. In contrast Graham Bellingham's office was super modern despite the dark wood cladding on the walls. He had a sleek glass desk, a large monitor taking up most of the surface.

The man himself was in his late fifties, his hair was fully grey, and he was thinning on top slightly. His suit was nicely tailored and did a lot to help mask the fact that his midriff was sizeable.

'How can I help you Ms McFarlane?'

'I want to talk to you about Simon Cummings.'

He interlaced his fingers, pausing for a moment before responding. 'You're a journalist.' He said as though it was a fact and not a question.

'No, I'm a private detective.'

He frowned as if he thought I was lying.

I handed him my business card, he looked at it then back at me before placing it on this desk.

'Either way I assume you know that I can't tell you anything, I can't break a client's confidentiality. You must have heard of GDPR at least.'

'Of course, and most of what I'm interested in should be public record anyway.'

'If as you say it's public record, why are you wasting my time asking me about it?'

'Because what I'm interested in isn't only the bare facts, I'd like to understand your client a little bit more, get a feel for him as a person.'

'I don't have anything I want to say, you should read the records.'

'I will. You don't seem surprised that I'm asking about him though.'

'Why would I, this case is one of the area's most infamous. It's not unusual for me to be contacted by reality true crime TV shows or journalists wanting to see if I can persuade Simon to do an exclusive.'

'Like I said I'm not a journalist. But I'm surprised he's not interested.'

'My client served his time for the murder of Ms Adams, why would he want to talk about it.'

'Are you able to tell me if it was Simon that's been trying to get hold of Harmony Adams?'

'I'm not able to disclose that sort of information.' His eyes twitched fractionally as he spoke making me think that it was unlikely it was Simon, and if it was, he hadn't told his lawyer about it.'

'Could you pass my business card on to Simon, that way he can make his own mind up about whether or not he wants to talk about the details of his case.'

Graham hesitated. 'Why are you so keen to talk to Simon, what are you investigating? It's been ten years since Simon was released, I would've have thought as sensational as the case was in its time it's old news now. Unless of course you've uncovered some new evidence.'

'No new evidence, but Harmony Adams has disappeared.'

Graham's jaw slackened and there was a look of genuine shock followed by concern on his face. He stood up from his desk and walked round to be on the same side as me. 'Are you suggesting that Simon might have done something to her?'

'Not at all, it's just that in the last couple of months she has been contacted by a charity suggesting that either your client or his accomplice wanted the chance to meet with her. That in addition to her receiving some anonymous mail regarding the death of her mother, the obvious place to start was with the men who committed the murder,' I paused. 'I'm sorry to have wasted your time, I'll be off.' I stood to leave, hoping that my last statement might encourage Graham to be more forthcoming with information.

'Ms McFarlane, before you go.'

I paused hoping that whatever he was going to say would be worth my time.

'I strongly suggest that you take the time to fully avail yourself of the facts of this case before you proceed any further and when you do you will discover that my client always maintained his innocence. He stated in his original statement that, while he and his companion did break into the house with the intention to commit robbery, they were in a different part of the house at the time Tabitha Adams was killed. When he heard the gun shot, instead of running away and thinking only of himself, he went to check on the woman he knew was in the house and when he discovered that she was injured he took the time to phone an ambulance before he left.'

'It was pretty unusual for someone to have a mobile phone back in 1995, especially someone his age with no job.'

'It was a gift. I'm sure you'll find that in the transcripts when you get round to reading them.'

'I have the transcripts from the case on order.'

'Ah.' He replied.

'Off the record, did you believe Simon when he said he was innocent?'

He smiled. 'I wouldn't have agreed to represent him in his appeal if I didn't think I had a decent chance of winning.'

'That's not what I asked.'

'I know but it's the best answer you're going to get from me.'

'Why did Simon and Patrick decide to be represented separately for their appeals?'

'I can't speak for Patrick obviously, but Simon felt that the provided representation at the time had been inadequate. It was Simon that had sought help for Tabitha for example and he believed that this should have been emphasised to help his defence.'

'And yet Patrick was exonerated and released with a pardon after ten years. Simon who ended up serving the longer sentence, before eventually confessing to the murder,' I replied.

'Patrick O'Brian got lucky with a technicality and that's all. I'm not sure what experience you have of prison life Ms McFarlane, but sometimes you find you're prepared to say what you need to in order to get your life back.'

'You're saying that an innocent man decided he would rather admit he was a murderer than maintain his innocence and serve a longer sentence?'

'I really hope you're not so naive to think that doesn't happen.'

'Not naïve, just confused.'

'I don't think I can help you with that.'

'Thanks for your time, I said. 'And please do ask Simon to get in touch, I would really like to hear his recollection of the incident.'

Graham shook my hand and walked me to the front door, perhaps he was trying to be gentlemanly or perhaps he was making sure I left and didn't detour past the receptionist to see if there was anything more I could find out.

The meeting had raised a valid question, why if you had just shot someone would you take the risk of phoning an ambulance? Surely the last thing you would want would be to be identified as the person pulling the trigger.

Chapter Six

Nate had told me about Harmony's grandparents and whilst I doubted they knew where she was, I wondered if they would be willing to talk to me so I could find out a little more about their daughter. I kicked myself for not asking him for their contact details when I saw him. I'd felt so disarmed by the way he made me feel and now I was annoyed with myself for not doing the bare minimum of my job.

I leant back in my office chair, phone in hand, thinking through what I would say when he answered. I was glad now that I had put his number in my phone, taking a deep breath I hit dial, hoping that I wouldn't be getting his hopes up that I had news on Harmony or that I'd changed my mind about the date that he'd suggested. I shook my head, who was I kidding, I doubt he'd given me a second thought. I'm sure he was just being friendly.

The phone rang, on the fourth ring I considered hanging up, but before I got the chance, I heard his voice.

'This is a nice surprise,' he said.

I felt my cheeks burn and I was glad there was no one to see me. 'I hope you don't mind me calling?'

'Not at all. Has Harmony turned up?'

'Not yet I'm afraid.'

'What can I do for you?'

'I meant to ask before, do you think you could give me Tabitha's parent's contact details, I'd like to meet them and find out more about what happened.'

'It's just Caz now, Rodger passed away a few years back.'

'Oh, do you think Caz would be okay with me talking to her?'

'She leads a pretty quiet life these days. But I go and see her most weekends. I'm going up this Sunday if you fancy coming with?'

I almost said yes but then I remembered we'd already said we'd go to Maureen's. 'I can't do Sunday, I'm having dinner with my grandparents.' Saying that still sounded weird to me.

'I'll give Caz a call and see if we can switch to Saturday.'

'I don't want to put you out.'

'It's no trouble, I'd do anything to help find Harmony and I'm sure that Caz will feel the same.'

'Okay that would be great, as long as you don't mind?'

'Not at all. I'll text you with the details.'

I thanked him and hung up, my sensible head reminding me that I couldn't rule out the thought that Nate wanted to be there when I met Caz because he was trying to control the narrative and wanted to make sure he knew everything I knew. I had a flash back to the first day of my private investigators course, Jack standing there with a packed lunch like it was my first day at school. He said, 'you're going to learn so much important stuff on this course but there's one thing that can't be taught and that's gut instinct and you've got that so never forget to trust your gut.' He had given himself three sharp pats on his own gut as he'd said it. My gut said that Nate wanted to help and had nothing to do with Harmony going missing and that wasn't just because I fancied him.

After all, why would Nate want to kill Tabitha, if he was going to kill anyone I would've thought it would have been Alistair. Then again Harmony would likely trust him, even after all this time, she would likely have gone to meet him willingly and I only had Nate's word for it that he only saw her that one time. I chewed gently on my thumb nail as I thought about why Nate might want to take Harmony and I couldn't come up with a good reason. Although he may have had access to some of Tabitha's old sketch books there was nothing connecting him to her murder, it felt unlikely that he was the person behind the anonymous letter.

I closed my eyes, 'what do you think Jack?' I whispered – obviously I didn't expect an answer, sometimes though it was good to try and make myself look at a situation the way I knew he would have. Was it possible that Harmony was with Nate, but voluntarily, was he protecting her from something and if so, what was it and why was he so reluctant to share this information with me? While this scenario was plausible I had absolutely nothing to back it up, until I did I intended to continue trying to find out more about what happened to Tabitha Adams and Harmony's life after her mother died.

Chapter Seven

The transcripts from the trial were shorter than I had expected and although Graham Bellingham had suggested that having joint representation had been particularly disadvantageous for Simon, as I read through the notes, I felt that it was Patrick that was most let down by this situation.

Neither of them had been model citizens prior to this break-in, they both had criminal records. Simon had spent time in and out of prison or juvenile detention since the age of 15, mostly for drug related charges, and then served six months for shop lifting.

Patrick had served one year for Public Affray two years earlier. There wasn't any detailed information about what the cause of the affray had been, but it was clear that for both men, having had previous run ins with the law had not helped them plead their case.

The lawyer mentioned several times that Simon had stopped to phone an ambulance before making his escape whereas Patrick had left the scene straight away. They both claimed they were in another part of the house when they heard the gunshot. Simon stated in his testimony that they had both gone towards the sound to find out what had happened and then when he saw Tabitha Adams lying shot on the floor Patrick had run away. He had then called 999 before following Patrick out of the house. In court Patrick had confirmed that this is what had happened.

The two men answered the questions on the stand with almost identical answers, so much so that when I compared the two side by side it appeared rehearsed.

Andrew Farquharson QC: You admit that you and your co-defendant broke into the house at approximately 9pm on the evening in question, believing the home to be empty. Is that correct?

Simon Cummings: Yes, we had been told that it was empty.

Patrick O'Brian: Yes, we had been told it should be empty.

Andrew Farquharson QC: And at what point did you become aware of there being someone else in the house?

Simon Cummings: When we heard the gunshot.

Patrick O'Brian: When we heard a sound like gunshot.

Andrew Farquharson QC: And what did you do then?

Simon Cummings: We went to investigate.

Patrick O'Brian: We went to investigate.

Andrew Farquharson QC: You would like the court to believe that upon hearing what you believed to be a gun being fired you went to investigate rather than leave straight away?

Simon Cummings: Yes.

Patrick O'Brian: Yes.

Andrew Farquharson QC: I put it to you that during the course of you committing burglary at the Lockland house you were disturbed by one of the homeowners, Mrs Tabitha Lockland, and one of you shot and killed her and you both then conspired to make up this ridiculous story.

Simon Cummings: No. We went to investigate, and I saw the woman on the ground and she was bleeding so I phoned an ambulance and then left.

Patrick O'Brian: No, we went to see what the noise was. I saw the woman on the floor, she had been shot, I shouted to Simon to tell him and then I ran away.

I could understand why the jury had found this version of events hard to believe – what was the likelihood that there was a third person in the house that night who broke in and shot Tabitha Lockland and escaped again without leaving any evidence at all.

Their own lawyer hadn't helped make it any more believable either, instead choosing to concentrate on the fact Simon Cummings had phoned for an ambulance, the lack of a murder weapon and fact that neither man had been convicted of any similar crimes in the past. No alternative theory was offered up.

It was little wonder that the trial was short, and the jury took only a few hours to come back with a unanimous verdict of guilty. I'd done a quick Google search for the man representing Simon and Patrick, he had it seemed taken early retirement shortly after the case concluded and then one year later died in a car accident.

And now Patrick O'Brian's current lawyer wasn't accepting or returning my calls and I wondered if he thought speaking to me was beneath him or if he, like Graham, simply assumed I was a journalist looking for a scoop. I'd already done a search of social media and hadn't been surprised to find no trace of Patrick O'Brian.

But someone had been trying to contact Harmony through an offender's charity. There were only two anywhere near Cuddieford. Although there were more in Edinburgh, it made more sense to start looking close to home. I read through their web pages with their mission statements all saying something along the lines of interactions between victim and perpetrator gave the opportunity to start a healing process leading to a level of closure and forgiveness which brought value to both parties and assisted in the rebuilding of lives. I couldn't imagine that I would ever be able to forgive Harry Aitkens for the part he played in Jack's death, and I was glad I'd killed Jimmy Murray, but I was sure there were people for whom it was the right thing to do.

If I wanted to speak to Simon or Patrick it was beginning to look like I would need to use some more underhanded tactics. I contacted both the charities claiming to be Harmony Adams and hoped that one of them would bite.

Chapter Eight

I was just about to get into the shower when I heard my phone ring. It was George.

'To what do I owe the pleasure?' I asked.

'You wanted to meet Amadeus?'

'Yep'

'We'll meet you at Sunshine Café in an hour.'

'We?' I asked, 'don't you trust me to speak to him by myself.'

'I trust you just fine, but I thought it might be better for us all if I was there to make the introductions and smooth the path, sometimes you can come across as…a little prickly. Especially with law enforcement.'

He wasn't wrong, although I thought I'd come a long way since the day we'd first met and that had everything to do with him.

'Fine, if it will make you feel less jumpy about the whole thing. I'll see you there.'

I hung up and dashed into the shower, I was ready to leave the house thirty minutes later. I would have preferred to have time to dry my hair, but I would have to do.

I was greeted by Billy when I arrived at Sunshine Café. 'Alright gorgeous,' he smiled. 'George is already here. I've shown him to your usual table.'

I glanced over his shoulder and saw the back of two men's heads. 'Thanks Billy, can I get my usual?'

He nodded and I squeezed my way through the tables to join George and Detective Inspector Amadeus McAvoy. I smiled at them and sat down.

'Amadeus this is my friend Rowan McFarlane, she's a private detective.' I held out my hand and he shook it firmly eyeing me more with curiosity than suspicion, I thought.

'You the one that found the body of that murderer last year?' his accent was hard to place but I would have said maybe Trinidadian with hints of Glaswegian thrown in.

'That's me.' I smiled.

'George says I should trust you, that you're all right.'

I looked at George who was suddenly very interested in stirring sugar into his coffee. 'That's high praise coming from DCI Johnston,' I mocked gently and saw him shake his head out of the corner of my eye.

Amadeus smiled. 'He also says you want to ask me some questions about Harmony Lockland?'

'She goes by Adams these days.'

He nodded his head slowly as if this meant something to him. 'She took her mother's name, good for her. George says you think Harmony is missing?'

I was beginning to like Amadeus already. He had a soft, gentle way about him and was clever at never really answering a question but lulling you into believing he had and then asking you a question.

'That's what I've been hired to find out.'

'What do you want with me?'

'I found the cards you sent to Harmony over the years. It seems like you were really concerned about her and I wondered why?'

47

'She found her mother's murdered body, isn't that enough of a reason?'

I shrugged, 'I guess that would explain the first couple of years, but you sent them well into adulthood. It's like you thought she might need you and I wondered why that might be.'

Amadeus took a sip of his coffee and looked past me at the wall behind my head. George looked like the effort it was taking not to interrupt proceedings was enough it might make him burst.

'I'm going to be honest with you because I care about you finding Harmony safe and well and because my boss insists you are a good person I can trust.'

I nodded.

'I was one of the first officers on the scene that night. I took Harmony's statement, and it broke my heart. She was the spitting image of her mother. She was frightened by what had happened for sure, she looked so lost and empty. I didn't get the best vibes from the father, he seemed much more interested in the mess that had been made and what had been taken in the break in than he did about his dead wife or the distress his very small child was in. If I'd had my way I'd have placed her in the custody of her grandparents.'

'Wasn't that where Harmony was meant to be that night?'

'Not them, Tabitha's parents.'

There was a lot to unpack in what he said. 'You kept in touch because you didn't think she was safe?'

'That might be putting it a bit strongly, but it didn't feel right in my gut. I went to the funeral and she just looked like a little empty shell of a person. I persuaded my boss at the time to let me check in with the family regularly during the court case. Her father had a lady friend with him on most occasions and Harmony wasn't allowed to speak to me at all.'

'Did you report your concerns?'

'I did but the reports came back saying she was safe and that she was grieving in an appropriate way and there was no further follow up.'

'Did you ever suspect that Harmony had seen who killed her mother?'

'No, I think she would've said that night when I asked her that, she kept saying sorry, like she thought she was going to get in trouble or something.'

'I told her she didn't have one thing to be sorry about and that her mama would be proud of her doing as she was told and keeping herself safe.'

'Why do you think she felt guilty?'

'I don't think it was guilt she was feeling. I think it was fear. I think that she was afraid that her father might blame her for not doing enough to save her mother.'

'But she never said that?'

'No, that was just the way it seemed to me.'

'Did you see her again after the trial?'

'Only once, I went to do a talk at her school. It was a couple of years afterwards.'

'Did she recognise you?'

'She did, but I almost didn't recognise her. She'd had her hair dyed dark brown and straightened.'

'A bit odd to dye the hair of such a young child.' I thought about everything that I'd learnt so far and this must have been just another way her father used to remove Tabitha from Harmony's life. 'Did she speak to you?'

Amadeus nodded. 'She told me she was grateful for the cards. I told her she could call me any time. And you know what, I used to wish that she would so that I could do something to help her.'

'She never called?'

He sighed, 'no.'

'Thank you for talking to me Amadeus. I really appreciate it. George is right, you can trust me, and I will do everything I can to find Harmony.'

'Is there anything I can do to help?'

I glanced a George, I knew that he would be annoyed with me for what I was about to say but I did it anyway. 'It would be really helpful if I could have copies of all the original case notes.'

Amadeus looked at George who glared at me, 'fine,' he said gruffly.

'Thank you. I can come by the station and pick them up when you're ready.'

'Don't bother, I'll bring them to you. I think we should keep this low key don't you.' George jumped in before Amadeus had a chance to speak.

'That would be great, if you tell me when, I can make dinner as a way of saying thank you.' I smiled.

'Not sure I'd trust your cooking,' he said, his tone softening.

'Hey, I'm a good cook I'll have you know.'

'We'll see. Anyway we'd better be going, we've got actual police work to do.'

'It was lovely to meet you Amadeus,' I said shaking his hand. 'Don't work too hard will you George,' I said teasingly. He rolled his eyes at me and they both left.

Chapter Nine

Nate text to say that Caz was happy to help and that he would pick me up on Saturday and could I send him my address. I closed the text and thought about how to reply. When I had made the decision to have my own detective agency Alana and I had sat down together and made some simple rules, to keep us both happy and safe. Rule one was don't see clients or anyone relating to a case at the house, don't give out our address unnecessarily. Not that it had always stopped people finding out where we lived but it was about limitation as much as anything. I didn't usually have any qualms about telling people that I wasn't prepared to give out my home address, so why was I suddenly worrying about it? So what if Nate thought I was being weird or rude and frankly if he did it would only serve as proof that he and I would not be a suitable match.

I replied saying that I don't give out my address and that as I'd be in the library doing some research in the afternoon anyway it would be easier to pick me up from there. As soon as I'd hit send on the text I pondered a little too long on what he would think when he received it before giving myself a thorough talking too.

I was interrupted by Ellie phoning me and I was immediately glad of the distraction.

'Hi, it's Ellie,' she said before I had the chance to speak. 'You asked me to go through Harmony's desk and see if there was anything there. Well, I did and, well I found some things I think you should see.'

'That's great, what did you find?'

'It would be easier if I showed you,' she said, then before I had a chance to reply Ellie continued. 'It's been really rough at work this week, Stephen, Harmony's boss, is being a complete dick about Harmony not coming into work. He said if she's not back at her desk by Monday then she's sacked. He's planning on getting maintenance to empty her office over the weekend, so I stayed late last night to go through everything before they had a chance. I don't think he knows that Harmony gave me a key.'

'That was good thinking,' I rushed my words needing to create a chance to speak.

'Thanks,' she said. I could tell she enjoyed being helpful.

'When would you be free for us to meet up?' The sooner I could see what she had discovered the better.

'Are you free this evening?'

I looked at my watch, it was nearly 4. Sunshine Café closed at 5.30 and my list of evening meeting places was limited.

'No problem, what time were you thinking?'

'Is 7 o'clock okay?'

'Yeah, that will be fine. Do you know Ruby Rouge?' Robbie's place would still be relatively quiet at that time and I was sure he'd find me a quiet booth out of the way.

'The Burlesque place, I've always fancied seeing what it's like inside. That would be fab.'

I would have enough time to go home, grab a coffee and catch up with Alana before heading back out. She was of course more than capable of coming home from school without me being there to greet her but lately spending time with her had begun to feel precious and finite. I was sure that by the time she left for uni she would be glad to see the back of me. There had been so much change and upheaval in the last couple of years you'd think I would've learnt to deal with it better but actually I think I'm worse.

Alana was sitting at the kitchen table when I came home.

'You had a good day?' She asked looking up from her laptop briefly.

'Productive.'

'What are we having for dinner?' She asked.

'Actually, I have a meeting at 7 this evening. Do you want to get yourself something or can you wait till I'm back?'

'I'll wait.' She smiled. 'Who's you're meeting with.'

She tried to sound casually interested but I always recognised when she was more concerned than merely curious. 'It's Ellie, the woman who hired me to find her friend. She's nice, I like her. We're meeting at Robbie's place.'

Alana's shoulders relaxed, comfortable in the knowledge that I would likely be safe this evening.

'I've got a meeting on Saturday evening as well; I might be back a bit late.'

Alana frowned, 'don't forget we have plans on Sunday, you said we could go clothes shopping and then we have dinner at Gran's.'

I smiled, 'I remember. I'll be back home Saturday night, it's just I don't know how long I'll be.'

'Where are you going?'

'I've got a lead. I'm going to meet the grandmother of the missing woman. I met a friend of the family, a guy called Nate, he keeps in contact so he's going to take me and introduce me to her.'

I could tell by the look on her face she wasn't keen on this arrangement. 'You're going in his car?'

'Yes.'

'He could take you literally anywhere, have you thought about that?' It never ceased to amuse me when Alana took on the parental role in our relationship.

'Yes, I have. He seems perfectly nice and I'll do that thing where you can track my location from my phone.'

'What if he makes you turn off your phone?'

'Why would he ask me to turn off my phone?'

'Because he's a murdering maniac who killed this woman and intends to kill you on Saturday as well, so you don't find out.'

Her concern was sweet although it nagged at me that she was saying all the things I would have normally thought myself.

'How about I ask George to run a background check on him, would that make you happier?'

'Much.' She said, her jaw tight and her expression steely.

'I'll phone him tomorrow.'

She looked at her watch, 'you've got time to do it now.'

I rolled my eyes and dialled his number. He was grumpy at first when I asked him to do the check but when I explained that it was at Alana's insistence he laughed out loud and said he would do it first thing in the morning. By the time I left to meet Ellie, Alana had been placated and her head was back in her books where I had no doubt it would stay until I returned.

I parked at the back of the club and waited for Ellie on the pavement outside. She wasn't easy to miss in a bright pink coat. She waved enthusiastically at me, her hand encased in a white glove. I smiled and felt immediately underdressed for our meeting in my jeans and jumper.

She ran across the road to meet me, 'I've never been in here before, have you?' She asked almost as soon as she reached me.

'I used to work here when it was Electric Nights.'

A look of confusion flitted across her face. 'The strip club?'

I nodded but didn't elaborate.

'Awesome. I've always though pole dancers are amazing, such strong cores.' She said patting her stomach. 'Don't think I'd manage it.'

'The owner Robbie is an old friend.' I said as we went in. Last year Robbie had hired Mel to make the place over and she had done an amazing job. It was now a beautiful, classy establishment with a 1930s Art Deco feel that had altered the place beyond all recognition from the club where I once worked.

'Hey Ro, you should have told me you were coming.' Robbie's voice boomed as he strode towards us. He enveloped me in a hug before I had the chance to protest. 'Who's this?' He asked when he let me go.

'This is my new client Ellie,'

He shook her hand and introduced himself. 'So, this is more business than pleasure?'

I nodded, 'now you're a classy joint you're on my list of places I can take clients,' I teased.

'How kind of you,' he grinned. 'What would you ladies like to drink, we have a great mocktail menu or there's coffee or tea?'

'Have you had any kick back since you stopped serving alcohol?' I asked

'A little in the beginning, but I think that was only because people remembered the old place, the clientele has changed a fair bit since then and if we get booked out for parties then I do a bring your own bottle thing. So far, so good.'

I was pleased that it was working out well for Robbie, he had told me before the makeover that he was beginning to think it was time to close up shop, Mel had persuaded him that he could turn the place into something else and she had been right.

'Have you got a quiet booth that we can chat in?'

'Sure, there's one round the back there that should suit you. I'll bring your drinks over, when you let me know what you're wanting.'

I ordered a cup of tea and Ellie a mocktail and we headed towards the booth.

'It's lovely in here,' she said looking around as she sat down. 'And your friend was the interior designer?'

'Yeah, Mel. She's very talented.'

'She should get into set design; she would be fabulous at that.'

'What did you find?' I asked, keen to turn the conversation in the right direction.

Ellie had a canvas bag clamped to her side since I first caught sight of her and now she moved it into her lap, carefully opening it and peering inside. She handed me a large brown envelope.

'I found this in her desk drawer,' she said.

I put my hand inside and pulled out the contents. There were some large, faded photographs of Harmony's childhood home. There were a few of the outside and one of them had a circle in marker pen around a downstairs window. When asked in court how they had got inside Patrick and Simon both said they entered through a downstairs window that had been left open. Looking at this photo I tried to decide if this was a picture after the fact showing the window or if this had been given to the duo before the break in showing them where to make their entrance. Then there was a single picture of the inside of each room with the exception of Tabitha's studio which had at least six of it taken from all different angles.

Ellie reached out and put her hand on mine stopping me from looking at the next photo. 'The next ones are pretty gruesome,' she said quietly, her face looking paler than usual.

I smiled and moved her hand, 'it's okay I've seen some pretty nasty things before,' my mind immediately flitting back to the house on the edge of Aviemore where I found the dead and decaying body of serial child killer Alexander Evans.

Ellie looked away as I turned my attention to the photograph that showed Tabitha's dead body lying in a pool of blood on the floor of her studio, paint brush still in her hand. I desperately wanted to be able to compare these photos to those in the police file. I examined them as closely as I could in the dimly lit booth before putting them back in the envelope aware at how increasingly uncomfortable Ellie appeared to be.

'Any idea how Harmony got hold of these?' I asked.

'No, she didn't mention them to me, but she'd been…off for a little while and I knew something was up. I assumed she would tell me when she was ready. She was like that, you had to wait for her to open up to you and I knew she didn't like to be pushed.'

'This isn't your fault Ellie; you couldn't possibly have known what she was dealing with. What else did you find?' I knew there must have been other things because the bag was still being held tightly in Ellie's hands.

'There was another one of those sketch books like the one that was delivered to Harmony's flat.' She handed it to me, I flicked quickly through the pages, stopping and going back to one of the pages. It was the sketch for one of the completed works I had seen at the gallery.

'I also found this at the bottom of her bin.' Ellie pulled a piece of crumpled up paper out of the bag. It was slightly coffee stained and had clearly been rolled into a tight ball before being thrown away.

'You were thorough,'

'I thought it was worth double checking and it was unlike her to throw something like this in the bin, nearly all her waste paperwork went straight to shredding.'

I took it from her, a message in bold typescript read:

Simon and Patrick did not kill your mother. They were framed and her killer walked free. You know what happened, you saw who the killer was, and you *will* make it right.

I looked up at Ellie, 'I thought Harmony didn't see her mother's killer?'

'She has always said she didn't, she was in a cupboard so her view would have been obscured. She wasn't keen to talk about it for obvious reasons.'

'You know her, do you think this is the sort of thing she would have taken seriously?'

Ellie sat quiet in contemplation, 'I wish I could say. I know she's tough, much more so than people gave her credit for but I think if she had truly been unconcerned, she would have told me about it and then shredded it. The fact that she balled it up and threw it in the bin makes me think she was angry but hadn't quite decided what she thought yet.'

I looked at the paper again, it was plain white printer paper, nothing discernible about it, 'is this likely to be Harmony's coffee stain?'

Ellie shook her head, 'no way. Harmony hated mess, her coffee was always in one of the reusable metal coffee mugs.'

'Well, that might be something then.'

'Do you think it was one of them that took her then?'

'You mean Patrick or Simon? I don't know, it needs more investigation.'

Chapter Ten

I left Ellie at the club to enjoy the evening and take in one of the shows and headed home a few moments after 9pm. I had called Alana from the car to let her know I was on the way home, she had told me not to worry about dinner, she'd sort it and I was delighted to be greeted by the smell of fish & chips when I walked through the door.

'Thanks, this is perfect,' I said sitting at the table applying lashings of tomato ketchup to the side of the cardboard container.

'I used your online account, so you paid for it,' she smiled.

'That's ok as long as I didn't have to cook, that's the main thing.'

'George came round whilst you were out and dropped some stuff off for you. I put it in your office. He also said he ran a check on that Nate bloke, and he came back clean.'

'Good, you satisfied now?'

'More or less, people slip though the net sometimes.' She said it in a jokey tone, but I knew that there was always going to be an underlying worry.

'I'll be fine. I know how to take care of myself and I have George on speed dial. How is your studying going?'

'Nice subject change there, mum, very subtle.'

After dinner I headed into the office to see what George had left me, I was hoping it was the notes from the Tabitha Adams case and I wasn't disappointed. On my desk were two cardboard envelope files, not much considering it was a murder case, but then again, they had caught the perpetrators fairly early on and after that there was not much need to investigate, I guessed.

Inside the top folder was a scrawled message from George telling me there hadn't been very much available and he'd printed off what he could find from the systems but much of the information had been archived and if I wanted anything else I would need to make a Freedom of Information request formally.

I sat back in the chair and pulled out the first document, Amadeus' report:

I attended the house following a 999 call from an unidentified male stating there had been a fatal shooting. Upon arrival we were met by Mrs Dean, a neighbour who was looking after a small female child, who was identified to me as Harmony Lockland, the child of the victim.

I was then directed to a room at the side of the house which appeared to be an art studio. On the ground I could see a woman and a considerable amount of blood. The paramedics attended and the woman was declared dead at the scene. My partner PC Elaine Lucas stayed at the doorway of the room to prevent further disturbance of the crime scene whilst we waited for DCI Williams to arrive.

I took Mrs Dean and Harmony Lockland into the living room and took an initial statement from the child, who stated that she was sitting with her mummy whilst she painted and then they heard a loud noise. The mother went into the hallway to investigate, ran back into the room and told Harmony to hide in the cupboard – she indicated to me that she had been told to be quiet by putting her finger to her lips. She got inside the cupboard and then she heard her mummy scream and a loud bang. She said she waited and after a short while she heard footsteps. She heard a man's voice but could not remember what they said and then footsteps that sounded like someone running away.

She climbed out of the cupboard and found her mother 'lying in some red paint and she wouldn't wake up'

Mrs Dean said she had heard the sound which she now realised was a gun shot and at first hadn't thought anything of it but became concerned when she saw a young man running down the street. She decided to check on her neighbour and when she arrived at the house she found the door open. She said she called out but could hear what she thought was crying so she entered the home and this was when she discovered Harmony lying on the ground next to her mother, crying.

Harmony had a considerable amount of blood on her clothes which likely transferred to her at this time.

Mrs Dean had called for Harmony's grandparents, Mr and Mrs Adams, to take her as it seemed her father Mr Alistair Lockland wass currently out of town on business and no contact details could be found for him.

I stayed with Harmony Lockland until Mr and Mrs Adams arrived on scene and were identified.

PC Amadeus McAvoy

No wonder Amadeus had formed such a strong attachment to Harmony, he had been the one to find her covered in her mother's blood, not able to understand what had happened.

I was looking forward to meeting Caz Adams, I wasn't sure how she would react to being asked to dig over some of her most painful memories, but it would be interesting to understand how those initial days after Tabitha's death played out.

Amadeus had mentioned to me that he had met Alistair Lockland and he had been wholeheartedly unimpressed with his behaviour and his lack of regard for his daughter, but I could not see any official report in the folder. It is possible that it was lost but equally probable that Amadeus had made his thoughts known to his superior officer and that his assessment had been discarded.

I had made a note of the fact that Amadeus' recording of Harmony's statement only mentioned hearing *one* man's voice. In the transcript of the court case Patrick had said that he shouted to Simon that Tabitha's body was there – it would have made sense that Simon had responded before Patrick ran off or before Simon realised that Patrick left. And then Simon said he made a phone call. Unless the two men sounded very similar surely Harmony would have said she heard men's voices? Maybe I was over thinking the recollection powers of a frightened seven-year-old girl.

Still, that and the fact that Mrs Dean said she only saw one man running away were points I'd like to follow up. If she had been looking out her window since the sound of the gun shot then surely she would have seen both men run away and not one. I'd flicked through the rest of the folder and whilst there was a further brief statement from Mrs Dean, she had only been comfortable saying that she had seen a man of average height and build running along the gravel path beside the Lockland house.

Chapter Eleven

DCI Vincent Williams, who according to George was a nasty bastard who was happy to blur the lines a little if it made for a quick conviction, had retired and was now living in sunny Benidorm. He had been the one to interview both Simon and Patrick

What did stand out when I read through Patrick's interview was that his story had changed between being arrested and appearing in court.

DCI Williams: The jewellery you had in your possession when we arrested you, did you know that it was the property of Tabitha Lockland?

Patrick O'Brian: No.

DCI Williams: Where did you get it from?

Patrick O'Brian: No comment

DCI Williams: You want to know what I think? I think you broke into Mrs Lockland's house and then when she disturbed you, you panicked and you shot her.

Patrick O'Brian: I didn't shoot anyone.

DCI Williams: Then why don't you tell me your side of the story then, because your mate Simon, he's telling my officers all sorts of things about you.

Patrick O'Brian: I'll confess to breaking into the house and nicking the stuff but I didn't kill that woman, I didn't even know she was there.

DCI Williams: Good lad, let's start at the beginning then shall we, how did you meet Simon Cummings?

Patrick O'Brian: We met in the pub, he was a mate of someone I used to know when I was young.

DCI Williams: How long have you know each other?

Patrick O'Brian: About six months.

DCI Williams: Tell me about the break-in, whose idea was that?

Patrick O'Brian: Both of ours, sort of.

DCI Williams: Because he says it was your idea.

Patrick O'Brian: I met this woman, we had a one night stand, things weren't going too well with the Mrs, anyway a few months later she comes into the pub and I'm thinking she's going to want...you know

DCI Williams: You thought it was a booty call, isn't that what people are calling it these days

Patrick O'Brian: Aye, something like that.

DCI Williams: But she wasn't interested in that?

Patrick O'Brian: No, she was, we went back to her place, and I had been complaining that my Mrs is always wanting money like she thinks it grows on trees and this lassie says she works as a cleaner in this big house and the wife has got plenty of expensive jewellery that she just leaves lying around, it's not kept in a safe or anything. She reckoned that it would be an easy job, she could find out when they were going to be away and then I could get in and out, sell the jewellery, get Natalie off my back and have money to spare for my bit on the side.

DCI Williams: Did you ask her to get you the information?

Patrick O'Brian: Not then no, I'd never broken into a house or anything, I thought she was being daft but she kept going on about it.

DCI Williams: You kept seeing this woman, what was her name?

Patrick O'Brian: Leah, and yeah, I've been seeing her on and off.

DCI Williams: Leah what?

Patrick O'Brian: I don't know, it wasn't serious. I told you she was the cleaner at the house, they'll have her name.

DCI Williams: When did you change your mind?

Patrick O'Brian: Natalie telt me that she was pregnant again. That meant two kids and she had her heart set on all this fancy nursery stuff that we could never afford. Anyway, I was complaining to Simon about it in the pub and Leah was there and she mentioned the break-in again and after that Simon wouldn't stop going on about it, reckoned it would be easier if we did it together, he told me he'd broken into a couple of houses and never been caught and I guess between them and Natalie they wore me down.

DCI Williams: You're saying that you committed a burglary because of peer pressure, interesting. And this Leah she told you that there would be no one in the house that night?

Patrick O'Brian: Yeah, she said they were away on a business trip and gave us a wee map she'd drawn of the place, she made sure there was a window that was open a tiny bit so we could get in easily.

DCI Williams: Tell me what happened when you broke in

Patrick O'Brian: Everything was going to plan and then we heard the gun shot, Simon said we should go check it out but there was no way I was staying around to get shot at.

DCI Williams: What did you do?

Patrick O'Brian: I stuffed the jewellery into my pockets and went back out of the window we came in through.

DCI Williams: And what about Simon, what did he do?

Patrick O'Brian: He said he was going to check it out but I didn't stay around to find out.

DCI Williams: And when did Simon tell you he had found the body of the homeowner, Tabitha Lockland?

Patrick O'Brian: The next day – he said he'd found a woman lying on the floor, shot. He said he called the ambulance and legged it in case the shooter was still in the house.

DCI Williams: Simon says that you went with him to check where the noise had come from and in fact that you were ahead of him and found the body first and then when he approached you ran off.

Patrick O'Brian: That's total shite. I never saw anybody.

DCI Williams: Why do you think he'd lie about something like that?

Patrick O'Brian: I dunno, you'd have to ask him.

DCI Williams: Do you want to know what I think happened? I think you heard a noise and the pair of you realised that you weren't in an empty house after all, you went to find out who was there and when Mrs Lockland saw you, one of you shot her. So

why don't you make your life a bit easier and tell me
which one of you pulled the trigger and where the
gun is now
Patrick O'Brian: I telt you I didn't kill anyone. I
don't have a gun; I've never had a gun.

The rest of the interview had gone back and forth over this
point before DCI Williams had ended it. What I didn't know was
what had happened between then and the trial that had made
Patrick change his story to match Simon's. It could be that he
had been lying all along, but he had seemed to answer without
hesitation when he was first questioned.

The gun had never been found; the theory was that it had been
tossed into a nearby river. Both men had been tested for gunshot residue but neither had come back with a positive result, this
was simply written off as being because they had been taking
forensic counter measures by wearing gloves.

Both men had been formally charged with Tabitha's murder
only five hours after they had first been arrested.

In the second cardboard wallet there were several
photographs of the scene of Tabitha's body lying on the ground.
I compared them to the one Ellie had given me earlier in the
evening. The photo from Harmony's office had shown Tabitha
lying in a perfect pool of blood whereas in the ones the police
had in evidence the blood was smeared across the floor and you
could see where Harmony had left bloody footprints as she left
the room.

Whoever took this picture had done so whilst Harmony was
still hiding in the cupboard, which meant I was looking at a
photograph taken by a murderer. Had Harmony seen that too?
Had she realised the danger she was in and run for safety or had

she been sucked into a promise of finding out the truth of her mother's death and been lured into a trap?

Chapter Twelve

The next day I emailed Ellie to ask if she knew how I could get in contact with Harmony's ex-husband. She gave me Harmony's old address and said that she thought he was still living there. It was only 3pm, it would be unlikely I would find him at home at this time of day but there might be some neighbours who remembered them as a couple. I drove to the address Ellie had provided and it took me to an estate of large sandstone houses with pillars holding up their front porches and driveways with large 4x4s that looked like they had never seen a puddle let alone any real off roading.

I parked my car on the pavement outside the house. As I got out I noticed a face in the front window of the house to the left. Clearly someone was already interested in my arrival so it made sense that I should go there first. The doorbell chimed loudly announcing my presence, but it was still a little while before the door was opened. A well-groomed woman in her late forties, early fifties stared at me. She had bobbed blonde hair, dark blue jeans with a crease ironed neatly down the front and a cream V-neck cricket style jumper on.

'I don't buy at the doorway,' she said pointing to the sign which said exactly that.

'I'm not…' I began.

'I don't do survey's either or discuss my political affiliations. This is a neighbourhood watch area, we're very careful here.'

'Very wise,' I said. 'My name is Rowan McFarlane and I'm a private detective.' Her head tilted to one side and I could tell that I had piqued her interest. 'I'm investigating the disappearance of Harmony Adams, she used to be your next-door neighbour I believe.' I shot a look at the equally grand house that Harmony had been happy to turn her back on.

The woman frowned, 'Harmony Adams? I'm not sure where you're getting that name from, but there can't be too many Harmony's about can there. I think you mean Harmony Clarke'

'Of course,' I agreed 'You knew her well?'

'I thought I did.' She paused. 'hold on did you say she was missing?'

I nodded.

'Well, she hasn't lived here for ages.'

'I understand she had separated from her husband, Martin isn't it?'

'Yes, she's been gone for a while now.'

'I was hoping to get a picture of who she was to see if it might help me find out where she might have gone.'

The woman looked up and down the street, 'you should come in, the longer you're on the doorstep the more people will notice and want to know what you're here for.'

I wasn't sure why that would bother her but the fact that she was about to invite me inside clearly meant she felt she had something to say. She opened the door, standing back to make way for me to enter, I hoped that the soles of my shoes were clean as I eyed her almost white plush carpet that flowed from the hallway to the living room. Thankfully she ushered me away and towards the large breakfasting kitchen and its tiled floor.

'Would you like a coffee,' she asked pressing a couple of buttons on a very expensive looking machine before sitting with me at the wooden table. 'I do hope everything is okay with Harmony.'

I knew she was fishing for gossip and I had no intention of helping her fuel those fires. 'So do I. Can you tell me how you got along with her, was she a good neighbour?'

'Oh yes she was lovely, well they both were. Such a smashing new couple.'

'You would have said it was a happy marriage then?' I thought about the way Ellie had described Harmony's situation.

'Well, that's how it looked on the outside anyway, but we live close, and sometimes you hear things even when you try not to.'

I nodded, although I strongly doubted that this woman had ever tried not to hear something going on in her neighbour's home.

'What sort of things?'

'Raised voices, smashing glass. Martin had said they were trying for a baby and that can take it out of you especially when it doesn't happen naturally.'

'They were using IVF?'

'Not sure if they had got that far, I think they were trying to figure out whose bits were to blame, if you know what I mean,' she smiled, amused by herself.

'Did you ever find out?'

'Well, I assumed it was him and maybe that's why she left. It can be more important to a woman, can't it, especially with time running out.'

'After she left Martin, my husband went round to check on him and apparently Martin had told him that she had left because it had become evident that they wanted different things from life.'

'Did he say what he meant by that?'

'No and he's been pretty closed up since she left. I really thought we'd see a for sale sign, but he's just kept living there.'

I listened to her gossip for another twenty minutes about the rest of the neighbours whilst simultaneously telling me that she hated gossip before I managed to leave. I wondered what time Martin Clarke got home from work. Ideally I would like to speak to him today before his neighbour had the chance to fill him in on my visit. I sat back in my car scrolling through my emails. There was one from Matthew Radley, Patrick O'Brian's solicitor telling me to stop trying to get in contact with him. He had no interest in speaking to me and instructed me not to try to contact his client either. The condescending tone of the email made it clear I wouldn't have gotten anything useful out of an interaction with him anyway.

By the time Martin arrived home I was kicking myself for not bringing anything to eat or drink with me. The coffee I had drunk earlier had only served to make me feel even more thirsty.

I walked quickly towards the driveway hoping to catch him before he got inside.

'Can I help you?' He frowned. 'We don't buy on the doorsteps here, this is a…'

'Neighbourhood watch area, yes I know. I'm not selling anything, I don't want you to sign up to a charity and I'm not a politician, I'm a private detective and I have been hired to look for your ex-wife, Harmony Adams.'

He froze, staring at me, his jaw sagging.

'I'd really like to talk to you, to see if I can find out more about her so I can try to find out what happened to her.'

'She said she was in danger and I, I sent her away. I was angry.'

'Harmony was here?'

'Yes, about a month ago.' He pressed a button on the keyring in his hand making his car bleep and flash it's lights. 'Let's finish this conversation inside.'

I followed him into the house which was architecturally an exact replica of his neighbours but decoratively very different. The hallway was painted a dark grey with a solid oak floor, the living room a dark green. I sat on the tweed sofa and waited whilst he made us coffee. He placed the tray on the table in front of me and I was relieved to discover he had brought a plate of biscuits, the kind you buy in M&S that are wrapped in foil indicating a thick layer of chocolate. I could have happily eaten every last one of them, but instead nibbled politely on the one I had.

'You were saying Harmony came to see you,' I said hoping that starting here would allow me to work backwards in their relationship.

'Yes, it was a shock to be honest, I've not seen her for over a year. I still play golf with her father, but she doesn't talk to him anymore either, so it was a shock to see her.'

'And she came here?'

He nodded, 'she must have taken a taxi or got a lift because her car wasn't outside, but she was sitting in the kitchen one day when I came home from work. She scared the crap out of me, she said I should've changed the locks.'

'Why had she come?'

'She said that she thought she was in danger, that she wanted to tell me to be careful.' He looked at his shoes. 'I'm not proud of how I responded. I told her I didn't believe she cared about what happened to me, I shouted at her.'

'Did she say why she thought she was at risk?'

'I didn't give her the chance. I told her I didn't want her here, that this wasn't her home, and she wasn't to come here again. I said if she was in danger then it was her own fault and that it wouldn't bother me if she wound up dead in a ditch.' He took a sip of his coffee. 'And now she's missing?'

'Yes, since last weekend.'

'I didn't... I wouldn't... what I mean is I don't know where she is. She hurt me, badly, but I wouldn't hurt her. Is that why you're here, because you think I might have done something to her?'

'I'm here to learn more about her that's all. Why did you get divorced?' I had considered trying to put it more tactfully but decided the direct approach would yield a better response.'

'Did my curtain twitching neighbourhood gossip not tell you,' he grunted.

'She told me some things but I'm more interested in hearing it from you.'

'Harmony left because I found out that whilst I was spending a bloody fortune on fertility doctors she was still on the pill and that was the real reason she wasn't getting pregnant.'

'That must've come as quite a shock?'

'You can say that again, I couldn't believe it after all the stress of trying to get pregnant and going to the best doctors.'

'How did you find out?'

'One of the doctors we'd been seeing called and said that he would like to see us as soon as possible and that he knew why we weren't getting pregnant. At first, I was delighted but there was something about the way he said it that made me concerned, honestly I thought there was something seriously wrong with one of us.'

'Did you go to the appointment together?'

'Yes, the brass neck of her coming along to the appointment as if she had nothing to hide and all the time she knew.' He paused and looked at me, tears forming in his eyes. 'I mean she must've known that she was about to be uncovered, but she was cool as anything.'

'The doctor told you she was still on the pill?'

'Pretty much. He suggested that we get some counselling.'

'What happened after the appointment?'

'It was lucky we had arrived in separate cars, by the time I got back here Harmony had her stuff packed and she was sitting in the kitchen waiting for me to come home.'

'Were you happy that she decided to leave?'

'In that moment yes, I hated her and I wanted her out of my life, I couldn't believe how much she'd hurt me and there was no sign of remorse or anything.'

'Did you talk about it at all, that night before she left or ever?'

'That night we had a huge argument, unsurprisingly.'

'Did she give you a reason for doing what she did?'

'She said she didn't want children, she said that she had tried to tell me that. I really thought that we were on the same page. I didn't understand why she had let it go this far, the amount of money it cost to get all these tests only to find out that she was sabotaging us.'

'Had she told you that she didn't want children.'

'I wouldn't have admitted it at the time, but she had, several times.'

'What made you think she had changed her mind?'

'Alistair, Harmony's dad told me that it was a phase, a response to losing her own mother so young, that once she got pregnant everything would change. He convinced me that she didn't really mean it.'

'Didn't you think it would have been best taking her word for what she wanted rather than her father's?' It was incredible arrogance on Martin's part to assume that he should ignore his wife in favour of his father in law on the subject.

He shrugged, 'It's easy to think that in retrospect, isn't it?'

I wanted to scream at him that it should've been pretty easy to figure out at the time by simply listening to his wife and believing what she said instead of asking her father and then taking his word for it. But I knew that wouldn't help me get more information from Martin.

'Your argument, did it get physical on either side?'

'Not really.'

'What do you mean, not really?'

'I threw a few things, smashed up a couple of vases, put my fist through the wall.'

'How did Harmony respond?' I asked.

'She didn't, and that made it worse. I wanted her to react, to show some sign of emotion, show me that she felt something, but she just sat there like a statue watching me and then when I'd finally stopped, she took off her wedding and engagement rings and put them down on the kitchen work surface, picked up her bags and left.'

'Did you try to find out where she went?'

'I called her a few times once I'd calmed down and thought about it, I realised that I would rather have her as my wife and have no children than not have her at all. I even suggested couples counselling.'

'She wasn't interested?'

'I got a letter from her solicitor a few days later saying that she wanted a divorce, stating 'irretrievable breakdown of the marriage'. I wanted to object and insist we go to counselling but when I spoke to Matthew, he said Harmony was offering me excellent terms, she didn't want anything from me, didn't even want the house. Her only condition was that I never try to contact her again, so I took his advice and agreed.'

'Sorry, is your solicitor Matthew Radley?' What were the chances of Harmony's ex-husband and one of the men convicted of her mother's murder having the same solicitor.

'Yes, ironically it was Alistair who introduced me to him, he's a friend of Karen.'

'Who's Karen?'

'Karen Lockland, Alistair remarried. I thought you would have known.'

'I knew he'd remarried.'

'She practically raised Harmony, although you wouldn't have known it, they weren't close.'

'How did you meet Harmony?'

'Alistair introduced us at one of his work functions, I used to work for him you see. We seemed to hit off and so a few months later we got engaged.'

'You were in love?'

'I thought we were, but now I'm not sure if Harmony married me to get her dad off her back.'

'Have you stayed in touch with Alistair and Karen since the divorce?'

'I still golf with Alistair and we have some of the same business associates and our paths cross from time to time, but I would say we're not as close as we used to be, obviously.'

'How did Alistair feel about the divorce?'

'He said that he was sorry, that he hadn't realised how like her mother she was. He said that Tabitha had been an unstable woman and although her death was a tragedy, he had hoped that Karen would have been a good influence on Harmony.'

'Did Harmony talk about her mother much?

'No and I didn't ask, Alistair said it was best not to.'

'Did you ever worry that Alistair was too involved in your relationship?' In the last twenty minutes he'd mentioned him so frequently you'd have been forgiven for thinking he was married to him not Harmony.

'You think I was a bad husband, a bad man no doubt, that I listened to him more than her. You'd be right, I was proud and self-righteous and I'm not sure I ever really stopped to think about what she wanted.'

I picked up a second biscuit, peeled back the red foil and bit into it as he continued telling me how much he regretted his actions, by the time I was swallowing the last bite he looked up at me.

'Do you know what the worst thing is?'

'What?'

'When she came here to see me, she was warning me, trying to keep me safe. She still cared about me.'

'That was nice.'

'It was. Even as I was throwing her out of the front door, she was telling me she was sorry she hurt me.'

'How did she get home?' I interrupted.

'I've no idea.' He looked deflated. 'I hope you find her.'

'Me too.'

'When you do can you tell her I said sorry.'

Chapter Thirteen

Amadeus was the only person who had bothered to put Harmony at the forefront of his mind when her mother was murdered, I wondered how much he'd kept an eye out for her over the years. Was it just friendly Christmas and birthday cards or had there been more to it than he'd wanted to admit to in front of George?

I dialled the number he had given me and waited until it rang out. I was about to try again when my screen lit up with the message that he was calling me.

'Thanks for calling me back.'

'You're welcome, you any further forward yet?'

'Not yet.'

'Maybe she decided that it was time for a completely fresh start and decided to walk out of this version of her life'

'Amadeus I would be the happiest person if that we true…but I highly doubt it.'

'You seem to be set on the idea that something bad has happened to her'

'I am and I'm fairly certain that it has something to do with her mother's death. Did you know Alistair Lockland remarried?'

'Yes, only six months after he buried Tabitha.'

'That was quick.'

'She was his secretary.'

'You think they were having an affair.'

'That was the sense I got, of course it was never followed up after they arrested the two men for the break in.'

'Are you at work?'

'Day off.'

'You doing anything?'

'Why?'

'I wondered if you fancied coming round to my house. I could really do with getting a first-hand account of what happened then and since. I'll cook lunch.'

There was a long pause and I wondered what he was mulling over, perhaps he was concerned that George would find out and think he'd spoken out of turn or he could even disapprove of George's attitude to working with a private detective.

'Honestly I know George said I was a bad cook but if it's food poisoning you're worrying about we can get take away.'

He laughed. 'I have a pretty strong constitution. I'll come but lunch had better not be some sort of salad.'

'I promise there will be no salad.'

'One o'clock any good for you?'

'That would be perfect.'

'All right I'll see you in a bit.'

I had made chilli last night when I got home from seeing Martin Clarke and there was plenty left over, I stuck a couple of potatoes in the oven, it was only 11am, by the time we were ready to eat they would be perfectly cooked.

It was strange seeing Amadeus dressed casually in jeans and a hoody, it had made him look ten years younger.

We went into the office and he sat on the chair across the desk from me. He looked around the room, his eyes pausing on the piles of papers and opened books.

'Looks like you're busy.'

'Research.'

'George said you were thorough but a little bit…unique.'

I was pretty sure that unique wasn't the word George had used, probably much more along the line of I was good but a pain in his ass. 'Do you like being in the police?'

'I do, just as well seeing as I've been doing it a long time.'

'What was it that made you care so much?'

'About Harmony, you mean?'

I nodded.

'Because she was vulnerable, and someone ought to have been looking out for her.'

'How old were you then?'

'19 years old, a PC not long out of police college and very idealistic.'

'You thought DCI Williams should have done more?

'He liked the easy option and those two were prime candidates, didn't bother looking any further.'

'Did you think the investigation should have been more thorough, turned over a few more rocks?'

'If I'm being honest the whole thing smelt rotten. Everyone knows when a woman is murdered you need to at least look at the partner.'

'Was DCI Williams not interested?'

'Not at all, he was happy with the burglary gone wrong theory.'

'What did you suspect?' I asked.

'Thing is, I'm not sure I really had enough experience to suspect anything, but there were too many things that bothered me. For instance, even if Simon and or Patrick did shoot Tabitha then who's to say they weren't paid to do it, also why you would shoot someone and then call an ambulance?'

'That's what Simon's lawyer said as well.'

'Neither one of them had any history with guns, the murder weapon was never recovered. If they were smart enough to ditch that successfully, how is it that they're also stupid enough to try and off load the jewellery so soon after when they would have had to have been absolute fools not to realise the police would've been looking out for it.'

'Do you think they were telling the truth when they said they had been set up?'

'I think there had to be more to it than met the eye. But the boss said the likelihood of having two sets of criminals entering a house to commit two separate crimes at the same time was not high and the jury agreed.'

'Tell me about their arrest.'

'We got a tip off that they were going to be trying to off load some of the jewellery they'd stolen to a local fence.'

'Where did the tip off come from?'

'Who knows, Williams was a bit cagey about that part, but he had the date, time, place, the whole lot and it went down like clockwork. They were arrested and then both their houses were searched and nearly everything was recovered. I might have been the new kid on the block, but it made me suspicious that it was that easy.'

'And what about the second wife, what do you know about her?'

'Not much, she was Alistair's secretary for about three years, it seems she was moved into the house about a month after the funeral, then they were engaged and married all within six months of putting Tabitha in the ground.'

'Did you run a background check on Karen?'

'I might've done a bit of digging, she wasn't some eighteen-year-old midlife crisis, she was in her early thirties, a little bit older than Tabitha. She was pretty enough, had been to university, business studies. From what I heard when I asked around her co-workers she was infatuated with Alistair.'

'Presumably it was mutual seeing as they got married?'

'I guess, but I'm not sure that man is capable of real love.'

I was leaning forward, elbows resting on the desk, my head supported by my left hand, Amadeus was easy to listen to and there was a passion about the way he spoke that made it feel like he and I had a very similar thought process.

The smell of baking potato wafted into the room, I stood up. 'I need to reheat the chilli, do you want to come through?' He followed me to the kitchen.

'Tell me about you' I said as I served the food.

'We all get together at my mum's house every Sunday, my sister Dorothy and her husband come round and now I have a little niece. They called her Blessing because that's what she is, they didn't think they could have children and then along she came.'

'What about you, do you have any children?'

He smiled, 'no, never found the right person to settle down with, the job isn't exactly a selling point for potential partners. It's hard, people think they understand and then after a couple of months they're complaining about cancelled nights out and anti-social shifts. I'm not saying you can't have both but frequently it ends in divorce.'

'What about your family?' He asked after a couple of minutes of silent eating.

'It's complicated.' I smiled 'most of the time it's just me and Alana but we discovered a bit of extended family recently and it's still taking a bit of getting used to.'

I wished I'd taken the time to get to know George like this, but our first meeting wasn't exactly conducive to it and now it felt like it would be awkward to bring up.

'I went to see Martin Clarke,' I said changing the subject. 'Have you ever met him?'

'No, I never had the pleasure. What's he like?'

'A bit strange, he seemed more interested in what his ex-father in law's opinions were than his wife's. They split because he wanted kids and she didn't. He did say one thing that was interesting though. He told me that Harmony had been to visit him about a month ago, she told him she thought she was in danger, and she was worried about his safety.'

'Did she tell him why she thought she was in danger?'

'He said he threw her out before she had a chance, but it was odd because earlier he'd told me that in the divorce, he got the house and the only thing she asked for was that Martin never contacted her again – so why would she go and see him?'

'Who knows, it's been a couple of years since they separated so perhaps she doesn't feel as strongly about it anymore.' Amadeus moved his empty plate away from the edge of the table.

'Maybe, but if they've not been in contact with one another for a couple of years then why would anything happening in her life now put him at risk?' I said.

'Unless of course it wasn't about her life now, if whatever was bothering her related back to when she was married then it's possible that she thought it might also come back to haunt him.'

'You know more about her than I do, is it likely that she'd worry about her ex-husband?'

'If I'm being honest, I felt a bit guilty when I heard that Harmony had gone missing. For the first few years I was able to keep track of her and make sure she was okay. But after she turned 13, I stopped paying as much attention. Not that I stopped caring, my life was getting busier, I was making a decent name for myself and getting promoted and there was no sign of any abuse. I contented myself with the idea that if I kept sending the cards, she would know I was here for her and that would be enough.'

'It must have meant a lot to her, she doesn't strike me as a sentimental sort of person, but she kept all of the things you sent.'

'I wish she had thought to call before it came to this.'

'Me too.'

Amadeus left promising that he would have a bit of a dig into the second Mrs Lockland and get back to me.

I looked back over the evidence file that George had given me, the only evidence that either man had been anywhere near the body were Simon's fingerprints on the doorframe of the art studio and against the wall opposite, and if he was telling the truth that he had found Tabitha's body and stopped to call 999 then it tied in with his story, and the now discounted contaminated DNA that had been used to prove Patrick had been in the vicinity of the body.

It seemed to me that DCI Williams had believed he had the people responsible and stopped looking. There was part of me that understood that mentality, but I hoped that if George had been in charge at the time he would've be more thorough. Still DCI Williams had managed to convince a jury to find them guilty.

The vibration of my phone against the wooden desk disrupted my thoughts, I moved papers around quickly almost toppling a stack of newspaper print outs trying to get to it before it went to answer machine.

'Hello, Rowan McFarlane.' I said trying to sound calm and professional.

'I hear you're looking for Harmony Lockland.' A female voice said.

'Who is this?' I asked grabbing a scrap of paper and a pen and taking down the number from the screen of my phone.

'She's not the only one who's gone missing,' the woman continued. 'my brother's gone too, and I think it's connected.'

'Who am I talking to and who's your brother?'

'My name is Sinead; my brother is Simon Cummings.'

'How long has Simon been missing?'

'Almost two weeks.'

That was longer than Harmony, but it was too much of a coincidence not to take seriously. 'Why do you think it's related and how did you know that Harmony has gone missing.'

'Because I knew he was trying to get hold of her, he wanted to tell her that it wasn't him that had killed her mum. Simon was convinced that she must have seen who the real killer was. He was talking about hypnotherapy. I told him he'd scare her off.'

'Did she agree to meet him?'

'Yes, they met once and after he was in such a strange mood and he didn't want to talk about it. The day he went missing he was supposed to be seeing her again. He left the house but he never came home, and I haven't been able to get hold of him since, his phone is off, and no one has heard from him at all.'

'Did you report it to the police?'

'They suggested I speak to charities that work with the homeless to see if they had seen him on the streets.'

'How did you know that Harmony was missing?'

'I tried to contact her but all I could find was her office number and eventually I spoke to her boss, Stephen, I think it was. He said she had vanished into thin air. He was raging saying she left him high and dry. And I wondered if they were together, you hear of weird things like that, but he wouldn't have done it. He wouldn't have abandoned his family.'

'Have you spoken to his friends?'

'He doesn't have much in the way of friends, after he came out of jail he kept to himself, got his head down and stayed out of trouble.'

I knew she wasn't being entirely honest with me; he'd been convicted of dangerous driving. 'What was he doing for work?'

'He'd done really well for himself, got a job as a car salesman, he was making great money, people like Simon you see, and they were happy to buy from him, the commission he made was impressive.'

'He was lucky to get such a good job.' I replied. 'Can I ask who told you I was looking for Harmony?'

'From a friend of a friend, word gets about.'

I felt my heckles raise slightly, her reluctance to tell me how she knew I was investigating Harmony's disappearance was a red flag, it implied that she had something to hide, how could I even know for sure that this was Simon's sister, or that he was missing. I made a note on the pad in front of me to ask George to double check her story.

'I have to be honest Sinead, when people aren't prepared to be honest with me about things, like where you heard I was investigating what's happened to Harmony, it makes me reluctant to trust anything they have to say.'

I heard her sigh. 'It's just that he made me promise not to say it was him that told me.'

'Who?'

'Her boss, he said that he had overheard her assistant saying she'd hired you.'

I still wasn't convinced, in fact there was something very off about the whole conversation, I just didn't know what it was yet. 'Do you know if Simon kept in touch with Patrick?' I asked.

'No.' she sounded angry. 'That little bastard led him into this and then let them both go down for it. They haven't talked since the original trial.'

'What do you mean he led your brother into this?'

'Robbing that house wasn't Simon's idea, I'm not saying he was an angel – I know that he wasn't and sure he broke into that house, but it wasn't his idea, he told me after that he'd had a bad feeling about the whole thing.'

'Why did he go along with it then?'

'He was young and impressionable, I know he'd told Patrick that he wasn't sure he wanted to go through with it, but Patrick was a nasty piece of work, he threatened Simon and he said that this was opportunity for them both to get rich. In the end I think greed won him over, he went along thinking what's the harm but then that woman was murdered, and his life was ruined.'

'I'm really sorry that Simon is missing, and I appreciate you letting me know, the background information is really helpful. If anything comes up about your brother whilst I'm looking for Harmony I'll let you know.'

'If you find him, tell him to come home.'

Chapter Fourteen

It was Saturday afternoon. I was getting ready to go to Caz Adam's House with Nate and my bedroom looked more like a teenage girl's than Alana's ever did. I had tried on almost everything I had in the wardrobe. I was overthinking this. This wasn't a date I reminded myself, this was a business meeting. The butterflies in my stomach clearly hadn't got the message. In the end I settled for a pair of dark blue jeans and olive-green V-neck jumper with my standard Doc Martens.

Alana cleared her throat from the doorway and made me jump, she was frowning.

'How long have you been standing there?' I asked.

'Long enough. Is there something I should know about this bloke you're meeting this evening?'

'No, he's just…a person who knew the mother of the missing person.'

'Then why all this?' She waved her hands around indicating the mess of the room.

'She's an artist type and so is he I wanted to make sure that I gave off the appearance of someone she'd want to talk to.'

'That has literally never bothered you in the past.'

'Yes it has.'

'Pft, do you fancy this guy, isn't he old enough to be your dad?'

'I do not fancy him.' I said, although I could feel my cheeks betraying me. 'And even if he was old enough to be my dad that wouldn't mean that he was too old for me.'

'Are you sure this isn't a date?'

'This is absolutely *not* a date, this is business, that's all. Why, would it bother you if I went on a date?'

'No, as long as you're happy.'

I wasn't sure she had been entirely truthful. I had never really dated, not that she would have known anyway. On the odd occasion I had met someone over the years, no one had met the standard that would have meant introducing them to Alana. I worried about it sometimes, how it would affect the dynamic of our relationship to bring someone into the picture. I liked the status quo and that had a lot to do with why no one had ever met my exacting standards.

'Thanks.' I responded.

'You'll text me when he picks you up?'

'Yes.'

'And you'll send me his car registration.'

'Why?'

'So, I can send it to George.'

'Fine.'

'And you'll text me when you arrive and give me the address?'

'Will do.'

'And then when you're leaving?'

'mmhmm.'

'where is he dropping you off?'

I had arranged for him to pick me up from the library so he wouldn't know where we lived. 'He's going to drop me at Sonya's house then we can come home together.'

'Okay.' Alana had been going to stay at home this evening but when Sonya had called and asked for Alana's help with some university lectures, she had jumped at the chance.

'You satisfied now?'

'I would've still preferred it if you were driving yourself.'

In truth so would I, as much as it was very endearing to have Alana give me twenty questions, it was a very valid worry. I liked Nate, maybe too much and letting my guard down with the wrong person could be disastrous. 'I'll be fine, don't worry.'

I'd not long reached the library when I got a text from Nate to say he was on his way. I replied saying I would meet him outside. The wind was bitterly cold, I wished I had worn a warmer jacket. Luckily, I didn't have long to wait until a black Volvo estate pulled up beside me and Nate rolled down the passenger window.

'Hi. Jump in, the door's open.'

I took a photograph of his registration and text it to Alana before I lowered myself into the car. 'This isn't what I was expecting,' I said.

'It's practical, if I fold down the seats I can get some pretty large pictures in here.'

That made sense, but it didn't stop me from thinking with the blacked-out windows in the back passenger area and the boot it would be pretty handy for transporting a body too.

'Fair enough.'

'Aw you're disappointed, were you hoping that I would turn up in a surf bus or something.'

'No, I just thought it would be something less functional.' I text Alana that we were on our way and stared out the window. I didn't like small talk and don't find silence awkward at all, Nate, however, clearly found it hard to not talk with someone sat beside him. I tried to listen intently to him talking about painting and how he really liked using pastels, but they made such a mess everywhere. But the whole time I was watching the road and looking at signposts, so I knew where I was.

'Sorry, I'm boring you,' he said after about twenty minutes.

'No, it's interesting, it's a bit hard to keep up that's all. I've never been much of an artist myself. My friend Mel is an interior designer though, I'm sure she would understand everything.'

'Okay,' he smiled and for a moment I chastised myself for being crazy enough to think that Nate was anything other than he appeared to be, an old friend of Tabitha, an artist and gallery owner. Then I thought about Alana saying he could take you anywhere and I reminded myself that a nice smile didn't make him any less of a suspect.

'So, how was your week?' He continued.

'Busy.'

'The case coming along well?'

'I think so.'

'But you don't want to talk about it?'

I shook my head.

'Fair enough, let's talk about something else then, what kind of music do you like?'

'Classical, piano, violins, that sort of thing, I find it very calming.'

He raised his eyebrows, 'I was expecting some kind of death metal.'

I smiled, pleased that I wasn't the only one with pre-conceived ideas. 'And you?'

'I like folk music, I like the lyrics to tell a story.'

Nate took a right turn down a narrow country road, the type that don't appear to be much more than a farm track but that regularly pass for 'B' roads in Scotland.

'I told you the house was a bit out of the way,' he said.

I smiled and tried to glance at my phone surreptitiously to check that I still had enough signal to ping my location to Alana so that she wouldn't worry. After about ten minutes he turned off onto a dirt road, a few moments later a large white farm house appeared at the side of the road. He parked in the driveway and as I got out of the car I sent my location and a quick I'm here text to Alana. Knowing that she was stressed had made me feel a lot jumpier that usual.

A tall slim woman with long grey hair bundled on top of her head in a loose, messy bun was stood waiting for us. She looked almost exactly as I had imagined her, an artistic hippy. She was wearing a long purple skirt and a black top. There was something about her that felt warm and safe even from a distance.

She put her arms out to embrace Nate in a hug. 'I swear you get taller each week.' She kissed him on the cheek, then she looked past him towards where I was standing awkwardly.

'Caz, this is the private detective I was telling you about.'

She gave me a long hard stare and I could tell she was trying to decide whether she liked me.

'Hi, I'm Rowan,' I said walking towards her with my hand out, finally shifting gear into professional.

She shook my hand briefly, 'well you'd both better come in.'

I gladly followed them out of the cold of the January evening. The kitchen was warm, heated by a large log burner. Caz indicated for us to sit down, and we did as instructed. A black Labrador roused itself from in front of the hearth and walked gingerly on what I recognised as arthritic legs towards me, stopping at my feet, slumping his whole body down on them and resting his head on my knee. I ran my hand along his soft head gently, he yawned and closed his eyes.

Caz joined us with a tray of drinks, she looked at her dog and then back at me, 'You've made a friend, I see,' she looked at me, 'Winston's a good judge of character,' she patted me on the shoulder and sat down in the chair opposite. 'Dinner will be about half an hour; Nate likes a roast, so I always make sure he gets one when he comes to visit.'

I could smell dinner cooking and my stomach growled appreciatively but loud enough to embarrass me. Nate laughed at me and suddenly the whole room felt more relaxed.

'Nate says you're looking for Harmony?'

'Yes, her friend from work hired me to find her. She's very worried about her.'

'We all are,'

'Did you keep in contact with Harmony after Tabitha died?'

'For a bit, she came to stay with us initially and to be honest we were hoping that it would become a more permanent situation. I was never a fan of Alistair, I want to be honest with you, I thought he was completely unsuitable for Tabitha, but she loved him and for a time they seemed to make each other very happy. With Tabitha gone I thought it would've been better for Harmony to live with us. He travelled a lot for work, and I didn't like the idea that she would always have to be staying with friends or neighbours. I knew we could give her the consistent loving home that Tabitha would've wanted for her daughter. It's not like I wanted to cut Alistair out of Harmony's life, I just wanted what was best for her.'

'But Alistair was against the idea?'

'That's the thing, we thought we were all on the same page then all of a sudden he's announcing he's engaged and of course we knew that he must've been having an affair with that woman whilst Tabitha was alive, but I thought he would have had the common decency to have waited a bit longer than a couple of months.'

'Is that when he changed his mind?'

'They said that they were going to send Harmony to boarding school, she was only eight and I told him that was too young so he said that Karen would take care of her. She'd have been better off at boarding school, because that woman is vile, she never cared one jot for Harmony.'

'You had arguments about it all?'

'I'll say we did, that's not surprising seeing as I had a telephone call from Harmony sobbing that all her mummy's things were being thrown in a skip! Everything, all her artwork, furniture, clothes. Well, we took the van and drove up there, but we were too late, Karen said it had already been picked up and taken away, she looked so smug about it, it was all I could do not to slap the stupid look off her face.'

'God that's awful, such a shame they didn't at least give you the opportunity to take your daughter's things.'

'It was a power trip for Karen I think, she definitely got enjoyment out of seeing how devastated we were.'

'She sounds awful.' I always tried to keep an open mind about people until I'd met them but I was struggling to imagine how there could be another side to this story that showed her in a better light.

'She is and then of course Alistair phoned us and started shouting about interfering and that Karen was only doing what she thought was best for all of them and that it wouldn't do any good to have reminders of Tabitha all around the house.'

'Poor Harmony,' I said trying to imagine how I would have felt if someone had removed every trace of Jack from my home. 'How was your relationship with Alistair after that?'

'We told him we wanted to see Harmony every other weekend, if they wanted to make it difficult, we were prepared to go to court. He agreed and in the beginning that's what happened, and it was lovely to see her and every time she had to go home she wept and it broke my heart. As she got older it was like her soul had been worn away by their extreme rules and she was afraid to do anything to rock the boat.'

'That must have been hard to watch.'

Caz nodded her head slowly, 'then when she was twelve, they said that it would be best if Harmony went away to school and this time I didn't protest because I actually agreed, I hoped that she would at least be able to have a good life during term time and that it might return some of the spark of the girl that I knew was inside her. It made it harder to spend any time with her though.'

'Did she like school?'

'I think so, it was going well until she was fifteen, she had met a boy from the local village and the next thing you know I hear she's pregnant. Alistair was on the phone raging asking me if I knew anything about it and of course anything I did know I denied. He dragged her out of school and locked her in the house and had her home schooled.'

'What happened to the baby?' I glanced at Nate. I presumed he would have known this segment of her history, but he had chosen not to tell me, and I wondered why.

'Well Harmony was adamant she was keeping it and they were adamant it was going up for adoption. In the end it was a moot point because she had an accident and fell down the stairs and miscarried.'

'That must have been very traumatic, how did Harmony cope?'

'It was particularly difficult with Karen crowing about what a relief it was and how she should be counting her lucky stars not to be burdened with a child at her age and what a narrow escape it was. Honestly no empathy or compassion for the poor girl.'

'Did they continue home schooling her after that?'

'No, but they sent her to a school much further away, it was very strict. She withdrew into herself, she stopped coming to see us. She concentrated only on her studies, did really well in her exams. She asked Alistair about going to art school, but he said no, and she accepted it. To be honest I thought we had lost her, she wasn't really a person anymore, just an empty shell, we didn't even get an invite to her wedding.'

'What do you mean 'you thought you'd lost her'? Have you heard from her recently?' I asked.

Caz smiled, 'Excuse me, I need to check on dinner, I'll be back in a moment,' she disappeared into the kitchen without elaborating further.

I looked at Nate who had been sitting so quietly it would have been easy to forget he was even there.

He leant forward and patted Winston's head 'It wasn't my story to tell, we had only just met, and I didn't think it was appropriate.' He said quietly.

It was a reasonable response, I doubted I would have told me either. 'Okay.'

'She must like you otherwise she wouldn't have told you so much.'

I stroked Winston's soft fur, 'I think I might have this fella to thank for that.'

'Five minutes,' she said before leaning down and man handling her dog off my legs, 'come on, there's a good old boy, you need to let your new friend get to the table.'

Over dinner the conversation turned to the gallery and how Nate was, Caz was particularly interested in whether or not there was anyone special in his life yet. She shot me a knowing look before saying, 'He's such a catch any woman would be lucky to have him, don't you think, Rowan?'

To my horror I felt my cheeks flush and my mouth go dry, 'Jury is still out on that I think.' Out of the corner of my eye I could see him looking at me, I tried not to look, the butterflies in my stomach making it hard for me to act like myself.

'Do you have him pegged as a suspect?' She asked, her tone only semi-serious.

'You never know, I need to keep my wits about me when I'm investigating.' I replied trying to keep the conversation light.

'Do you have family yourself?'

'I have a daughter, she's seventeen.' I saw the look pass across her face, the one I'd seen a hundred times before when someone is trying to discreetly work out how old I was when I had her. 'I was sixteen when she was born,'

'Ah,' was all that Caz said before moving the conversation on to her garden and art. The food was delicious, and I was grateful for the home cooked meal, it reminded me that we had been eating far too much takeaway lately and as soon as this case was over I really had to start cooking more again.

We had our coffee in the conservatory because Caz said I should see how beautiful the sky looked over the hills and she was right, it was stunning. With very little light pollution the stars looked brighter than I had seen for a long while.

'She contacted me about a month ago you know,' Caz said as we all stared out of the window.

'Harmony,' Nate said, turning to face Caz. This time he hadn't been holding out on me.

'Yes, she phoned me at first and said that she wanted to get back in touch, rebuild our relationship, I didn't know she was divorced, I was delighted to have to opportunity to have her back in my life. She was sad that she didn't know Rodger had died.'

'And did you meet up?'

'Yes, she came up here and we had a lovely time, she did say something weird though and now I wish I had asked her to explain herself more.'

'What did she say?'

'She said she felt safe for the first time in a long time.'

Chapter Fifteen

I could have happily dozed off a couple of times as Nate drove me home, but all my instincts had taught me not to fall asleep in a car with a man a barely knew. It wasn't like me to feel this relaxed, but it was dark and I was full of food. He pulled into Sonya's street and stopped, I had been deliberately vague about which house was hers.

'Thanks for taking me to meet Caz,'

'You're welcome, I know this might sound weird, but I had a really nice time.'

I swallowed hard, I could feel him moving closer towards me and part of me hoped he would lean in and kiss me.

'Yes, it was really useful.' I said pulling away and opening the car door slightly.

He sat back clearly embarrassed, 'I'm sorry, I am not very good at this kind of thing, I didn't mean to…'

'It's fine, it's me. I didn't intend to give you the wrong impression, I do like you,' I surprised myself by admitting it, 'but this is not a good time.'

'Yeah, you did say that already didn't you.'

'I did,' I smiled. I leant forward and kissed him on the cheek. 'After we've found Harmony, okay?'

'Okay.'

I got out of the car, pleased to be met by the cold winter air helping me to clear my head. I stood on the pavement and watched him drive out of the street and out of sight before going to Sonya's. Her door opened a crack as I approached.

'Everything okay?' She asked.

'Yeah,' I said not wanting to tell her in case Alana was lurking somewhere she would hear.

'I'm sorry I'm a bit later than I expected.'

'That's okay,'

I followed her into the living room where Alana was zonked out on the sofa, her blonde hair covering her face, making her look almost like a child again.

Sonya smiled, 'I think I've worn her out. Do you want a drink?'

'You got any camomile tea?'

'Sure,' she said disappearing into the kitchen.

Alana's deep peaceful sleeping breaths made me feel much calmer, I wondered how I would feel when she was living in halls. I knew university would be a good experience for her, she needed her independence. Maybe it would be good for us both, I thought, trying to ignore the churning in the pit of my stomach.

Sonya handed me the cup and sat down on the armchair next to mine. 'So, how was it?'

'Interesting. I learnt a lot about her but nothing that helps me to know where she is now.'

'And Nate turned out not to be a kidnapper or serial killer then,' she laughed.

'No, well not yet anyway. I really hope he's not involved, he seems nice.'

'Nice?' She tilted her head and raised her eyebrows, 'how nice?'

'He tried to kiss me.'

Sonya's jaw dropped a little, 'and did you want to be kissed?'

I didn't reply straight away.

'Do you like him?' She asked.

'Maybe, he's very easy on the eye and he seems kind and interesting but he also can't be ruled out as a suspect in this case so I can't even think about it and honestly I don't know if I'm having some midlife crisis because Alana is going to be leaving home soon.'

Sonya laughed at me. 'Maybe a relationship is just what you need,' she said taking a sip of tea.

'I don't know, I've always liked my own company and you know I'm pretty set in my ways and besides, apart from how he fits in to Harmony's life I don't know that much about him.'

'Well, we know he likes you.'

'What if he doesn't, what if he has Harmony tied up in a basement and he's hitting on me to deflect?'

'Is that likely do you think?'

'From all the evidence I've found so far no, he hadn't seen or spoken to her for years before she came to see him at the gallery. Tabitha was like a sister to him and he clearly has a great relationship with her mum. But it's not professional, is it?'

'Maybe you should wait until after you've finished investigating then decide if it's something you do want to explore. Anyway, I have a gift for you.' She smiled and handed me a brown cardboard file. 'It's Tabitha Adams' post mortem, not that there's much in it to be honest, she had a clean tox screen, she was shot in the head at reasonably close range, she died instantly. But I thought you'd like to see for yourself anyway.'

'Thanks,' I tucked it into my bag and finished my tea. 'I'd better wake this one up and take her home.'

'You're both welcome to stay the night.'

'Thanks, but she has big shopping plans for us tomorrow, so we'll need an early start.'

I shook Alana gently trying not to startle her. She made a gasping grunting noise before opening one eye. 'When did you get home,' she asked in a muffled half yawn.

'A little while ago, but I've been chatting to Sonya. Come on, time to wake up so we can head home.'

Chapter Sixteen

The next day I hardly had time to think about the case. Between taking Alana shopping and having dinner at Maureen's I didn't have a moment to myself. Nate did text me mid-morning to say he was sorry that he overstepped the mark and that he hoped I was okay. I thought about not replying at all, I didn't want to have to think about him at the moment, but in the end I sent a quick reply 'don't worry about it speak soon'.

On Monday morning I drove to the train station and took the train into Edinburgh. I had considered dropping in on Alistair Lockland unannounced, after all it was my preferred approach. I hated giving people time to concoct a story, but taking into consideration all I had discovered about him, not only would he be unlikely to take kindly to that, he might shut me down and refuse all further contact. Instead, I'd phoned his office and spoken to his secretary whilst trying to give away as little as possible and after a ridiculous length of time on hold I was finally granted an audience with the man himself.

His office was in one of these large glass fronted buildings that look impressive from the street but once you go through the door they are just like any other place. This building housed six other business, one of them a bank which took up two floors, but the name that really caught my eye was Radley & Jones solicitors. It couldn't be a coincidence that Patrick's lawyers' office was in the same building as Harmony's father's company.

The receptionist answered the phone and glanced across at me, when she put down the handset, she waved me to come to the desk.

'Do you have an appointment?'

'I have a meeting with Alistair Lockland,' I replied

'One moment,' she said and pointed towards a small seating area.

I didn't sit down, partly because standing meant I could be closer to her and catch a few words of the conversation and partly through the bloody mindedness of not wanting to be told what to do.

She cleared her throat, 'you'll be collected in a moment, this is your visitor badge, please don't lose it, you need it to get through the secure doors and don't forget to return it before you leave.'

I nodded and took the well-used lanyard with a plastic square hanging from the end with the word 'visitor' enclosed inside and hung it round my neck. I looked up at the staircase beyond the glass wall that separated the reception area from the warren of offices beyond. After a few moments I heard the clip, clip sound of high heels on the floor. A tall woman appeared dressed in a burgundy trouser suit, with cream blouse, her dark hair neatly contained within a tight bun. She was by far the most put together woman I had seen in a long time, there wasn't a thing out of place.

She smiled towards the receptionist, 'thanks Claire,' she said before turning her attention to me, she looked me up and down and regarded me with something that looked close to disdain. 'Ms McFarlane?'

'And you are?'

'I'm Fiona, Mr Lockland's PA'

She shook my hand then led me through the door. She sped up the stairs at a speed I wasn't anticipating, and I was verging on being out of breath by the time she stopped. She opened the door with a pass card that was attached to the waist band of her trousers on an elasticated cord. The large floor was broken up by offices all the way around the outer walls making the most of the glass exterior. The rest was split into clusters of desks.

She continued to walk briskly until we reached the back of the office space, where a large office took up most of the wall, she led me into the first section which was hers.

'Take a seat, I'll let Alistair know you're here.'

The seats in his personal waiting area were a good deal fancier than the ones in the general reception, this time I decided creating a good impression was important and did as requested. The seats had carved wooden backs and a square of padded leather to sit on. It rather reminded me of waiting to see the head mistress at school.

Alistair Lockland was tall, grey haired and smartly dressed. He smiled appreciatively at Fiona, and she returned a warm smile back.

'Ms McFarlane, if you'd like to come through.'

His office was big, and his view was nice, although significantly restricted by all the other buildings in its surrounding area. He sat behind a modern glass and wood desk, leaning back slightly in his chair. He said nothing, starting out with what I assumed he wanted to be an awkward silence. I would have to up my game, he was prepared for my visit, and we were on his turf, giving him the upper hand.

'Thank you for making the time to see me, I know Fiona said you have a very full schedule.'

'When she said it was pertaining to my daughter you piqued my interest, so I pushed back a meeting to accommodate you.'

'Thank you, that was very thoughtful.'

'I understand that you are a private detective, Ms McFarlane, what is it that Harmony has engaged you to detect?'

I tilted my head and looked at him, he didn't know. Perhaps I had been too judgemental of Martin, and he hadn't run straight to his father-in-law and told him about our encounter.

'I wasn't engaged by Harmony; I was hired to find her.'

He leant forward, the back of his chair making a strange cracking noise, 'find her, is she lost?' His tone slightly higher in pitch than it had been a moment ago.

'Not so much lost, more missing and I believe she has been taken.'

He laughed, 'I'm sorry Ms McFarlane but I'm not sure who has set you up on this wild goose chase, but I can assure you my daughter is not missing, nor has she been taken.'

'Great, you know where she is then?'

'If you are a half decent detective, of which I have my doubts, you should know that my daughter cut me out of her life the day she lost her mind and left her husband.'

'If you had properly prepared for this meeting, you would know I'm an excellent detective with an impressive track record. And given that I was very much aware of your strained relationship I'm perplexed that you're so ready to scoff at the idea that your daughter has been kidnapped.'

'You're actually serious, aren't you?' His superior expression had slipped, and the colour was draining from his cheeks slightly.

'I am, she vanished, didn't turn up for work, just disappeared. And what's more she had been receiving correspondence from someone who purported to know the truth about her mother's death, indicating that the people who were arrested and went to jail for the crime were in fact set up.'

He turned a shade of grey, his growing concern was a surprise to me. I had expected him to be generally dismissive, but this new attitude was different.

'What do you mean correspondence? Who sent it?'

'It was sent anonymously. Do you have any idea who might have sent it?'

He ignored my question, 'do you think whoever it was who sent her this letter is the same person that abducted her?'

'I don't know, it's certainly a line of enquiry I'm looking into.'

'And you think that her going missing is in some way connected to Tabitha's death?'

'Is that possible?'

He opened his mouth and then closed it, I couldn't be sure, but it looked like he was on the brink of tears. He rubbed his chin with his right hand.

'Mr Lockland, if you know something then you should tell me, it could be the difference between finding her alive and not.'

'I am sure Ms McFarlane that everyone you have spoken to has told you what a monster I am, what a terrible father I was and perhaps they are right, but I assure you that despite our differences I love my daughter and all I have ever tried to do is keep her safe.'

'Then help me, tell me who would gain from trying to open up the investigation into your first wife's death?'

'No one, the correct people were punished. The idea that it was something else is frankly ridiculous.' He sat back in his chair.

'Patrick O'Brian was released after his appeal provided evidence that he wasn't involved in your wife's death, do you think that was a mistake?'

'He was let out on a technicality, evidence was handled incorrectly, that doesn't make him innocent though.'

'Simon Cummings has also disappeared.'

'I don't care about either of those men. I know that sounds callous, but they ruined my life, if you are as you say an excellent detective I'm sure that you'll find a way of getting in contact with Patrick O'Brian.'

'I have to say I was surprised to discover that the very lawyer that represented Patrick in his appeal has his offices in the same building as yourself and furthermore is a friend of your second wife, seems a bit of a conflict of interest if you ask me.'

'I don't believe you.'

'Look it up for yourself, it's on record. Mathew Radley represented Patrick O'Brian at his appeal.'

He frowned at me. 'I hope you find Harmony, I truly do, but these men you think might be innocent are very dangerous, before the trial they had their cronies sending us death threats.'

'You and Harmony?'

'Me and Karen.'

'Did you report it to the police?'

'No, Karen thought it wasn't a good idea.'

'I'd like to speak to Karen actually. After all she moved in with you not long after Tabitha died, she probably knew Harmony pretty well.'

'My wife and daughter never really saw eye to eye, so I can't think she'd be able to help you.'

'Still, I like to be thorough, do I need to book an appointment or would it be okay for me to swing by your house?'

'You can go this afternoon. I'll let her know to expect you.'

'Thank you,' I handed him my card. 'In case you decide you actually want to share the information you're holding back.'

He got up and hurried behind me to his office door. Fiona looked up. 'Is everything okay Alistair?' She asked.

He nodded and walked me to the door. 'You should be very careful, Ms McFarlane.'

'I don't take kindly to being told what to do.'

As I walked away I looked over my shoulder and back into the office, Fiona was by his side holding his arm in a way that gave the impression of lover more than concerned PA. Perhaps Alistair Lockland simply couldn't resist his secretaries, there are plenty of men like that after all.

Chapter Seventeen

When I had discovered that Alistair hadn't thought it was a good idea to move from the house his wife was murdered in, I was astounded. I couldn't imagine how awful it must have been for Harmony to have to walk past the spot she discovered her mother's body. But as I pulled up outside it was Karen I was thinking about, how could she have stepped into a dead woman's shoes and felt comfortable.

The house's appearance would have aged, of course, but it looked incredibly similar to the photographs I had seen. The fence was painted grey and looked reasonably fresh, the fondness for grey was a current trend, several other houses in the street had followed suit. The grass was neatly trimmed with border plants that I'm sure looked pretty in spring.

Karen Lockland was not what I had imagined, her hair was dyed a pale brown and she wore tight black trousers with a white top. I imagine she had intended to look classy, but the oversized top gave a her a plump, boxy look. She looked thoroughly unimpressed to have to entertain me.

'I'm sure there is absolutely nothing I can do to assist in your little investigation,' she said before the front door was even fully closed.

'You never know, even the smallest things can be helpful.'

'Do you want to see where it happened.'

'Okay,' it was like being on a ghoulish ghost walk, I wondered if she had given this horrifically inappropriate tour before.

'Of course, the room has completely changed. We use it as our formal dining room now.'

She opened the door to reveal a large room with a long mahogany dining table and a large sideboard. The floor was wooden laminate and the walls a pale grey. I looked at the floor imagining Tabitha's body lying in an ever-increasing pool of her own blood and then across to the opposite wall where the art supplies cabinet was that Harmony had hidden in. I imagined the horror that poor child had to endure every time she was forced to eat in this room.

'It certainly has changed.' I agreed.

'Thank you, I can't stand it when people make their home a shrine to the dead, you have to move on after all.'

'Indeed.' I said already finding it hard to tolerate this awful woman.

'I know a lot of people said we should have waited, but you see Alistair and I we were already in a relationship. It was unfortunate that his first wife died but he was going to leave her anyway and so this would have been my...our house anyway.'

It had been more than unfortunate for Tabitha and Harmony, I held my tongue, 'You wouldn't have lived somewhere else and let Tabitha and Harmony stay here?'

'Oh, Tabitha wouldn't have kept Harmony. No, she was an entirely unsuitable parent, in the end in a roundabout way it worked out for the best and Harmony thrived under my care.'

It was all I could do to keep my tone neutral; I'd have gladly bitch slapped her into next week. 'Oh, I thought the two of you weren't at all close and that she went away to school at twelve?'

'Define close,' she laughed awkwardly.

'I understood you didn't see eye to eye,' I replied using Alistair's own words.

'Children need discipline, it's how they know you care for them, and Harmony needed that in bucket loads. She was a wild, unruly child that needed to be reined in. I did what was best for her and in the end, she was grateful to have me as a mother.'

'She was only seven,' I said before I could help myself.

'Perhaps you are one of these modern types that think that children need to have freedom and creativity to discover themselves. But I believe in discipline, accountability and working hard.'

It sounded more like a boot camp than a home to me, it was no wonder that Harmony had issues forming attachments to people and no wonder that the way she was brought up plus the miscarriage had put her off the idea of having children of her own.

'But you and Alistair didn't have any children together?'

'No, it just never happened for us,' she sighed. 'Anyway, if you're looking for Harmony, you won't find her here. She hasn't graced us with her presence since she pulled that stunt with poor Martin.'

'Martin said the two of you got along well and that you had been very kind to him, helped him find a lawyer to handle the divorce.'

'I still consider him family even if she doesn't't'

'Did you get to know Mathew Radley when you were Alistair's secretary, their office is in the same building as his after all.'

'Actually no, my father was friends with one of the founding partners of the firm and they regularly acted for my family and became good friends, and that's why I knew they would look after Martin.'

'Did you know they were acting for one of the men that killed Tabitha?'

'How could I, it's not the sort of thing they'd be likely to discuss with me, is it.'

'I'm curious Karen, you're a well-educated woman with a degree in business and I know you had the opportunity to move up the company, but you chose to stay Alistair's secretary, why was that?'

'Love can make you do all sorts of daft things, but the truth was I didn't want to build a career, I wanted to marry Alistair and be his wife, have a family.'

'It must have hurt when Harmony got pregnant so easily at fifteen?'

'Stupid girl, I couldn't believe the audacity of her, not a care for the shame that she brought on her father. I tried to be kind, I said her father and I would adopt the child and raise it as our own. And do you know what she said to me, she said she would rather they both die than let me raise it. How ungrateful after everything I had done for her.'

'The miscarriage was tragic though.'

'Again, her own fault, she shouldn't have been trying to be so independent, she wasn't supposed to be wandering around the house, she tripped on the belt of her own dressing gown. It was devastating for me,' she smiled, 'I knew in the end she would see my point of view and give the baby up to me.'

I wanted to push *her* down the stairs, there was no empathy in her face, if anything she looked smug, everything about her disgusted me.

'What about with Harmony as an adult, has your relationship improved?'

'I would say it improved after the miscarriage; I think she was finally able to put things into perspective. She settled down, there was a slight wobble when she suggested going to art college. But we put her back on track and I think in the end she really appreciated that.'

I bet she bloody didn't, I thought. 'The night Tabitha was murdered Alistair was away on a business trip, were you with him.'

'Yes. I was, as his secretary.'

'And his lover?'

'It certainly was nice to be able to spend more time together.'

'Whose idea was it that Harmony should spend the night with his parents?'

'Alistair was never comfortable leaving Harmony in Tabitha's care; she could get caught up in her art and forget what time of day it was and then before you knew they were eating cake for breakfast or pancakes for dinner.'

She clearly thought I should have been shocked by that, but frankly not only did I think that sounded brilliant, I was absolutely sure that it would have done Harmony no harm at all.

'Any chance I could look at Harmony's bedroom?'

Karen looked confused, 'You can see the room, but I redecorated when she went to university. It's a guest room now.'

I decided instead to cut the visit short, glad to be away from the house. It had been expertly decorated but felt entirely soulless. I've been in show houses that felt more personal. Honestly, after meeting Karen Lockland I almost felt sorry for

Alistair, I couldn't imagine she was pleasant to live with, but he made his bed and he deserved to be uncomfortable in it.

I phoned George from the car. 'Hey, are you about for a cuppa?'

'Sunshine Café?' He responded.

'Perfect.'

I was relieved to be back on home turf for once, this case was taking me fully out of my comfort zone. Star's face lit up when I jangled the door chimes.

'We haven't seen you for ages.' She wrapped her arms around me.

'Sorry, I've been working.'

'That's okay, you want your usual?'

'Yes please, and a coffee, George is joining me.'

'No problem, will Mel be with him?'

'Mel?' I frowned 'Why would she…' I trailed off, Star's face revealing that she had realised too late that she was betraying a secret.

'Are you saying George and Mel are an item?' I asked.

'I'm not saying another word,' she smiled and headed back to the kitchen.

I sat in my usual table, trying to decide why I could feel anger and annoyance brewing in the depths of my gut. I wasn't jealous, George was nice but I'd never thought about him in that way. I should be pleased, he was a good guy and Mel was my oldest friend and one of the best people I knew, she deserved to be with someone great. It was the being left out that had got to me, Mel and I were close, I thought. And I knew that our lives had changed, and my circle of friends and family had grown, but this was pretty big news, and she hadn't wanted to share it with me.

Star put a mug of camomile tea and a slice of raw carrot cake in front of me. 'Don't go making a big deal of this thing between Mel and George, the only reason I know is because I saw them together at the market.'

'I wasn't even thinking about it.'

'If you say so.' She patted me on the shoulder and walked back through the café.

A couple of moments later George walked in, Star handed him his coffee as he passed, and he worked his way through the tables. He pushed his large black coat off his shoulders on to a spare chair and sat down.

'You look well, you met someone new,' I asked, annoyed with myself for being so childish even as the words were coming out of my mouth.

'Star told you, didn't she?' He sighed.

'You can't blame her really, it's not like it wouldn't be normal for someone's best friend to know who they were dating.'

'I'm sorry, we should have told you; we weren't going behind your back, I promise. It's…it's new and we were trying to keep it on the down low for a bit.' I could see that he was genuinely concerned about having hurt my feelings.'

I softened my shoulders, trying to let go of all the tension I'd been building up over the last few days. 'No, I'm just being a bit of a bellend, ignore me.'

He snorted, spraying coffee across the table and we both laughed as he mopped up the mess. 'That's very honest.'

'Mel's awesome though so please be nice to her.'

He smiled, 'it's very sweet you want to look out for her, but do you honestly think she'd entertain being with me if I was anything but nice? Anyway, as I'm certain you didn't ask to meet me to discuss my dating life, what can I do for you?'

'Sinead Cummings told me that no one took her seriously when she reported her brother Simon missing.'

'Isn't he one of the men that killed your missing woman's mother?'

'Yep, he went missing just before she did. Sinead says that Simon and Harmony met and that he was convinced that she would remember who really killed her mother and clear his name. About the same time Harmony was reaching out to her grandmother and her ex-husband to say that she thought she was in danger. No one took her seriously though.'

'Who's to say they're event related events, ex-cons walk out of their lives on a much more regular basis than you can imagine. They struggle to cope on the outside.'

'He's been out a while though, he even had a job as a car salesman, so he doesn't exactly strike me as the walk out on your life kind.'

'Sometimes things can catch up with people and it sounds like if he wanted Harmony to help clear his name he wasn't in a good place.'

'Yeah, that was pretty much what she was told when she reported him missing? Don't you think your lot should be doing something to find Harmony?'

'It's down to missing persons.'

'And what, you have no influence at all?'

'Is that what you want. Me to go putting my size nines into their cases on your behalf, because they'll know it's you who's asked trying to use my authority to get them to take a case they think is not a real missing persons? You have to understand they need to put their resources into looking for missing children and vulnerable people, adults who walk out on their own lives without any sign of a struggle can't be top of their list.'

'I guess we'd both better hope that I find her alive then.'

'Look Rowan, it's not that I don't believe you, I agree there does seem something fishy about the whole thing, it's just that you haven't found out anything that would suggest she's actually been kidnapped or that she's really in any danger. If that changes, I'll back you completely, pull out all the stops to help you find her, but until then my hands are kind of tied.'

I showed him the note that Ellie had found screwed up in the bin in Harmony's office, 'doesn't this help?'

'It's not enough. I don't understand, normally you'd be delighted to not have me breathing down your neck telling you to stay out of my way and now you seem to want that.'

'All I want is to make sure Harmony's alright.'

'I know and I have every faith in you.'

George glugged the rest of his coffee, 'I'd better be off,' he said.

I'd really hoped that a bit of police involvement might have spooked whoever had Harmony into making a stupid move. Instead, I'd have to do it the hard way and shake the trees myself and hope I could do it hard enough that something comes loose. I was surprised that neither of the charities that I had found specialising in bringing criminals and their victims together had got back in touch with me yet.

I scrolled through my phone and found Sinead's number. 'Hi, it's Rowan McFarlane, the private detective, we spoke earlier.'

'I wasn't expecting to hear from you so soon.'

'I know, I'm sorry to call like this, but I was wondering is there any chance you had a spare key to Simon's flat? I thought I could have a look around and see if there was anything that might help?'

'Yeah, I suppose, any chance you could leave it till tomorrow though, I'm looking after my grandkids and I don't really want them asking questions about who you are and that. No offence.'

'None taken, about 10am okay?'

'Aye, that would work.'

Next, I phoned Ellie asking if she could give me the keys to Harmony's apartment, I wanted to go back and have a more thorough search.

'Can I come with you?' She asked.

'Won't you be at work?'

'Nope, I quit, Stephen is unbearable to work with, he's already gutted Harmony's office and given her job and her client list to someone else. He said if she couldn't be bothered coming to work then he didn't have time to wait for her. Honestly Rowan he's the worst. It means I'm at a bit of a loose end and I'd be happy to help in any way I can.'

'Okay, that would be great.' I would have preferred to have gone alone but Ellie seemed more invested in finding Harmony than anyone else. I knew in theory I should have at least taken a moment to consider if Ellie was a suspect, wanting to come back to the apartment could be seen as inserting yourself into an investigation, but my gut told me that she just wanted to help find her friend. 'If you're free now I'll meet you there shortly,' I said.

I stopped by the house to pick up my full kit including my proper camera, I wasn't sure what I was hoping to find but perhaps I'd missed something the first time.

Ellie was already there when I arrived. 'Hi, sorry I was a bit longer than I said.'

'That's okay, a weird thing happened when I first arrived though.'

'Weird how?'

'I was parking up and there was a man at the door pressing the buzzer to be let in, but then this other couple came up to the door and the man said something to him and there was a bit of an argument. The first man seemed to be saying he was trying to deliver a parcel but the second man didn't seem convinced and then the first man walked away back to his car, he looked really pissed off.'

Sometimes I found Ellie quite hard to follow, 'The first man, did you recognise him.'

'No, but he looked a bit shifty.'

I was cursing myself now for not coming straight here and then I would have been able to see for myself.

'I took some photos on my phone in case it was important, I took some of his car as well and wrote down the number plate.'

I grinned. 'I could kiss you right now.'

Ellie blushed. 'It just seemed sensible.'

She showed me the photographs, it was hard to make out his face properly, but I recognised him from somewhere, I couldn't think where, though. I would get George to run the number plates for me.

'Well done, honestly what quick thinking.'

She shrugged, 'The whole thing didn't feel right, who knows, it might be nothing.'

'But it might be the something we need.'

We went inside the building and climbed the stairs to Harmony's apartment. There was some mail behind the door. I pulled on some latex gloves and gave a pair to Ellie. I sifted through the letters discarding the ones that were either circulars or junk mail. There was one from her bank, I opened it and scanned my eyes down the list of transactions. Her debit card hadn't been used since the date she disappeared.

But there were two transactions that caught my eye. The first was a payment to Process Forensics in Dundee and the second was a cash withdrawal of £10,000.

Chapter Eighteen

Other than the bank statement, there was nothing of interest in Harmony's apartment. Ellie had offered to come back with me and look through the information that I had gathered so far, but I'd told her I would be fine and I'd let her know if I needed her to help with anything else. She had looked disappointed and for a moment I had felt bad, she had got photographs of the man trying to get into Harmony's building, she had been savvy enough to know that what she was watching was worth taking note of.

I needed some time by myself though, I'd spent the last few days working hard to find out not very much, I wanted to phone Michael from Process Forensics and see if I could persuade him to tell me what they were doing for Harmony.

I thought about going home first, but instead decided to call from the car.

'Hello, Michael speaking.'

'Hi Michael, I'm not sure if you remember me from last year, it's…'

'Rowan McFarlane, how could I forget?' He interrupted. 'What can I do for you?'

I wasn't sure if I should be flattered or offended that he remembered me so quickly, either way I was hoping it would work to my advantage. 'Well, I'm really hoping that you'll agree to help me with a case I'm working on.'

'We're relatively quiet at the moment so I could probably get a rush job on some tests if that's what you're hoping for?'

'Thanks, I might need that, but actually I was calling about something else. I'm investigating a missing persons case and I can see from her bank statements that she sent something to be tested at your lab and I was hoping you might be able to tell me what that was.'

'You know I can't do that, it would breach the data protection rules.'

'I understand, it's just that I think something really bad might have happened to her. Sending you something for testing was one of the last things she did before she disappeared.'

'I would help you if I could, but it's out of my hands.'

'I understand. Is she scheduled to pick up those results in person or were they being sent out to her?'

'I'll check that.'

I gave him Harmony's details and waited for him to look on the computer.

'She's due here in two days to collect.'

'Thanks, listen Michael any chance you could let me know if someone turns up to collect the results?'

'I can't see why not,' he replied.

It wasn't quite the result I was hoping for, but it would have to do. George, however, had come up with a lead for me from the car registration that Ellie had taken down. The car, a 2007 Vauxhall Astra had been scrapped 6 months ago according to the DVLA and should be languishing in a scrapyard on the outskirts of Dunfermline.

I checked my watch, if I left now, I should be able to get there in plenty of time. The roads were quiet and I arrived with time to spare before closing.

Piles of crushed cars were stacked on one side of the large fenced in area, on the other side were various bits of metal that I couldn't have identified. I drove through the open gates and parked next to a Portakabin beside a sign that said visitor.

I was surprised to find the inside of the cabin quite office like. A young woman, maybe 17, sat behind a desk, wearing a full face of makeup including bronzing and contouring powders, all things that I was more used to seeing when I worked at the club. She had about 3 sets of fake eyelashes on, and when she looked up at me, I wondered if they felt heavy.

'Can I help you?' She asked.

'I hope so, I was wondering if you knew this man.' I showed her the photograph that Ellie had taken.

She looked at me and frowned. 'Who's asking?'

'So, you do know him, does he work here.'

She stood up, 'I think I'd better get my dad.' She leaned out of the door and when she couldn't see him, she returned and picked up her mobile phone from the desk. She walked back outside, phone pressed against her ear. I stood as close to the open doorway as I could without drawing attention to myself and strained to hear her conversation.

She was too far away to hear it all, but I picked out bits and pieces, including 'she's got a photo of Patrick'. I looked back at the picture, that's why he looked familiar, the photo was a bit grainy and he'd aged but if I squinted my eyes I could see the resemblance to photographs of a young Patrick O'Brian.

'My dad will be along in a minute,' she said when she came back inside and slumped into her seat. A few moments later a man appeared dressed in overalls and a bright orange high visibility jacket.

'Hi I'm...'

'What do you want.' He cut me off.

'I want to know if you know this man.' I said showing him the photo.

'Nope, never seen him before in my life.'

From the corner of my eye, I could see shock on his daughter's face.

'Okay, thanks.'

'Was that it?'

'There was one other thing. If you don't know him how come he's driving around in a car that you took in for scrapping six months ago.'

'I have all the paperwork for every car that comes in here, everything is done by the book.'

'Great, so you won't mind if I get some people in to check that, then, would you?'

'Who did you say you were?'

'You didn't give me a chance, my name's Rowan and I'm a detective.' I deliberately missed out the 'private' part in the hope he would confuse himself into thinking I was with the police.

'What do you want with him, this man in the photo?'

'He's a person of interest in a case I'm working on, that's all. So do you know him?'

'Maybe.'

'Look either you know him or you don't, why not save us both time and effort and tell me.'

'Aye alright, I do know him.' He sighed. 'He did some work for me until recently. I thought it was him that took the car, but he smashed up my CCTV cameras which cost me a fucking fortune and meant I couldn't prove it. His name is Patrick O'Brian.'

'How long had he worked for you.'

'A few years.'

'Why did he leave?'

'Your guess is as good as mine. I turn up here one morning to find the CCTV smashed in like I said. The car was gone, and bit of petty cash missing, then Patrick doesn't come into work, so I figure he's got himself in a spot of bother.'

'You didn't report it?'

'Where's the point, I'd probably be told it was my own fault, I knew his background.'

'Do you regularly employee ex-convicts?'

'I do as it happens. They've served their time and need a second chance. I was inside myself once and I know how hard it can be when you get out. I was lucky my Granddad owned this place, so I had somewhere to go, I try to offer those less fortunate the same opportunity.'

'Fair enough, not bothered that he was a convicted murderer though, given that you've got your daughter here all the time?'

'He never had anything to do with Stacey and besides his conviction was overturned at appeal, so he wasn't a murderer at all, was he.'

'When was the last time you saw him?'

'About two weeks ago.'

'Okay thanks for that.'

I didn't leave him my card. I was pretty sure he would have kicked off if he realised that I wasn't with the police. The question was, what was Patrick doing at Harmony's apartment and why did he look so shady. Perhaps, he had some evidence regarding Tabitha's murder. But why wait all this time, what had happened that had brough Simon and Patrick out of the woodwork to Harmony's door.

At home I Googled the scrapyard. Ian Stewart had been in jail for GBH, he served four years in the end, but he would have been in prison during the time that Simon and Patrick were serving their sentences. I looked up what had happened, Ian had got into a fight outside a pub, it had turned nasty and he had slashed another man's face with a broken bottle and then punched him so hard he broke his jaw.

His defence had been that he had seen the other man trying to hit on his younger sister earlier in the day and that he was trying to warn him off when the other guy started the fight.

Following his stay at Her Majesty's pleasure though he appeared to have cleared up his act, there were articles from local newspapers showing the charitable work he was involved in, he supported his local food bank and employed ex-offenders, working with the charity 'AMB, Accountability and Mending Bridges', which was one of the charities I'd reached out to pretending to be Harmony.

This case was full of almost connected dots, but I couldn't tell what the picture was meant to be yet. Patrick was connected to Karen through her lawyer, but he was also connected to the charity through Ian.

And Patrick was the only person I couldn't get hold of to ask about what happened in that house and that couldn't be a coincidence. If I could find Patrick, perhaps I would also find Harmony and Simon.

My phone rang, it was Nate. I hit ignore. I was busy, whatever it was he wanted to talk about it would have to wait. It rang again. I sighed, 'Hi Nate, I'm a bit caught up in things right now…'

'I think you're going to want to hear this,' his voice wavered slightly.

'Are you okay?'

'No, actually I'm not.'

'What's happened? Where are you?'

'I'm at the gallery, someone came here in a ski mask and smashed up the windows. He said I needed to stay away from things that don't concern me, or she'll die. 'They're going to kill Harmony if you don't back off.'

'Oh God, I'm so sorry Nate. Have you phoned the police?'

'Yes, they said they'll get someone here as soon as they can.'

'Okay, I am going to give a friend a call so we can get to you sooner, you haven't touched anything have you?'

'No.'

'Great I'll be there as soon as I can.'

As soon as I had hung up, I phoned George.

'Is this enough for you to get involved?' I asked.

'Okay, I'll send my team over and I'll meet you there.'

I was glad that he was getting involved and for once we weren't going to be at odds with one another.

Chapter Nineteen

By the time I got to the gallery Nate was drinking a coffee, and although his complexion was ashen, he looked quite composed. The place had been pretty badly smashed up. I knew he would be devastated if any of the original work had been damaged.

'How are you doing?' It was a stupid question, but I needed to say something.

'I'm okay. I can't believe this has happened.'

'It probably looks worse than it is, broken glass has that affect.'

'How would someone even know I had anything to do with trying to find Harmony?' He looked at me and I could see the accusation in his expression.

'I don't know, someone must be following me, they must've seen us together and thought you were more involved in the investigation.'

'Doesn't this bother you?' He waved his hands around the space. 'Aren't you scared of what these people will do to you if they catch up with you?'

'I'm sorry that this has happened to you, but this is my life Nate, I couldn't do this job if I was easily scared off.'

'You're not going to stop then?'

'No. How would that help Harmony? Do you think if I back off then they'll let her go and everything will be okay?'

'I don't know what to think, this is more than chatting to people and following clues, perhaps you should leave it to the professionals.'

I sighed, I felt bad for what had happened to the gallery, I really did, and I knew it was probably just a reaction to what had happened, but still I was disappointed by what he had said.

'I *am* a professional, Nate. This is my job and yes sometimes it's scary and sometimes it's dangerous, but I'm really, really good at it and I don't back off at the first sign of trouble.'

'Not interrupting are we,' George's voice came from the doorway ending my conversation with Nate.

I turned and smiled. 'Not at all, what took you so long.'

'Had to get the team together.'

A woman in jeans and a green jacket stood behind him, her short hair tucked neatly behind her ears. 'Rowan, this is DC Liz Collins. I think you know everyone else.'

I smiled at Liz, and she returned a half smile, half frown.

'Is there somewhere we can talk Mr Wallace,' George asked.

'Call me Nate,' he said as he took us to the staff room and made us both coffee before sitting down.

'Can you to talk me through what happened here today?' George said.

'I'm not here every day, how would someone know that I would be here?'

'It might have been lucky timing for them, or it's possible that they've been watching the gallery. I know it's distressing, but anything you can tell me might help.'

'It was a pretty normal day, we'd had a few customers and I was at the counter reading whilst the shop was empty and then the door flew open. I jerked my head up because it was like it had been blown open by a strong wind and we almost had our door taken off the hinges last year with the weather and I wanted to avoid it getting damaged.'

'And is that when you saw the person?'

Nate nodded. 'Not that I saw much of him though, he was wearing a ski mask thing that covered about all of his face.'

'Was there something about the person that made you think it was a man straight away?' George asked.

'I just assumed at first, but when he started talking it was obvious.'

'Did you recognise the voice at all?'

'No, I'd say localish, certainly east coast of Scotland but other than that I wouldn't know.'

'What happened after that?'

'He had a baseball bat and I thought we were being robbed and I told him we don't have much cash here and that was when he said they didn't give a shit about the money. I was confused, the art work we keep here is valuable but not so much that I imagined someone would rob us for it. Then he said I needed to keep my nose out of things that didn't concern me.'

'And what did you think he meant by that?'

'I honestly didn't know what they were talking about at first.'

'Did he say anything else?'

Nate glanced in my direction then looked away, 'he said you and that bitch detective need to stay away or else she'll die, and that's when I knew they must be talking about Harmony.'

'Did you say anything to them?'

'I asked why he had taken her and if she was alright.'

'Did he answer?'

'He repeated that I needed to stay away and that's when he started smashing the windows up.'

'Did you see where he went when he left?'

'Not really, he went down the street, but I've no idea if there was a vehicle or anything waiting for him.'

'And are you helping Rowan with her investigation?'

I tried not to notice George's 'you never let anyone help you, what's going on here' expression.

'Not really,' Nate said looking awkwardly at me again.

'I came here to look for Tabitha's artwork and see if I could find out any more about her,' I interrupted, 'I got chatting to Nate and found out that he grew up with Tabitha and that he was still in touch with Caz Adams, Tabitha's mum and Nate kindly arranged a meeting between us and did the introductions, but you know me George. I work alone.'

'Okay.' He said frowning. 'I'd get on to your insurance company and then get those windows boarded up. I'm sure it was nothing but empty threats but is there somewhere you can go for a few days?'

'You think they know where I live?'

'It's doubtful but you might want to be away whilst our investigation is going on.'

'No, I'm going to stay.'

'Okay, but please if you notice anything unusual then give me a call.' He handed Nate his card then stood up, 'do you and Mr Wallace need some time alone before we continue?'

I felt my cheeks warm and cursed myself for reacting. 'No, we're good, thanks.' I smiled briefly at Nate before following George out of the room.

'We need to spend some time together so you can get me up to speed,' George said.

'No problem, I'll give you a lift and we can catch up in the car, I'm parked outside.'

We drove in silence for the first few moments, and it was unusually uncomfortable. I knew what he would eventually ask me about Nate, and I had no idea how to answer.

'Tell me what you've found out so far?' George said.

I filled him in on everything that I knew.

'The bloke trying to get into Harmony's building is this Patrick O'Brian and you think that he might have something to do with her going missing?'

'I don't know. That's the thing, nothing makes sense at all. Harmony has always maintained that she didn't see anything that night and both men have been out of prison for a while, so what's changed?'

'Someone took that photograph that Harmony was sent, and whoever it was could well be the person who shot her mum.'

'But they're not likely to be offering up that information though are they, if it wasn't Simon or Patrick then someone else has got away with murder all this time and I can't see why they would want to change that situation.'

'True,' George replied

'I'm picking up the key to Simon Cumming's flat tomorrow, you fancy coming with me for a nose about?'

'Wish I could, but with Harmony Adams now an official case I'm going to be busy with news bulletins and dealing with press etc.'

'No problem, I'll let you know if anything interesting turns up.'

'Thanks. So, what's with you and this Nate bloke?'

'Nothing.'

'The colour of your face would tell me otherwise, what happened to the cool as a cucumber, don't show any emotion other than anger Rowan that I've come to know and love?'

'Ha ha. I did sort of liked him, I mean he's easy on the eye, he has a job he's passionate about and he seemed like a decent bloke.'

'Why all the past tense, what did he do?'

'He didn't *do* anything, it's that…' I paused; I knew that George would likely share Nate's opinion of who should be dealing with this case. 'When I told him I was a private detective, he acted like he got it and then today not so much.'

'His art gallery was just smashed up because someone saw the two of you together and assumed that he was your sidekick. It's natural that would have an effect on him, very few people are as tough as you, maybe you should cut him some slack.'

I shrugged and frowned, 'I don't know, with Alana leaving after the summer for uni I'm worried that it's a knee jerk reaction to being alone. And besides, until I know what's happened to Harmony I don't know if he's involved and I've no intention of being played for a fool.'

'I'm glad you keep your guard up, and you're right getting involved with someone connected to a case whilst you're investigating is not a smart move, but when Alana goes to uni you're not going to be alone. For a start I don't think Maureen will let a week go by without having you round for dinner.'

I smiled, he was probably right, sometimes I still forget how much my circle of friends and family has grown over the last three years. 'I know, it's a big change that's all'

'She's not going to the moon you know, only Dundee. And if you're really feeling down, I'm sure Mel would be up for you third wheeling us occasionally.'

I pulled a face of mock horror. I dropped George back at the station and headed home, dark clouds made it feel even later than it was and for once luck was on my side and I managed to get indoors before the rain started.

Chapter Twenty

I had Harmony's bank statement on my desk, she'd kept a fairly high balance for a while and even after taking the £10,000 out she still had £9,000 left. She had a good salary and there were no signs of an extravagant lifestyle, it looked like she let the money build up in the account. But why take that much in cash when every other transaction was done digitally.

Best guess was someone had information for sale and Harmony had been so drawn into the thought that there was more to her mother's death than she had thought that she was prepared to pay for it.

My phone rang, it was Nate. Last time I had ignored his call he had been trying to tell me that his gallery had been trashed, it was possible that something else had happened, but highly unlikely. I let it go to voice message. A few moments later it rang again, I glanced down irritated, couldn't he take a hint, but it wasn't Nate, it was Ellie.

'Hey how are you doing?' I said.

'I've had better days, I just got home, and someone put a brick through my window.'

'Oh God. I know this is going to sound weird but was there a note or anything?'

'Yeah, it said 'back off bitch'.'

'And there wasn't anyone hanging around when you got home?'

'I didn't see anyone.'

'Have you called the police?'

'No, I called a glazier, they've boarded it up and I need to call my insurance to see if they'll cover the repair.'

I filled her in on the events of the day.

'At least the Police are taking it seriously now, not that I think that we need them,' Ellie said.

'They can get doors to open that are harder for me and if it helps to find Harmony, I'm all for it. Are you alright, I know things like this can be quite frightening.'

'I'm bloody angry, that's what I am. Like a brick through my window is going to scare me off, if anything it confirms I was right to be worried and that Harmony needs our help. Anyway, there's glass everywhere and if the police are going to have to come and have a look I probably shouldn't touch anything. I'll pack a few things and check into an hotel.'

'Good idea, I'll give my friend in the police a call and he'll arrange to get his team out to yours, take a statement, that sort of thing.'

'Okay, perhaps we can meet up after?'

'Sounds good, let me know when they've left and we'll catch up.'

I hung up and called George to tell him about Ellie's window.

'How well do you know this woman, any chance she could be behind the attack on the art gallery today and then did this to her own place to stop suspicion falling on her?'

'I don't know her well, but she seems legit, genuinely worried about Harmony. I've no reason to believe that she's anything other than what she says she is.'

'Okay, I'll do some digging and let you know if anything flags.'

Alana opened the front door as I ended the call to George. 'Hey mum.'

'Hiya, I'm in the office.'

Alana appeared in the doorway a few moments later looking like a drowned rat, 'it's proper chucking it down out there,' her blonde hair looked mousey brown and dripping wet.

'Have you not heard of a hood or an umbrella?'

'I know, rookie mistake,' she laughed and sat down opposite me. 'How's your day been?'

'Busy and I'm going to go out and meet my client again in a bit as well.'

'Is that the actress woman?'

'Ellie, yeah. We'll probably go to Robbie's.'

'I doubt he'll be open tonight, the bus home had to take a detour because one of the drains was overflowing and flooding the road he's on.'

'Bugger,' I slumped back into my chair racking my brains to think of where else I would be comfortable meeting with her to discuss anything.

'She could come here if you like.'

I frowned, 'are you sure? You're always the one reminding me about keeping work and home separate.'

'I know, but I mentioned her to Becky the other day, no details I promise, and she said she thinks she knows who she is. When she was at school, she's sure the drama department had a theatre group in and she said that Ellie sounded like one of the women from that'

It was unlikely there were two people as distinctive as Ellie, 'I still don't see why that makes any difference though.'

'Well, if they came to the school, they'd have all been vetted wouldn't they.'

'I suppose. I don't want to do anything that would make you uncomfortable though.'

'You said she was really nice, and you like her right?'

'Yep.'

'And you don't think she's involved in her friend's disappearance.'

'Not a chance.'

'Then you should tell her to come meet you here, we could get a takeaway for dinner.' Alana smiled.

'We really need to stop eating takeaway food and start cooking more.'

'Probably, but let's not turn over a new leaf tonight.'

'Fine, I'll phone Ellie and let her know.'

Ellie had been delighted when I suggested that she head to the house for our catch up and join Alana and I for some dinner. An hour later she arrived at the front door wearing a large yellow raincoat and matching wellies.

'This is so nice of you to have me for dinner,' she said as she took off her coat.

'It made more sense than trying to find somewhere we could chat in this weather.' Alana appeared in the hallway, and I made the introductions.

'We're having take-away, would you prefer Indian or Chinese?'

'Indian.' Ellie replied.

Alana smiled approvingly and led Ellie through to the kitchen. I was about to join them when I notice the PIR at the front door flicker into action, moments later there was a knock at the door.

'Package for Rowan McFarlane.' The delivery driver looked drenched as he offered up a small shoe box shaped parcel wrapped in brown paper, spots of rain starting to soak into it.

'Okay, thanks.' I reached out to take it from him.

'Need a signature for it please.'

I obliged by scribbling on his electric screen something that in no way resembled my signature, but he seemed satisfied and handed it over.

The brown paper, despite being slightly soggy from the rain had a faint smell on it, something I'd smelt before but couldn't quite put my finger on. I sniffed again and felt the hairs on the back of my neck raise, I searched my memory to locate it, a cold feeling creeping up my spine, but still couldn't place it.

I glanced up the hallway to where I could hear Alana and Ellie laughing. I should go and join them but instead I went into my office and sat down and placed the parcel on the desk in front of me. I took out my phone and photographed it, then pulled on a pair of latex gloves and carefully removed the paper packaging and put it into one of the evidence bags I keep in my desk drawer. I took some more photographs of the plain white box before gently lifting off the lid.

The first thing I saw was a lock of red hair with an elastic band around it. I took my time unpacking it, photographing it at every stage. Under the hair was a plastic tube with what looked like a cotton swab inside. At the bottom was a photograph and a folded sheet of paper. I looked at the picture first. It was Harmony, her hair pulled back into a tight ponytail revealing a cut on her left cheek and a black eye. She was only wearing a vest and a pair of knickers; I hoped that she is being kept somewhere warm. At this time of year overnight temperatures can drop below zero. In her hands was a newspaper. I could just make out that it has yesterday's date on it.

I opened the folded piece of paper and read the message.

Stop looking for Harmony. If you don't believe I have her then the DNA swab and photograph should satisfy you. No one else needs to die. If you don't back off the next thing I send you will be her severed finger.

The handwriting didn't look familiar. I was almost finished bagging everything up when Alana opened the office door.

'Are we going to order...' her voice trailed off and she looked at the evidence bags on the floor beside me. 'What's going on? What's all that stuff?'

'Nothing for you to worry about.'

'I'm not a child, if it's not anything to be worried about why do you look worried?'

'A package was delivered a moment ago, and it had stuff to do with the missing women. I think it's from the kidnappers. And I'm not worried, I was concentrating that's all and before you ask, I'm about to call George and let him know.'

'Good,' she paused. 'You're not in any danger are you?'

I stood up and walked across to the doorway and put my arm around her shoulder. 'Nah, it's just someone who thinks they can scare me off the case.'

She laughed, 'Clearly they haven't done much research on you then. On the plus side that must mean that they think you know something, otherwise why would they bother.'

'That's a good point. Do you want to put the order in while I finish up in here, you can pick me something you think I'll like.'

I phoned George to let him know about the package, he complained a little about me opening it, reminding me that I should've waited, etc but I could tell his heart wasn't really in it. He said he was caught up with something and he would send Amadeus over to collect it.

We were waiting for our food to be delivered when Amadeus arrived. I took his rain-soaked jacket and hung it up to drip in the hallway. He looked different, more relaxed in jeans and a green jumper

'The boss says I have to pick a package up from you.'

I led him through to the office and showed him the delivery.

'We know she was alive yesterday at least.' He sat back in the chair, 'What's the end game here, the note says no one else needs to die. Do you think that means they don't intend on killing Harmony and if that's the case why take her in the first place, unless of course her father has been asked for a ransom and he isn't forthcoming about it.'

I shook my head, 'I doubt it, he seemed genuinely shocked when I told him Harmony had disappeared and that I thought she was in danger.'

'Hopefully the kidnapper will have made a mistake and left a little trace of himself on something.'

'Fingers crossed. Do you know if we have a DNA sample on file for Harmony that we'll be able to compare the swab to?'

'No, but we might have for Tabitha so we could do a test against that.'

'Are you going back to the station tonight?'

'Yeah, in a little bit, I was heading home for something to eat and a freshen up.'

'We've just ordered takeaway and there's always plenty left over, you're welcome to stay and join us.'

He smiled, 'thanks for the offer but I need a shower more than I need the food, I've been on the go since early this morning and who knows how long I'll be in for this evening.'

'Fair enough, you'll let me know if you get anything useful from this lot?'

He shrugged, 'not up to me I'm afraid, ordinarily I'd say no but you and the DCI have an…interesting relationship.'

It wasn't surprising to me that George's colleagues didn't approve of us working so closely together, although I doubt they minded when they were taking the credit for arresting people. All the same I hoped that Amadeus didn't think of me in that way. 'We help each other.'

'All for the greater good then,' he smiled. 'Well, I'd better be off, enjoy your takeaway.'

I walked him to the door and handed him his coat, a small puddle of water had formed underneath the spot where it had been hanging. He looked at it and then back at me. 'I'm sorry about the mess,' he said.

'It's only water, don't worry, tell George I'll catch up with him tomorrow.'

'Will do, you mind and stay safe now, okay.'

'I'll do my best,' I replied wondering why for the first time someone suggesting I stay safe hadn't irritated me.

I watched from the doorway until he was back in his car and driving away before shutting the miserable night out.

Chapter Twenty-One

I had felt guilty last night when Ellie ordered a taxi, part of me thought about inviting her to stay with us the night, but I like my space and besides the only spare room is Jack's old bedroom and despite everything, I still wasn't ready to let anyone sleep in there. She had seemed quite happy to be heading to the hotel for the night though, giving George the chance to have a forensics team check out her broken window. Perhaps she too liked her own company.

After Alana went upstairs I pulled out the case file on Tabitha Adams' murder, I wondered if there was anything in it that might give me an insight into the man whose flat I was going to be poking around in soon. I tucked it back in the drawer feeling uninspired.

The next morning I headed out to meet Sinead. Her house was on the outskirts of the Robert the Bruce estate, a place which at one time was filled with memories of Mark's betrayal and Jimmy Murray's criminal gang. These days though I associate it more with family roast dinners with Maureen and Eddie. Sinead had an end terrace which provided her with what I would imagine was an enviably large garden. I rang the doorbell then took a step back and waited.

A tall thin woman answered the door in a white vest top and very pale skin tight jeans. Sinead's excellent figure and long dark hair would I'm sure mean that from a distance she passed for a lot younger than she was, but the lines around her mouth gave away a lifetime of smoking and the skin under her eyes looked puffy.

'Hi, it's Rowan, we spoke on the phone,' I said. Her frown gave way to a brief smile.

'Here's Simon's keys,' she thrust a small bunch of keys at me and then handed me a piece of white paper, 'that's his address.'

'Thanks, have you checked on the place since you last saw Simon.'

'No hen, I've never been in it. Simon wasn't keen on me going round to his.'

'Okay…'

'Listen can you chuck the keys back through the letterbox when you're done.'

'Of course, thanks again.'

'Aye, no worries,' she sighed, gave me another fleeting smile and closed the door.

I walked back to my car a little taken aback, I wasn't sure what I had been expecting but that definitely wasn't it. She'd asked me to come this morning, so she didn't have to explain my visit to her grandkids and now she had barely opened her front door to me.

I unfolded the slip of paper she'd written Simon's address on, and I half expected it to have 'Help Me' written on it. I recognised the address immediately as being not far from the apartment Mark had lived in.

The drive to Dalgety Bay was quiet, the streets are a little bit of a warren and it's easy to find yourself on the right street but wrong section. Simon's flat was on the top floor, this wasn't a new block, but it was in a nice area, the sort of place that has someone come and clean the stairwell every week and smelt perma clean. Sinead had said that her brother had done well for himself, and he would have needed to have, to be able to afford this place.

I opened the front door, the hall floor was covered in a plush beige carpet, with cream walls. Leading off the hallway were five immaculate white doors, all closed. There was the smell of stale smoke and cannabis in the air but luckily not the smell of rotting flesh I had encountered last year when I was working on the Sally Mitchell case. I hadn't allowed myself to think about it beforehand, but it must have been circling my subconscious because I could feel myself relax.

I opened the first door on the left to reveal a living room/dining room, the view from the windows over the Forth was spectacular. In the dining room end there was a small oak table that looked like it was rarely used. On the wall of the living room an enormous TV had been mounted and I wondered if it was strong enough to hold it. There were a number of games consoles on a shelving unit and a fancy leather chair that I knew people used for driving games.

There were two two-seater black leather sofas, one of the cushions looked like it was considerably more used than the others. There was a sleek Bang & Olufsen slim line, tall speaker near the television. I was no expert but even I knew that was expensive kit. I did a quick Google search only to discover you wouldn't get much change out of ten grand.

The next door led to the bedroom where there was a leather bedframe, the type that has a TV installed in the foot of it. I opened the wardrobes, Simon Cummings had expensive tastes, most of the things hanging in there had designer labels and some hadn't even had the tags removed. A couple of the shirts had cost £500 each. I opened the next set of doors, the contents of this wardrobe looked like it belonged to a different man, Adidas tracksuits, trainers, high street stuff.

I wondered if Simon had branched out in to selling drugs, I struggled to believe he could live like this on car salesman wages. The expensive car he'd been caught speeding in was starting to make more sense. The spare bedroom was half office, half music studio with an iMac, a MacBook Pro and recording equipment and a small sound booth. If I knew anything about how to use the equipment I would have checked to see if there was anything to listen to.

The expensive gadgets didn't stop there, in the kitchen there was a Smeg fridge, toaster and kettle and Sage coffee machine that looked like it would be more at home in a hipster coffee shop. Whatever Simon had been doing before he disappeared, I doubted very much if it was legal. I tried to imagine the look on Sinead's face if she saw this place, no wonder he hadn't wanted her to visit, Simon Cummings was leading a double life.

I opened the fridge, there wasn't much in the way of food, plenty of beer though, and a carton of milk that looked like it was already going lumpy. I would guess that Simon hadn't been here in a while. I lifted the lid on the bin, it was empty.

Empty bin, clean house, it didn't look like he'd left in a hurry or that he'd intended to come back and hadn't for whatever reason. I walked back into the spare bedroom, sat down at the desk and switched on the iMac, it sprung quickly into life and requested a password, the MacBook did the same. I could've taken a couple of guesses of what it might be, but I knew the likelihood of me getting it right was slim to none.

I searched around the flat for any sign of a mobile but all I could find were chargers that indicated he had one. I did a walk through a final time, photographing every room and the inside of each cupboard. I hoped that George would consider this to be worthy of a bit more investigation. I was finishing up in the kitchen when I heard a key turn in the front door.

I considered hiding, but short of contorting myself into a cupboard, that wasn't going to be possible. My heart pounded, not sure how an unsuspecting Simon Cummings would take to finding a stranger in his home.

A petite woman walked into the kitchen and opened the cupboard behind the door, she hadn't seen me yet but as soon as she turned around, she would. I cleared my throat, she whisked round then stumbled backwards.

'Who are you?' She asked, her voice breaking slightly as she spoke.

'I'm a friend of Sinead's, she asked me to come and check on Simon.'

The woman frowned, 'who?'

Whoever she was I wasn't shocked to discover she didn't know who Sinead was. 'Simon's sister.'

'I don't know anyone called Simon or Sinead.'

She was still slightly off balance and clinging to the Vax to keep her from toppling over all together.

'Simon Cummings,' I said. 'The man that owns this flat, who are you.' For a brief second my mind was panic stricken imagining I'd come into the wrong flat, but Sinead had given me the address and the keys and I knew I wasn't wrong.

She paused before she spoke, 'my name is Beth, the man that lives here is called Alistair Lockland.'

Chapter Twenty-Two

What kind of sicko was Simon Cummings that the pseudonym he had chosen to live his other life under was the husband of the woman he had served time for murdering?

'Do you want to have a wee seat Beth,' I motioned towards the breakfast bar and sat down. She was a little hesitant but after a couple of moments she joined me. 'Beth my name is Rowan McFarlane and I'm a private detective. I'm looking for a missing woman called Harmony Adams, have you heard of her?'

Beth shook her head. 'What's that got to do with Alistair?'

'Can you describe Alistair to me.'

'Sure, he's kind of average height, I'd say mid to late forties, he's a music producer I think, he doesn't talk about his work much.'

I showed her the most recent photo I had of Simon, it was a few years old, he looked nothing like Alistair Lockland. She took her time examining the picture before she confirmed that this was the occupant of the flat.

'What's your relationship to this man?' I asked.

'I don't have a relationship with him, I just come once a week and clean.'

'When was the last time you saw him?'

She thought for a little while, 'It's hard to say but I think it's been about three weeks.'

'And since then, would you say it looks like the place has been lived in much?'

'I noticed last week that the bin didn't need emptying or anything and to be honest there was hardly any mess.'

'Is there usually mess?' When I had looked around originally I had assumed that he was one of those excessively neat people.

'I don't really like to talk about my client's homes,' she said looking at the work surface.

'I completely understand, they trust you to do a good job and be discreet and I'm sure you take that very seriously.'

'It took me a long time to build up a good list of clients with nice houses you know, where they pay you a decent amount to keep their homes looking clean.'

'I promise that no one will ever know you've spoken to me, I really need your help. I've been hired to find this woman, Harmony, who went missing recently...'

'I still don't understand what that has to so with Alistair, do you think he did something to her?'

'The man that you know as Alistair Lockland is really called Simon Cummings. And Simon went to jail for murdering a woman called Tabitha. Tabitha was the real Alistair Lockland's wife and Harmony is their now adult daughter.' I glanced at her to make sure she was following.

Beth had clapped her hand across her gapping mouth, her eyes now considerably wider than they had been.

'Oh my God. I can't believe it. Why would he do that?'

I wasn't sure if she was referring to killing Tabitha or lying about his identity, so I said nothing.

'I don't get it,' she continued. 'He was a bit of pig to be honest.'

I was relieved that my revelation had loosened her tongue as I had hoped it would.

'Often, I would come in here and he'd be passed out in the studio, the place would stink and there would be takeaway containers with half eaten food strewn about the place and empty beer cans on the floor.'

'That doesn't sound very nice.'

'It wasn't the worst of it – you should've seen the state of the bathroom,' she pulled a face.

I hoped that she charged him a lot, there was no way in hell I could do her job. 'Did you ever speak to him?'

'He spoke at me, he treated me like I was his servant and it annoyed me because I have my own business, I employ fifty other women and I do alright thank you very much. I know some people think it's weird, but I like cleaning, I always have. My dad said I was daft, said I'd done well at school, should've gone to university, but I knew it wasn't for me. I spent a summer working in the local Tesco when I was sixteen and I knew then that I didn't want to work for someone else.'

I could tell I was on the precipice of hearing her whole story and as much as I was sure it would be interesting, I really wanted to find out more about Simon Cummings. 'That's amazing, I don't think I was so sure of myself at that age.' It was a lie of course; I'd always been head strong and knew what I wanted in life. 'It must have been really frustrating to have him treat you like that, how come you didn't tell him to sod off and find someone else to clean up after him?'

'It was difficult but I'm not daft, I charge a lot because of the state of the place, and he never complains he pays up every month without fail.'

'What sort of things did he say to you?'

'Nothing specific, weird stuff. He told me he did a job years ago and he was going to live off that for the rest of his days. I assumed he'd done some advertising jingle or written a Christmas song, you hear about that don't you.'

I agreed that you did. 'He never said what the job was?'

'No, he did say something about danger money once, but he was pretty wasted at the time, so I assumed he was being a twat.'

'Did he tell you he was a music producer?'

She didn't answer straight away, she frowned, 'you know I don't think he told me that directly.'

It had been a lucky coincidence meeting Beth today, God knows what state the place would've been in without her, although I would've liked the opportunity to look through his rubbish. I'd asked Beth if she had noticed anything unusual last time she emptied the bin but she couldn't remember. It had been a long shot, after all with the state of the place I doubted she was keen to poke through what he actually bothered to put in the bin himself.

Back in the car I called George to let him know it might be worth digging into Simon a bit more to see if he could find out where he was getting the money to live the high life and to see if Simon owned or rented and either way in what name.

Chapter Twenty-Three

It was already one o'clock; my stomach growled. I considered going home and grabbing some lunch but decided instead it would be nicer to go to the Sunshine Café. I phoned Ellie. I still had a small pang of guilt for waving her off to a hotel in the heaving rain.

'Hey, I'm heading out for some lunch if you fancy joining me?'

'Would love to, see you in about fifteen minutes.'

We said our goodbyes and I drove into town, parking in the designated staff area at Robbie's place, because I knew at this time of day there wouldn't be many dancers in and he wouldn't mind. I walked the short distance to the café, thankful that the rain had eased off and was little more than a light drizzle now.

I was glad to be in the warm café, the smell of incense heavy in the air, but it was busier than I would've liked, I was relieved to see that my usual table was empty and made my way quickly across to it.

Billy practically bounded over to greet me. 'I was going to call you later. Chantelle and Mohammed's flight gets in tonight. We're going to do a dinner for them at the weekend, will you be free?'

I smiled. 'Wouldn't miss it. I was hoping I could borrow you for a couple of minutes if that's okay, tap into your knowledge.'

He sat down. 'Why do I get the impression it's not my knowledge of the menu you're after?'

'I know, I'm sorry to ask.'

'Anything for you, you know that,' he said, half a smile flitting across his face.

'Thank you. I just wondered if you know either of these men.' I showed him the photographs of Simon & Patrick from the time of their arrest.'

'I don't know him,' he pointed at Simon's picture, 'but I know Patrick. He used to live on the estate back in the day. His misses and kids lived there for a while after he went to the jail but then they moved.'

'Any idea where they went?'

'I'm not sure, I know she wasn't from here originally. Pretty certain her family were from Aberdeen area.'

'Thanks, you think she might've gone back there?'

He shrugged, 'would make sense, the kids were proper small when Patrick went to jail and she didn't really know anyone I don't think.'

'Thanks a million.' I put my hand over his and gave it a little squeeze.

'You want your usual?'

'Actually, I was hoping for something more substantial, I'm starving, but I'm waiting for a…' I paused, what was Ellie. I should say client, obviously, but I'd found myself thinking of her more as a friend over the last couple of days. 'A client,' I said.

Ellie appeared, dressed as colourfully as ever, before Billy had left the table. He stood up and resumed his professional waiter/café owner pose. 'The soup today is curried parsnip and I happen to know for a fact that Star baked bread this morning and it's still warm.'

'That sounds perfect.' I looked at Ellie.

'That sounds good for me too,' she smiled.

Billy patted me on the shoulder and left.

'How do you know him?' Ellie asked.

'It's a long story, all you need to know is that Billy is one of the best people I know, and he risked his life to save Alana's'

Ellie's draw dropped a little. We made small talk, mostly about the weather, as we waited for our food to arrive. I took a couple of mouthfuls of soup soaked bread before doing anything else.

'How have you been getting on?' Ellie asked.

I considered telling her about Simon's house, but something held me back. 'I've been looking at the transcripts from the murder case. Simon said that as soon as he heard the gun shot, they ran towards it and found Tabitha lying on the ground and then phoned the ambulance.'

'It's a bit of an odd thing to do if you ask me.'

'I agree, why when you've broken into a house, you've already bagged yourself quite a haul in expensive jewellery would your instinct not be to get out of that house as fast as you could.'

'You mean in case it was the homeowner and you've been caught.'

'Whatever the reason, self-preservation would normally take precedence. If it were me, I would've got out and then gone to ground, waited until things had quietened down and hoped I hadn't been seen.'

Ellie sat forward in her seat, 'I would've been crapping myself if I was them.'

'You're right, even if you do rob houses regularly, you would still be scared by the prospect of getting shot. Patrick was always painted in a worse light because he wanted to leave.'

'But in reality, he was just doing what you'd expect.'

'In the transcript of the court case Simon says that upon hearing the gun shot he ran through the house to the studio and found Tabitha, but he saw no one. Which if the house had been huge you might understand.'

'I always imagined the house Harmony grew up in to be quite grand.'

'It was a decent size. A bigger than average five bedroom detached house, and that's the other thing, how did Simon find his way across the house so easily, although according to him they had been given a floor plan of the house so maybe he'd studied it really well.'

'He must have a better sense of direction than me,' Ellie said

'And it would be worse if you were frightened, which is making me wonder if Simon, at least, had been inside the house before,' I sighed. 'God this is so annoying, nothing makes any sense.'

Chapter Twenty-Four

Karen and Alistair were supposed to be in Perth the night Tabitha was murdered, at a fund raiser. Alistair's firm had bought a table and by all accounts it was a prestigious event. The hotel that had facilitated it was long gone and luxury apartments had taken its place, but events like these were usually documented in the local papers. With a bit of luck there might be some archived photographs.

The library reference room held newspaper archives that went back more than 100 years. After half an hour of searching I found a front-page article from the Perth Gazette. The fund raiser had been in aid of disadvantaged children in Scotland. I scanned the information, £250,000 had been raised. The photograph was grainy but there was no mistaking that Alistair was in it. He had been a handsome man, he was smiling and looked genuinely happy.

There was no sign of Karen, I was about to give up looking at the picture when I caught sight of another face. In the background I saw Matthew Radley. It bothered me that he was always there, lurking in the background, like a fly on the wall at every major event in this case.

I printed the article. The Perth Gazette was still in publication but when I called none of the staff had been there in 1995 and they didn't know where the journalist or photographer worked now. It had been a long shot and whilst Perth wasn't that far away, I doubted that Alistair would have managed to get away from the event for the hour and half he would have needed to drive home, shoot his wife and then drive back again without being missed.

The original police investigation had ruled him out almost before it began and then when Simon and Patrick were arrested no one else was even considered a suspect. I phoned Alistair Lockland's office to arrange another appointment. Fiona, his PA offered me ten minutes at the end of the day tomorrow. I took it, if I needed more time to talk to him what would he do, have me thrown out?

I'd missed three calls from Nate whilst I had been in the library. I was reluctant to call him back. His behaviour yesterday had taken the sheen off of how I felt about him, but I had the feeling he would keep calling until I relented and spoke to him. I waited till I was back in my car then called.

'Hey Rowan, thanks for calling me back.'

'No problem, I was in the library.' I didn't want him to think I'd been ignoring his calls through pettiness, even if that were partially true.

'You still working on the case?'

My heckles raised, I took a deep breath. 'Yes.'

'I mean not that you shouldn't or anything, it was just that I thought now that the police are involved…'

'That I would leave it to the professionals?'

There was a moments silence, I hated that he'd got under my skin enough to illicit such an emotive response.

'I'm sorry. I didn't mean to offend you, I'd had a huge shock, you must understand that.'

'Why?' I asked

'Why what?' He responded.

'Must I understand that you having a shock would suddenly mean that you think I'm no longer capable of doing my job.'

'I didn't say you weren't capable of doing your job, it's just that a brick through a window is pretty serious stuff and the police are trained for this kind of thing, it's not the same as proving someone's husband is cheating on them.'

'Is that all you think my job is, running around chasing cheating spouses?'

'I don't know, but it's one thing asking a few questions, it's another getting involved with someone who is clearly dangerous.'

I laughed. 'Are you taking the piss?'

'No, why would I...'

'In the last two years Nate, my daughter has been kidnapped, I killed a man to protect her, and I've helped crack a case of a serial killer that was targeting teenage girls, honestly a brick through the window and being told to back off is fairly inconsequential for me.'

'I didn't know.'

'All you would have needed to do was Google my name and you would have been able to see the headlines. You know what the most disappointing part for me is, I was excited that I had met someone who didn't find the thought of me being a private detective ridiculous, who I presumed would support me and not assume I wasn't capable. And now I don't know what to think, was it all lip service because you thought if you boosted my ego I'd sleep with you or were you patronising me with your understanding of my job?'

'I've really fucked up here, haven't I?' I could hear him sigh.

'Yep.'

'I honestly didn't mean to offend you and for the record I wasn't just trying to get you to sleep with me, I really like you.'

'No you don't, you can't. You barely know me and you sure as hell don't understand me. It was a physical attraction and I'm flattered and I thought there might have been something in it, but I haven't got time to waste on someone who doesn't believe in me.'

'There must be something I can do to make it up to you. When this is over let me take you on that date we talked about, and I can get to know you properly.'

'No thanks. I think it would be better if we didn't talk again unless I need to speak to you in the course of my investigation. And I would really appreciate it if you stopped calling me as well. Whatever this was or could have been it's over and I think it's best for both of us if you accept that.'

'Okay. I won't bother you again, but can I ask one favour. When you find Harmony, would you mind letting me know.'

'Of course,' I said. 'Right, I've got to go. Goodbye Nate.' I hung up before he had the chance to say anything else.

I sat in the car park for a few more minutes staring out of the windscreen replaying the conversation in my head, trying to decide if I had been too hard on him, asking myself if I was using this as an excuse to reject him because frankly the idea of being in a relationship freaked me out.

Chapter Twenty-Five

Fiona was waiting in the reception chatting to the receptionist when I arrived, I wasn't sure if it was by coincidence or design. She signed me in with barely a good afternoon and said nothing until we started to walk up the stairs.

'The police came to see Alistair,' she said glaring at me. 'Was that your doing?'

'His daughter is missing and some of her friends have been threatened, it's their job to investigate.'

Her face softened slightly. 'He's been worried sick you know.'

'I can imagine,' except I couldn't, Alistair Lockland hadn't really given me the impression of someone who was inclined to worry.

'I've cancelled so many meetings for him, it's really not like him at all.'

'He must rely on you a lot,' I said.

Her cheeks went a deeper shade of pink, 'it's my job.'

'But you're fond of Alistair?' I asked.

She paused before we went through to the main office. 'I know what you're thinking, but it's not like that. He wouldn't do that to Karen.'

'What do you think of Karen?'

'I can't stand the woman, she makes his life miserable. I don't understand why he stays married to her. She's always spending money, but she's never worked a day since they got married, and then she wants luxury holidays and to fly first class. And I know you're probably thinking that he can afford it and it's true, he does have money but only because he works so hard. I think she would be happy if he dropped down dead and then she could have all of his money.'

'You think she's a gold digger?'

'I do. And I know that you'll say it's because I'm jealous, but it's not that, she's rude, she comes from a wealthy family and I don't believe she doesn't have some sort of trust fund or something. But worse than wanting his money I don't think she loves him, and I can't imagine she ever did. I think she took advantage of him when his wife had died, and he was alone and vulnerable.'

'There were rumours that they were already involved before the first Mrs Lockland died.'

She shrugged her shoulders, 'before my time. I'm only telling you what it looks like to me.' She opened the door and led me through to the office.

This time Alistair seemed smaller than before, all the pompousness had left him. He stood as I entered the room.

'It's nice to see you again Ms McFarlane.'

'Fiona tells me that the police have already been to see you?'

He nodded, 'I've told them everything I could.'

Now, as I sat down across the table from him, I could see how grey and tired he looked. 'That's good.'

'DCI Johnston was full of praises for you. I understand you're the reason that we have such a prestigious officer in charge?'

'George and I have a good working relationship, he trusted me when I said that Harmony was in trouble and we're going to work together to try and find her.'

'Good.' He looked away from me to his left, out the large window that looked out on to other office buildings. 'What else can I do to help with your investigation?'

'I'm looking into the possibility that whatever has happened to Harmony might have something to do with the murder of your first wife.'

He stiffened in his chair, 'I can't see how what happened to Tabby could be related.'

'I want to make sure that every angle has been covered. You were in Perth at a fundraiser that night, weren't you?'

'Yes, we did a lot of them back then. There was value in being seen to be being active in your community. It gave me the opportunity to network and if I was lucky, get my face and the business name in the papers. I don't do it so much these days, with social media etcetera there's not the same need.'

'I saw that the Perth Gazette were there that evening, there was a nice photo of you and Matthew Radley on the front page. How long had you known Matthew by then?'

'I'm honestly not sure, perhaps a couple of years. It's not like we're friends, more business acquaintances.'

'And Karen, she came with you that evening?'

'Yes.'

'How come you didn't ask Tabitha to go with you, it looked like other people had brought their wives.'

'It wasn't really her kind of thing.'

'Raising money for disadvantaged children? I would've imagined that would be right up her street.'

He sat back in the chair. 'Karen wanted to come.' He paused, 'I'm not proud of the fact that I was with another women the night Tabby was killed. I don't expect you to understand, being with Karen made me feel…important, she hung on my every word and told me how amazing I was. I can tell from your expression that you think that makes me pathetic, and you're right.'

'Tabitha didn't make you feel like that?'

He looked down, 'Tabby was out of my league in more ways than one and I knew it. We came from such different worlds, but in the beginning I didn't care, I thought we would make it work. But it was hard, she was feisty, and we had so many disagreements. I honestly didn't think our marriage was going to last and I felt sorry for myself, Karen boosted my ego. I'm sure I was a rotten husband in the last months of her life, she didn't deserve to be treated like that. No doubt people will tell you I wasn't kind to Tabby,' his eyes met mine for a brief second. 'They'd be right. I was stupid and pig headed, I wanted to change her, which was madness because she was perfect the way she was. If I could go back and do things differently then I would in a heartbeat, I've spent the rest of my life paying for my mistake.'

'What do you mean?' I asked.

'Nothing, why are you asking about that night?'

'I was surprised that I couldn't see Karen in any of the pictures the newspaper took.' He didn't need to know that the front-page snap had been the only one I'd seen.

'That surprises me, obviously we couldn't be seen together constantly. It wasn't the sort of place I wanted rumours to get around. But we were at the table together for dinner. Karen had arranged a meeting with a prospective client the next again day to make it look better that she was with me and not my wife.'

'How did Tabitha react to you taking Karen?'

'She just looked at me and said nothing.'

'Do you think she knew about you and Karen?'

'I'm not sure. I thought I was being careful, but if I'm being honest I wanted to provoke a response from her. I needed to know that she still cared about us.'

'Would you have left Tabitha for Karen in the end do you think?'

'I don't know.' He sighed.

'Would you have fought Tabitha for custody of Harmony if she left you?'

'Tabitha was a wonderful mother, she gave Harmony the sort of parenting I wasn't capable of, I knew she would have been better off living with her mother, but that doesn't mean I was prepared to give up being a father, no matter what happened in my marriage. I know it might not seem like it to you, Ms McFarlane, but I love my daughter and I would do anything to have the opportunity to repair my relationship with her.'

'Thank you for giving me some of your time.' I said as I stood up.

'Do you think she'll forgive me?' He asked as I started to move.

'Who?'

'Harmony, do you think she'd be willing to give me another chance?'

'I don't know.' I looked at Alistair Lockland sitting back in his chair, his face pale, his eyes sad as if he was only now realising the gravity of the situation.

Fiona was still at her desk when I left, it was half past five. 'You working late?' I asked.

'I leave when he does,' she replied.

'That must make for some very long days.'

169

'I love my job.'

Personally, I thought she loved more than just her job, I couldn't see the attraction myself, but then I was hardly an expert in relationships.

On the way home I phoned Sonya, 'any luck with the DNA swab the forensics team took from the package I received?'

'There was nothing on file for Harmony or Tabitha.'

'That's frustrating,' I replied.

'Well, it would be if you hadn't mentioned that Harmony had sent something to Process Forensics for testing before she went missing.'

'I suspect you had more luck persuading Michael to tell you what it was than I did.'

'I am the police pathologist, which usually helps.'

'That's true – so what was it?'

'A DNA test.'

'Why was Harmony doing a DNA test?'

'According to Michael she had asked for a paternity test against a sample that she provided. He said he thought it was a bit strange though, she provided a normal cotton swab for herself and for the potential father she provided a cloth handkerchief with blood on it.'

'Whose DNA was it?'

'A Nathanial Wallace.'

'Nate?' I said, shocked. 'And what was the result?'

'Is that the bloke who tried to kiss you the other day, the one that Tabitha's parents took in?'

'Yes. And is he her biological father?'

'No, he's not.'

I didn't know why, but I felt a sense of relief immediately. 'Interesting.'

'How's that going by the way?' Sonya asked.

'It's not.' I briefly explained what he had said and how things had ended.

'Oh well, probably best not to complicate the case,' she said. 'Have you found out anything that would have made Harmony think Nate was her father.'

'Nope, but it could have been wishful thinking. She has a strained, barely existent relationship with her father. Perhaps she would like not to be related to someone like him, then when she met Nate, she felt like they had more in common. He was clearly very fond of Tabitha, it's possible that she read more into that than existed.'

'Maybe you should ask him.'

'Hmm.'

'Well, you can't avoid him altogether, not until this is over. Anyway, it's not like you were in a relationship, it was a bit of flirting.'

I laughed, glad that I could rely on Sonya to bring me back down to reality. 'I'll see what I can find out. Did Michael say why Harmony arranged to go and collect the results in person? Isn't that the sort of thing that's usually sent in a letter?'

'Mostly, he said she very specifically asked if it was possible to come in person to collect the results, even offered to pay extra.'

'Strange. I can only think of a couple of reasons why she'd do that, either she was concerned that someone was interfering with her post or she didn't expect to be at home when they were ready.'

'I'll leave that for you to figure out, but at least it means that we know that the DNA swab you were sent was genuine, so it makes sense that whoever took it, has Harmony.'

'I take it they weren't helpful and left us any fingerprints or anything?'

'Sadly not. The photograph has been authenticated and the hair is human but there wasn't enough to prove that it's definitely Harmony's, but I'm working on the assumption that it is given that everything else that came in your package is legitimate.'

Chapter Twenty-Six

The image of Harmony, cold, injured and frightened had swum around my mind most of the night, making getting anything close to restful sleep next to impossible, which meant that when a withheld number called my mobile at 5.30am I was already dressed and in my office drinking coffee.

'Hello,' I answered, expecting it to be an automated message telling me I'd been involved in a car accident that wasn't my fault.

'This is Patrick O'Brian, I think we should talk.' He spoke in a whisper.

'Where are you?' I asked.

'I'm moving around so they don't find me.'

'Who?'

'I'll answer your questions, but not on the phone. Do you know the caravan site out by the beach just before you get into St. Andrews?'

'Yes.'

'Good, before you get to that there's a turning, a farm track. Drive down there and there's a small cove. I'll meet you there at 9am. Don't bring anyone with you.'

He hung up before I had the chance to ask him anything else. I considered telling George where I was going, but he would have wanted to come with me or have people standing by. If Patrick saw police, he would be bound to bail on our meeting, and I doubted he would give me a second chance.

I left a voice message for Sonya. She would contact George if she hadn't heard from me by the end of lunch time and then at least he would know where to start looking. Traffic would be busier at that time of day, I would need to add an extra half an hour to my journey time. I'd leave at quarter past seven to make sure I'd be in plenty of time and cross my fingers that the A92 would be free of breakdowns and collisions. I waited until just after six to try and wake Alana. Eventually, after what felt like endless cajoling, she was awake enough to understand what was happening.

'Have you turned on find my phone?'

'Yes, and I've told Sonya where I'm going.'

'And you'll message me as soon as you're heading home and again when you get home?'

'Yes.'

Loosing Jack and all that had followed had forever altered our dynamic and whilst I wasn't sure she would ever be completely comfortable with the situations I sometimes had to put myself in to do my job, we had at least worked out a process that helped her feel more at ease.

'Do you think he's dangerous?'

'He sounded more scared than anything.'

'Could be an act?'

'Possible, but I don't think so.'

Breakfast was a bit more of a subdued event than normal. This would be the only benefit of Alana going to university, I wouldn't have to sit and watch her pretend not to worry as she ate toast and marmalade. She'd be slightly removed from it all and there was an element of protection for her in that which I welcomed.

The traffic was lighter than usual, getting on the road early had made all the difference. I took the turning off the main road, it was little more than a dirt track and it didn't seem like it was in regular use at all. I looked out for any sign of Patrick, but I didn't see anyone. The fields either side were empty, waiting to be planted for this year's crops. I passed a derelict farmhouse on the right-hand side but other than that there were no buildings.

At the end of the track there was a pull-in near the field gate. I pulled my car in tight out of the way of any other vehicles, not that I was expecting any. It was 8.30am. I considered sitting in my car for the next thirty minutes but instead decided to go and check out the meeting spot.

The wind was cold, I was glad that I'd taken to keeping a warmer jacket in the boot of my car. Now suitably wrapped up I began the decent to the beach, I wondered how Patrick had even known about this spot. You would never have guessed from the track that it would lead to a small exclusive beach cove. And that must be how the landowners wanted it otherwise it would likely be very popular in the warmer weather.

Parts of the path down were lose under foot and a couple of times I stumbled, catching my balance by grabbing hold of some sturdy looking long grasses. I slid the last metre or so and landed awkwardly on the pebble beach. I quickly brushed myself down and began scanning the space.

The cove was tucked in between two rock faces making it feel protected from the wind that had made me feel so cold earlier. Confident that I was the first to arrive, I strode from one end to the other. There was nowhere to hide and no sign of anyone camping. I took my phone out my pocket and was surprised to see that I still had full signal.

A crunch of pebbles behind me caught my attention and I spun round to see a man walking towards me. He was tall and slim, wearing jeans and a grey hoodie with a denim jacket over the top.

'Patrick?' I called to him.

He nodded.

He was only a couple of steps away when my phone buzzed.

'I telt you to come by yourself,' he said, he turned to look behind him anxiously.

I looked at my screen, 'it's my daughter letting me know she's got to school okay.' I replied holding it out to him to see for himself.

He glanced at the screen and the partial message from Alana, his shoulders dropped. 'It's hard to know who you can trust.'

'I promise you I came by myself, like you asked. Is this where you've been staying?'

'No, this whole beach disappears at high tide.'

'Why did you want to talk to me?'

'I saw it in the news that Harmony Lockland has disappeared, and the police think she's been kidnapped.'

'So why aren't you talking to the police?'

'I don't trust them, they just want an outcome that makes them look good and I'd seen you sniffing about Harmony's place with that weird friend of hers, so I found out who you were, and people have some pretty good things to say about you.'

I would have loved to ask which people and what they had said but this wasn't the time to stroke my ego.

'You didn't know Harmony was missing?'

'No. I figured something had happened to her because she was supposed to be meeting me and she didn't show up. I sat outside her flat for a couple of evenings, not to scare her or anything, I wanted to check on her and when she didn't show for days I started to think something wasn't right.'

'Why was she meeting with you? Was it you that was trying to contact her through the charity?'

'No, that Ian bloke at the scrap yard, he kept going on about someplace that he was involved with and that I should reach out to the family and say I was sorry and all that shite.'

'You're not sorry?'

'I'm sorry for breaking into that house that night, but I can't be sorry for something I didn't do.'

'The police file said that you were the one that wanted to break into that house though.'

'I was desperate, I'd been in and out of the jail since I was a teen and I swear I was trying to make a go of it, getting a normal job and that. Trying to do right by my missus and my kids. I was working as a bricky on this building site, and I hadn't fully disclosed that I'd been to jail so when the bosses found out they gave me the sack. I don't blame them but I had promised Michelle that I'd get a job so that she could have the fancy nursery she wanted for the new baby, we'd just found out she was pregnant you see, but getting a job wasn't as easy as I hoped it would be.'

'How did you find out about the house?'

'I started spending a bit of time in the pub, that's where I got to know Simon. Anyway I met this girl, Leah, she was dead pretty so I was surprised when she started coming on to me, I thought she would've been into Simon, he was the good looking one of the two of us. She worked at the house, I'm not proud of mysel' but I started having an affair with her.'

'Was it her idea that you rob the house?'

'Yeah, she made it sound like such an easy job, no one would be there, she would tell us where all the good stuff would be so we didn't have to waste time looking around. It was supposed to be get in, get the stuff, get out.'

'Did you ever worry that she was using you?'

'It's easy to have twenty-twenty hindsight, but at the time it felt like it was the answer to my worries. I'd do this last job, take the family on holiday and then I would be done and I'd find a proper job.'

'So how did Simon get involved?'

'He had overheard Leah talking to me about it and asked what was going on, so I told him everything, by this point it was getting close to the night Leah said we needed to do it and I was getting cold feet. Simon though, he thought it was a great idea and wanted to get involved and I knew there was going to be plenty in it for us both and I was grateful I guess that I would be with someone so we could watch each other's backs.'

'You want to tell me what happened that night?'

'Everything was going to plan, we were almost done. I couldn't believe the stuff we'd got, and I was feeling a bit smug that we'd pulled it off. Had even started thinking about seeing how much Euro Disney was. Then the gun shot happened and out of nowhere Simon was off running towards it and I was shouting after him that we needed to get out, but he wouldn't listen. So, I legged it out of there, I figured if he wanted to get himself killed or caught that was his problem.'

'You never saw the body then?'

He shook his head. 'Nope. I went home and laid low. Next day I got a text from Simon wanting to meet up. He told me that he'd found the woman and called the ambulance, but that she was already dead. He seemed pretty shaken up. He was desperate for us to off load the stuff, I told him we needed to wait until all the heat had died down but he said he couldn't wait. I held him off as long as I could but then arranged to sell it all on and that's when we got arrested.'

'Were you angry with Simon about that?'

'Fucking raging, but I wasn't expecting to be done for murder. I'm not that type of man. I know people think if you'd break into someone's house and rob them then you're scum and I get that, but there's a big leap to murder.' He took a packet of cigarettes out of his pocket and took one out. 'Do you mind?' He asked.

I shook my head.

'I've been trying to give up, but it's not going so well.' He paused to light the cigarette, trying to hide it inside his denim jacket to stop his match being extinguished by the wind. 'I didn't kill that woman and Simon was with me when we heard the gun shot, so he can't have either.'

'But in the end your appeal was successful though,' I said.

'For all the bloody good it did, my lawyer thought there might be a chance of some compensation, you know from the police, but it never came to anything. And everyone still thinks I done it and I just got out on a technicality because the police screwed up the evidence. It's not the same as having your name cleared.'

'Is that why were you in contact with Harmony now, did you think she could clear your name?'

'Nah, too late for that, I've done the time now. My girls grew up not knowing me. Michelle moved away, met someone else and got married. Probably just as well for them but it's too late to change the past. It was her that got in touch with me.'

'What did she want?'

'She wanted to know if I'd kept any of the jewellery, there was a necklace that had been her great grandmother's that wasn't recovered by the police.'

'And had you?'

'I kept a couple of bits back, stuff that Simon didn't know I had.'

'You still had it all this time?'

'Yeah, I'd left them somewhere safe when I went away, cos I knew I'd need cash when I got out and over the last few years, I've sold a bit here and there when times have been rough. It was coincidence the necklace was the last thing I had.'

'What was so special about the necklace?'

'It had a little spider on it in some dark blue/black stone, I wasn't sure if it was worth anything, but I liked it. I'd almost given it to one of my daughters last year, but I worried that it would be recognised one day and then it didn't seem like such a good idea.'

'That was lucky that you still had it.'

'Well, you see that was the thing, I didn't. I'd taken it down to the pawn broker. I hadn't realised it was worth so much, but the dude at the pawn brokers eyes lit up when I showed it to him. Gave me five grand for it, she started crying when I told her, I still had a couple of days left on my ticket and I told her if she had the cash she could get it back. Next day she met me outside the place, we went in, she got the necklace and left. She wasn't angry or anything, totally threw me to be honest.'

'How did she pay for it?'

'She had cash, the guy in there is a right con artist, gave me five for it but wanted seven to get it back – she didn't even bat an eyelid, just kept counting the notes.'

'What happened after that?'

'We went for a coffee at a café round the corner, I told her I didn't kill her mum and she said that she knew that. She asked me if anyone had taken any of her mum's sketch books. I hadn't seen anything like that, we'd been told to keep away from the art studio and that's where I'm guessing they were.'

'How many times did you meet up?'

'Four, always her that contacted me.'

'What did you talk about?'

'At first she asked me what happened, and I told her the same as I've told you and after that she talked about her mum, and I listened. I know it sounds dead weird, but for some reason she liked talking to me and I liked listening. There was nothing else in it, just friendship.'

'Okay, let's fast forward. Harmony doesn't show up to your meeting, you're a bit worried, how did you go from that to smashing up the CCTV in the scrapyard and stealing a car, to hiding from someone.'

Patrick took a drag on the cigarette and frowned. 'I haven't stolen anything, I bought that car off of Ian. He wrote me a receipt for the bloody thing. It'll be in the car somewhere, charged me £1,000.'

'Is that what you spent the money on from the pawn brokers?'

'No, I sent most of that to my girls for my grandchildren, I'm hoping one day they'll let me meet them. Harmony gave me the money for the car. I didn't ask her, I was telling her about it and she volunteered. And now Ian is saying I nicked it and smashed the place up?'

'That's what he told me.'

'He's a liar. And I ran for it because I knew something was off. Simon had been trying to get in touch with me. He said he had something to tell me. To be honest I wasn't keen to see him, we hadn't exactly kept in touch, and I was trying to put everything behind me, but he was insistent. Eventually I gave in and agreed to meet at some pub, but he never showed up. I was coming out of the bog and I saw these two guys at the bar, big muscly mean looking bastards and they were asking if anyone had seen me, showing the barmaid my photo. I snuck out through the beer garden and that's when I knew that something wasn't right.'

'No one has seen Simon in a while, the police are thinking that whoever has Harmony might also have taken him.'

'Yeah, well maybe, I'm sure as hell not going to give them a chance to get to me,' he stubbed his cigarette out and put the end back in the packet. 'Bad for the environment to throw them in the sea.' He said when he noticed me watching him. 'I had a lot of time to read when I was inside, I took courses. Not that it matters when you've been in jail for murder though.'

'You've no idea who might have taken her?'

'If I did, I would tell you, I really liked the girl. She had this lovely way about her, she made me feel dead calm and positive, she'd had a really hard time of it and that scum bag of an ex-husband hadn't helped.'

'I heard she went to see him before she went missing.'

'Not that I know of.'

'She didn't mention visiting Martin to you?' I asked.

'Look, that guy is an absolute bellend, he might come across all white collar and middle class but from what Harmony told me he was nasty to be around.'

'Interesting, so you think the likelihood of her visiting him for a chat because she was scared by all of the stuff she was being sent about her mum is pretty low?'

'I'd say it was zero, and if that's what he's saying he's a liar. Do you know what he told her the last time he saw her? He told her he hoped she ended up in a pool of her own blood just like her mum.'

'I can see why he wouldn't want that coming out now that she's missing.'

'I think he's one of those men that want everyone to think he's this nice, charming person, he needs everyone to think that Harmony was in the wrong.'

'It sounds like you got to know her pretty well.'

He shrugged, 'I don't know, but she seemed able to open up with me and talk and I know that she has her friend from work, but other than that she hasn't got anyone.'

The tide had started to come in and the available part of the pebble beach was receding. We climbed back up to the road and walked to my car.

'Do you want a lift somewhere?'

'No thanks.' He pointed into the corner of the field where I could make out a car carefully camouflaged by the bush it was parked under.

Back inside my car I wish I'd brought a flask with me. Back when Jack and I were talking about me joining the agency he told me that you should never leave home without a chocolate bar, a bottle of water and a flask. I'd laughed at him then, but now I could imagine him looking down on me and saying I told you so. I text Alana to tell her that I was fine and about to head home. I rubbed my hands together trying to get the circulation going and was about to reverse when Patrick appeared at the side of the car and knocked on my window.

I opened the window, 'everything okay?'

He pushed a crumpled piece of white paper at me. 'It's the receipt for the car, I knew I had it somewhere. You take it, you can show it to the police so they can see I didn't steal it.'

I unfolded the page. Despite being a bit worse for wear for kicking around the footwell of a car it was still easy to read. The page was torn from the headed receipt book of the scrap yard. The car, registration and amount of the sale were all detailed and it was signed by Ian. I had nothing to compare the signature to, but it wouldn't be hard for George to get it analysed.

I placed it into an evidence bag. 'Thanks.'

Patrick said nothing and wandered back to his car.

The rain started when I was about halfway along the farm track making the ground instantly boggier and more difficult to drive on. Back on the A92, my windscreen wipers at full speed, I thought about Patrick. I should have asked him about the lawyer and his connection to Karen, but I had been more interested in hearing about the unexpected friendship that he had with Harmony. It would've been easy to assume he was lying, but when he spoke about their meetings it had a ring of truth to it. Obviously, I would double check his story about the necklace at the pawn shop, but my gut was telling me that he'd been telling me the truth about everything.

Chapter Twenty-Seven

It would have been good to be able to speak to Simon and compare his account of that day with Patrick's, but that was never going to happen. George had phoned as I was on my way home, a farmer had found a body hanging in one of his barns. The first officer on scene had identified the man as Simon Cummings from the wallet in his jeans pocket. George had offered me the option to come with him to the crime scene or wait and look at the photographs later in the day. I told him I'd be with him as soon as I could.

Sonya and the forensics team were already there when we arrived, Simon's lifeless body was still attached to the rafters. I had taken deep breaths of fresh air before entering the barn in the hopes it would take the urge to vomit away. We stood in silent observation as he was carefully lowered onto a white sheet on the ground. George rocked backwards and forwards on the balls of his feet, waiting for Sonya to look over and indicate she was available to talk.

I saw Detective Constable Liz Collins, the newest member of George's team walking towards us, she looked at me disapprovingly, I smiled. I didn't care whether she liked me or not, but I did expect a little bit of respect.

'The farmer says he only comes out to this barn once or twice a week,' she looked at her notes, 'he said the last time he was in here was four days ago and obviously the deceased wasn't here then.' She turned her body slightly making it evident that she was only addressing George.

'How many ways can you get to this location?' George asked

'The main way is past the big farmhouse, but the farmer is pretty sure that no-one has been that way. There's an old farm track that hasn't been used in a long time, if you walk around to the back of the barn you can see it, there are some tyre tracks there that look fresh, only trouble is with the rain we've had this morning it's going to be difficult to get a good moulding from them.'

'Any sign of the vehicle?'

'None, but he could have got someone to give him a lift.'

George frowned at her.

She blushed and looked away. 'We'll keep looking for a car.'

'Any cameras on this stretch of the main road?'

'DS Hargreaves is checking, boss.'

'Okay let me know if you find anything interesting.'

Liz paused for a minute before walking towards her colleagues.

Sonya stood up and looked across. 'You want to come over?'

'How long has he been dead,' George asked before he'd come to a standstill.

'Best estimate, I'd say he died at some point in the last twelve hours. I'll need to wait till I get back to check the temperatures over night to be sure, but definitely within the last twenty-four hours.'

'Suicide?' He asked.

Sonya wrinkled her nose, 'not impossible I suppose but highly unlikely, there's significant fingernail markings around the ligature, which indicates that he was trying to get free. And if you put that together with the fact that the ladder we found on the ground underneath him, whilst tall enough, the wood looks rotten and I seriously doubt it would have withheld the weight of a grown man climbing up it. I'll send it away to get checked though to be certain. But my initial thoughts are murder made to look like suicide.'

'Thanks Sonya,' George said.

'No problem, good to see you two playing nice for a change,' she laughed.

'I'm a consultant for the police so I have to behave,' I replied

'You say consultant, I say apprentice slash pain in the arse.' George added.

'Whatever,' I replied. 'The question is what has happened in the couple of weeks since Sinead last saw her brother. Did you go to his apartment yet?'

'It was on my to do list but given everything else wasn't very high up it, that's changed now of course. We need to find his elusive partner in crime Patrick O'Brian as well, could be that they had some kind of disagreement that got out of hand.'

'About him, not so elusive as it turns out. I met with him this morning.'

George threw his hands in the air, 'Is there ever going to come a time Rowan when you trust me enough to involve me in these things?'

'I wasn't excluding you, it's just that he was really nervous about meeting up and has a strong dislike of police. I was always going to tell you about.'

'For fuck's sake Rowan, I thought we were working on this together. I've put my neck on the block bringing you in on this. There are plenty of senior officers who think it's a terrible idea, but I convinced them that collaborating with you would be worthwhile. That's why I brought you here.' He shook his head making me feel like I'd disappointed a favourite teacher. 'This has to stop. From now on it's a two-way street or I'm going to cut you off completely.'

Working with George was significantly better than working against him and I was grateful that he was including me in everything. 'I'm sorry. I made a bad call, you're used to working as part of a team, but I'm not and it doesn't come easily.'

'I know and I'm not saying I would've insisted I came with you to meet Patrick, but it would have been useful to know that he'd contacted you. Anything come out of it?'

I told him everything Patrick had told me and that I was planning on heading over to the pawn shop tomorrow.

'Okay and I'm going to send Amadeus over to the scrapyard, he can get a sample of the owner's handwriting and we'll see how it compares to this receipt he gave you.

'We also need to find out where Simon's been since he left his sister's house. And we need to see if there's anything that links him to Harmony's disappearance,' I said.

'It's feeling less likely now,' George replied.

'There has to be some connection though, don't you think it would be too much of a coincidence for them to be unrelated?'

'Based on everything you've said about Simon's apartment, it looks likely that he wasn't leading a squeaky clean life, these things have a way of catching up with you. I'm guessing that he managed to piss off the wrong person.'

'I would agree with you, but mostly when you piss of drug dealers and the like they want the world to know it was them that took you out, to make an example of you in case anyone else has any bright ideas to follow suit. We're looking for something different, whoever it was who did this wanted us to think it was suicide.'

'True, hopefully they left some trace of themselves behind for us. They were careless with the ladder, so perhaps they were careless with other things too.'

I looked around the farm and out into the field adjacent to the barn, 'this is a strange location to take someone to murder them, I mean how would you even know this was here? I know the farmer said he isn't out at this barn very often, but how would anyone else know that?'

George called Liz over, 'can you ask the farmer if he's noticed anyone hanging around over the last few weeks or if he's seen a vehicle he doesn't recognise. And make sure we don't just check the CCTV for the last couple of days, I want us to go back a couple of weeks and see if there's anyone who looks like they might be heading up near the farm on several occasions.'

She nodded, 'no problem.'

As she walked away I said, 'I'm not sure your newest recruit likes me very much.'

'She's ambitious and passionate about the job, I would imagine that she thinks I'm a bit nuts letting you be involved,' he smiled. 'She might be right.'

I left the scene promising to let George know the outcome of my visit with the pawn broker tomorrow. By the time I got home, Alana was already back from school sitting at the kitchen table studying. My stomach growled when I opened the fridge, I hadn't eaten since breakfast and my hunger plus my terrible night's sleep had left me feeling exhausted, so I was delighted to see a large container sitting on the shelf.

'You just missed Gran,' Alana said. 'She said to tell you she knows you're busy working on a case and she was worried we wouldn't have time to eat properly, so she's brought round a casserole. She said it should last us two days and to let her know if you need anything else dropping off. There's also a chocolate cake on the countertop. She left the instructions for re-heating as well.' Alana held up a folded piece of paper.

I took the paper from her hand and glanced over the instructions, 'seems straightforward enough. Can you pop it on to heat up, I could really do with catching the news?'

Alana glared at me and sighed, but she took back the instructions which I took as her agreement and headed into the office.

> **Reporter:** 'The body of Simon Cummings was found today in the Dunfermline area; Police say they are treating his death as suspicious.' The news reader began. 'We have Detective Chief Inspector George Johnston joining us.'

George appeared on another screen. He was standing outside the police station.

> **George:** 'Good evening.'
> **Reporter:** 'DCI Johnston, Simon Cummings was one of the men convicted of murdering local artist Tabitha Adams, is that right?'
> **George:** 'That's correct.'
> **Reporter:** 'We reported recently that Ms Adams' daughter Harmony has disappeared and that there are concerns for her safety, do you now suspect that this is linked to the murder of Simon Cummings?'

George: 'There is nothing to link the two matters at this time, but we are looking into every angle.'
Reporter: 'Do you think it's only a matter of time before you find Harmony Adams' body?'
George: 'We have evidence to indicate that she is still alive, and we are working on that basis and will continue to do so until we uncover something to the contrary.'
Reporter: 'What evidence do you have?'
George: 'I'm not able to share that with you at this time, but we'll update you when we can.'
Reporter: 'We've seen an increase in kidnappings in the last three years ,would you suggest that people need to be more careful leaving their homes now.'

The news reader was trying to goad him, and I hoped that he would retain his calm.

George: 'I would always recommend that everyone behaves in a way that keeps their personal safety at the forefront of their actions, however we do believe that this was a targeted abduction and therefore do not anticipate there being a heightened level of risk to the general public.'

The news reader thanked George and ended the interview.

Reporter: 'We've been lucky enough to talk to Harmony Adams' employer and it will be interesting to hear him shed a more personal light on the current situation.'

The screen that George had vacated was now filled by Stephen Kennedy, Harmony's former boss.

Reporter: 'You have worked with Harmony for a number of years, this must be very harrowing for you.'

Stephen used what I imagined was one of his stock responses.

Stephen: 'It's been extremely distressing for myself and her other colleagues. Harmony was a well liked member of our little family.'

A text pinged on my phone – it was Ellie:
'OMG are you watching the news right now, I could happily punch that little twat in the face. I bet he's not going to mention that he's sacked her for not coming into work.'
'I know, he looks so smarmy.' I typed.

Reporter: 'Would you say you know Ms Adams well?'
Stephen: 'We're a close-knit team and I would say that Harmony and I were good friends,' he paused looking at the camera, implying that there might be more to the relationship. 'I'm very worried about her, she is really missed.'

Ellie sent a vomiting emoji.

Reporter: 'Had she spoken to you about her mother's murder, that must have had a huge impact on her.'
Stephen: 'Like I said we were friends; she had a really difficult childhood. She didn't like to talk about it much.'

The news reader thanked Stephen and ended the interview.

Ellie sent another vomiting emoji followed by; 'I don't understand why they were talking to Stephen. Harmony hates him.'

I didn't reply, every time he talked about Harmony, he'd done it in the past tense. It could be a slip of the tongue or maybe he knew she was already dead.

Chapter Twenty-Eight

I had expected the pawn shop to be some seedy place filled with people's treasures, each with their own sad story. Instead it was a large, modern, well-lit shop with a foreign exchange booth in one corner, the staff wearing a uniform of a pale grey suit and a sky-blue shirt. I had called ahead and spoken to a woman named Diane who said she would arrange for the records to be available for my visit.

The door made an electronic beep-boop noise announcing my arrival. I walked to the counter and waited.

'Hello there how can I help today, are you thinking of buying or selling?' She smiled.

'Neither, my names Rowan McFarlane, I spoke to Diane earlier.'

'Oh yes, you're with the police, that's right she mentioned it. My name is Tina, I'm the deputy manager, we can go through to the back office to talk if that's okay.'

She unlocked the counter barrier to let me through, her eyes darting around until it was secured once more. She led me through to an office with a couple of desks and a large filing cabinet.

'Would you like a coffee; we've got one of those fancy pod machines.'

'Yes please, that would be lovely.' There was very little to see while I waited for Tina to make us coffee, the room was windowless, large strip lights illuminated the space in a glare of yellow light that I imagined would be migraine inducing if you had to work in here for too long.

'There we go,' she said popping a white mug with the store's logo printed on the side on the desk in front of me.

'Thanks. I mentioned to Diane that I was interested in one particular piece.'

'The spider necklace?' She opened the drawer in the desk, 'I printed everything out. The gentleman brought it in, he said he had inherited it from his grandmother but needed the cash.' She paused, taking a sip of coffee and reading some of the text on the paper. 'Looks like our in-store jewellery expert was in that day, it was him that put the value on it.'

'You gave Mr O'Brian £5,000 for it, is that right?'

'That's what it says on the receipt.'

'How long do you usually give people to come and buy their possessions back?

'30 days. Sometimes we offer extensions, but we didn't need to on this occasion, he came back with his sister just in time.'

'You charged her £7,000 to get the necklace back?'

'No, £5,800. It had fallen into a new interest charge period.' She looked at me before continuing. 'I know people think it's a lot, but we take all the risk, especially with jewellery. We could end up with a right dud and then we're out of pocket.'

'They paid cash?'

'Yes. Why did you think it was £7,000?'

'Mr O'Brian told me that's how much they were told it was. His sister was much closer to their grandmother and the necklace had a lot of sentimental value. Who served them?'

'It was Gary, our jewellery expert. There's a note on the file that says after closer inspection he thinks that it's worth nearer £15,000 and that he had a potential buyer to contact when the 30 days were up.'

'Can you tell me who the buyer was?'

'It just says M Radley and a telephone number, I can give you a copy of everything away with you if that would be useful?'

'That would be great, thanks. Had Mr O'Brian sold anything else to you recently?'

'Are you able to tell me what this is all about?'

'No, sorry.'

'It's just that the boss is worried about bad publicity, and she just wanted to make sure it's nothing to do with stolen goods.'

'Have you had problems with that before?'

'Not in this store, at least not since I've been here and that's nine years now, but last year in the Aberdeen store, two members of staff were sacked and one arrested because they took in stolen goods. One of them, the one that got arrested, knew but the others didn't follow protocol. It was in the papers and the big boss was raging. And now Diane, who you spoke to yesterday, is frantic that someone here is doing the same.'

'I can't go into detail, but I'm not investigating stolen property.' It wasn't a lie, and I had no idea if George would do any follow up on the store.

'Well at least that's something.'

'You were going to check if Mr O'Brian had sold anything else to you,' I reminded her.

'Oh yeah. I'll need to check the computer records for that.' She glugged down the rest of her coffee and wheeled herself in the chair towards the screen. She tapped and scrolled for a couple of minutes before coming out from behind the screen back to the edge of the desk. 'Three pairs of earrings, one with a small set diamond, one plain gold and the other with a blue stone which Gary had noted as sapphire but with a question mark, although that was over two years ago.'

'What happened to them?'

'All three pairs sold after the thirty days and all to different buyers, we paid out £900 on the lot, made £1,000 so not really very much in it for us on that occasion.'

'Do you have CCTV in the store?'

'Yes, but we don't keep it long enough to cover all the transactions.'

'Would you have the one where Mr O'Brian came in with his sister to buy the necklace?'

'Should do, I can get a copy for you if you like.' She didn't wait for my response before picking up the telephone and asking someone to make a copy and bring it through. We sat in silence for a few moments. 'Was there anything else you wanted to ask?' Tina said.

'No, I think that's everything.'

'Do you mind if we go back through then, it's just we're a bit short staffed today. Gary phoned in sick this morning, food poisoning from some dodgy prawn toast he says.'

'You don't believe him?'

'I shouldn't say this, but he often goes out on the lash on a work night and then calls in sick the next day. He's had more bouts of food poisoning than all the people I've ever known collectively.'

'I'm surprised you keep him on.'

'We've found it quite hard to get a decent jeweller, and his family are friends with the manager's family so he thinks he can get away with it and he's right, if any of the rest of us tried that we'd be out on our ear.'

I made a mental note to suggest to George that he should get someone to check into Gary. Even though he had a habit of calling in sick, it seemed too much of a coincidence that the day someone was coming to talk about the necklace he was not here. It was the downside to calling ahead yesterday, the upside was that I hadn't had to waste my time waiting whilst Tina located information for me.

Tina placed the flash drive with the copy of the CCTV into the poly pocket with the other documents and handed them to me. 'Thanks for all your help.' I put everything away in my bag and left.

I had missed two calls from Ellie and one from George. I called him first.

'You ignoring me again,' he said.

'Not this time, just finished at the pawn brokers.'

'How did you get on?'

'Good, they gave me a copy of the CCTV and I think their jeweller is a crook.'

'What do you mean?'

I gave him a brief overview of my conversation with Tina.

'I'll get someone to look into him.'

'Your turn, what were you calling for?'

'I've had a couple of officers trawling through the cameras on the A92. There's a white van that turns off in the direction of the farm and then comes back about an hour later. Plates were false though so that doesn't really move us any further forward.'

'What were the plates for?'

'A scrapped Ford Focus.'

'Have you checked where it was scrapped?'

'Yes, our not so friendly scrap merchant Ian Stewart. Amadeus went out to see him and he tried to make a run for it.'

'Did he find out much?'

'He finally admitted that he did sell the car to Patrick. Apparently he was paid by Mathew Radley to say that Patrick had wrecked the CCTV and stolen the car.'

'Interesting. Have you talked to Radley yet?'

'No, he's proving very difficult to locate at the moment.'

'And the van, who did he give that to?'

'He didn't see who took it, his instructions were to have a van fuelled up, keys in the glove box and it would be picked up. Then once it was returned it was to be crushed and disposed of ASAP.'

'Not much chance of getting any evidence from that then.'

'Sadly not, what are your plans for the rest of the day?'

'I'm going to see Ellie and then I thought I might pay the ex-husband, Martin Clarke, another visit.'

'I wouldn't be putting too much trust in what Patrick said, don't lose sight of the fact he was convicted of murder, and if I had a quid for every time a criminal had told me they were innocent I would have already retired.'

'Still think it's worth poking around a bit more.'

'Alright, call me when you're done if there's anything to report.'

Chapter Twenty-Nine

Ellie wasn't picking up when I called back, she had left me a voice mail which said. 'I hope everything is okay, I hope I didn't overstep the mark with my texts last night. Call me back when you get a chance.'

I left her a message saying everything was fine and that I'd got distracted, that was all and that I would be in the Sunshine Café for the next hour or two if she wanted to have a catch up.

A twenty-minute walk took me to the jingling door of the café where I was greeted by Star, who despite being one of the busiest people I'd ever met, never looked flustered or stressed. 'There's someone at your table, but I think they're nearly done.'

'Typical.' I knew it was ridiculous to expect it to be free every time I came here, but it's like your favourite spot in the car park, you're always a bit miffed when someone else is in it.

'You're looking a little weary,' she said. 'Are you making sure you're getting enough rest.'

'What do you think?' I smiled.

'I think the people at your table just left, I'll come and wipe it down for you.'

I was on my second cup of camomile tea when the jingle of the door announced the arrival of Ellie, although it wasn't so much the door I noticed, more her bright yellow coat. She waved enthusiastically at me.

'So sorry I didn't pick up earlier, I was at an audition and I left my phone in my bag.'

'Did you get the part?'

'No, too young to play Lady Macbeth apparently. Anyway, I'm sorry if I over stepped with my texts yesterday. I shouldn't let Stephen bother me like that but he's such a twat.'

'Honestly it was fine, I meant to reply but I got distracted.'

'By the case? Are you able to tell me what's been going on?'

'Honestly not sure I'm any closer to finding Harmony than I was at the beginning. There's plenty of information, but it's hard to see how it all fits together. I wanted to ask you about Stephen actually.'

'Why?'

'Him being on the news last night got me thinking, that's all. I know you don't like him, but Harmony had worked with him for a while, had they ever been close?'

'When she was married, Stephen and Martin became friendly, played golf together, that sort of thing. I think that it always rankled her that Stephen continued to stay in touch with him after. He'd say things to her about Martin having a new girlfriend or remodelling the kitchen in the house. He was trying to get a rise out of her.'

'Did she care about those things?'

'No, it wasn't that, it was more that it stopped her from being able to move on fully because he was always going on about Martin.'

'Why do you think he did that, do you think Martin put him up to it?'

'I don't know. Harmony was really unhappy in her marriage, but afterwards she didn't talk about it much. I think for Stephen it was a power play, he got promoted not long before I started there and everyone in the office thought it should have been Harmony. She was more competent, better at her job and even though she expected everyone to give their all and work super hard, everyone would rather that.'

'How come he got the promotion then?'

'Bad timing, Harmony was strong when she oversaw a team, she was a great leader, but Martin really held her back, didn't like the idea of her climbing the career ladder. There were a couple of times when she was late for work because Martin left the house before her and took both sets of house keys so she couldn't lock up, or her purse went missing only to magically turn up after she'd spent ages looking for it. '

'And all this started the same time that she was up for promotion?'

'I don't know if it only started then, but it was certainly worse then.'

'Did you ever ask Harmony about it?'

'Nope, she wasn't really into discussing the past, she wanted to focus on moving forward. I really think that one of the reasons she hired me in the first place was to annoy Stephen.'

'Have you ever seen Stephen lose his temper?'

'Umm, I've seen him get annoyed, get angry, but not totally lose it no. He's more of a snake, so if you piss him off and don't do what he says he likes to try and undermine you in the background, spread rumours or sabotage your career.'

'Have you ever been afraid of him?'

'No. He annoys me and makes my skin crawl, but I've never thought he might do me actual harm. Why, do you think he has something to do with Harmony's kidnapping?'

'I don't know, it's just yesterday on the news when he spoke about her, he used the past tense every time, 'we were friends' etc. It just struck me as odd that's all.'

Ellie put her hand over her mouth, 'Oh my god, I didn't notice. If he's hurt her then so help me, I'll kill him.'

I nearly laughed, the thought of Ellie actually murdering anyone was hard to imagine. 'I don't think that will be necessary and besides I'm not saying that he has anything to do with it, just that it was strange, that's all.'

Ellie checked her watch, 'better run, I'm helping out with an amdram production of Les Mis and between you and me they need all they help they can get.'

I could have happily sat in the café for the rest of the day, but I wanted to pay Martin another visit. He'd played the perfect part for me last time, the wounded but understanding ex-husband that wanted nothing more than to move on with his life.

I walked past his car in the driveway and hoped that it was a sign that he was home.

'Oh, it's you,' he said when he opened the door.

I smiled. 'Any chance I could come in? I have a few follow up questions.'

'I suppose.' He moved out of the way enough to let me into the house. 'The police came to my work,' he said turning to look at me, 'was that your idea?'

I glanced back to the front door, considering making an excuse to leave, I wasn't sure anything productive could come from a conversation with him in this mood.

'I asked you a question.'

'Your ex-wife is missing and we have reason to believe that she's in danger, so of course they came to see you. I would have thought you would've been happy to help.'

'I don't understand why they needed to come to my place of work, it was humiliating.'

I said nothing whilst we stood in awkward silence half-way along the hallway. He sighed and shook his head before continuing through to the kitchen. I followed.

'When we spoke last time, you said that you saw Harmony about a month ago, she was worried for your safety?'

'That was the cock and bull story she was peddling on that occasion, yes.' He took a bottle of whisky from the cupboard and poured himself a large measure without offering any to me. He took a large gulp. 'I get it, this is the point in the proceedings where everyone comes out of the woodwork to say what an angel she was, butter wouldn't melt in her mouth.'

'Are they wrong?'

He finished the whisky and poured another. 'She was a manipulating, evil bitch.'

'How so?'

'I'm happy to admit that I went out with her at first as a way to get noticed by Alistair. He seemed to be pleased that we were dating and I hoped our relationship would put me in a good position for promotion, but I actually fell for her in the end and by the time we got married I was pretty smitten.'

'I don't understand what you think she did wrong?'

'Let's just say if she was a product, I would have returned her as being not as advertised.'

It was a disgusting way to talk about the woman he had been married to, but I sensed that he was trying to be provocative.

'Are you saying you don't think your love was reciprocated?'

'She knew that I had a great career, that I was going to make it to the top. I have a good salary, she could've gone part time or not worked at all and done something worthwhile with her time.'

'But you knew Harmony had a career when you married her, why would you think things would change after you were married?'

'I told her I wanted a wife and children and when she said she didn't want children I assumed that she would come round, most of you do in the end don't you. You know when the old biological clock starts ticking.' He waved the hand with the almost empty whisky glass in the direction of my abdomen.

'There's nothing manipulative about telling you she doesn't want children, if that was a deal breaker and you stayed then that's on you, not her.'

'Shock. Bitches like you always stick together.'

'I see you've given up on the concerned ex-husband act, to be honest if this is how you behaved when you were married there's little wonder Harmony left you.'

'Who the fuck do you think you're talking too?' Martin replied.

'I know you think you're something special, but newsflash – you're not. You say you've got a good career, but I think you knew that Harmony was doing better than you, that's why you were so desperate to derail her promotion chances. I bet you and your little friend Stephen thought you were so clever.'

'I bet you're just jealous, I can't imagine any man would want to be with a miserable man hating bitch like you.'

I laughed, 'I'd rather be single than be with a pathetic excuse of a man like you.'

'You're just like her, if she'd only done as she was told, had a baby and stayed home where she belonged, we could've been happy.'

'You mean you would've been happy. I can't see how that was a good deal for Harmony.'

He shook his head, 'Fucking feminists, we're not equal. Your job is to stay home, have babies and take care of your man.'

'I bet when you first met Harmony you thought all your Incel dreams had come true.'

He took a step towards me, the smell of whisky heavy on his breath. 'I'm not one of those useless bastards who sits on the internet in their parent's basement complaining. If I want something I take it, I always get what I want.'

'But you didn't did you, Harmony left you, that must've bruised your fragile ego. Did it make you mad that she humiliated you like that?'

Martin lunged at me grabbing me by the throat, he laughed and squeezed, I thrust my knee hard into his groin. He let go of my neck and doubled over. I took the opportunity to head for the door.

'You whore, you'll pay for that,' he shouted as he dashed after me. I was halfway between the kitchen and the door when he caught me, taking hold of my wrist and pulling me round to face him. 'We are *not* done.'

'I think…'

He slapped me hard across the face, forcing my head round. I punched him in the gut, he stumbled backwards.

'Bitch.' He lifted his arm, fist clenched.

I tried to move but the punch caught me square in the mouth. I could taste the blood before I felt it. I punched him back but he moved with it and returned with a back hand across my cheek catching me just below my eye with his knuckle. I yelled out, he laughed.

'We're done when I say we're done.' His face was so close to mine that I felt tiny droplets of saliva land on my lips as he spoke.

I curled my lip in disgust. I thrust my fist upwards, the uppercut connecting with his jaw, throwing his head backwards, the clashing of his teeth together audible.

I was almost at the front door when Martin barrelled into me sending us both crashing to the floor through the open doorway into his cream carpeted living room.

'I said I wasn't finished,' he spat at me.

'How do you think this is going to end?' I asked. 'You think there's going to be no consequences for you attacking me?'

'I'll say you came on to me and that when I rejected you, you went berserk, started wrecking the place. I'll tell the police you had a weapon, and it was self-defence.'

I snorted a laugh. 'You think anyone will believe that?'

His face was purple, he'd loosened his grip on me, I pulled myself to my feet, pushing past him into the hallway. I felt his fingers on the fabric of my jeans. I flicked my foot away from his grasp kicking him hard in the face at the same time.

I ran down the driveway and into my car, locking the doors and sped off at a lot more than the twenty speed limit, not even stopping to put on my seatbelt.

Chapter Thirty

I pulled into a side street, parking under a streetlamp, searching through my bag for my phone.

There were seven missed calls from Alana and three voice mails, two from Alana, the other from Sonya. The first message from Alana was a simple 'hey I'm home, do you want me to make dinner'. The second was a more panicked 'Where are you mum, I'm getting really worried now.' Sonya's message was half in a whisper. 'I'm at your house, where the hell are you, Alana is freaking out, she says she can't get hold of you. I'm going to stay with her until I hear from you.' I would call her back, but first I needed to speak to George.

'To what do I owe the pleasure…' he began.

'I've just been attacked by Harmony's ex-husband, I'm fine, don't worry just a few cuts and bruises.'

'Are you somewhere safe now?'

'Yeah, I'm in my car. I don't think he followed me.'

'Okay I need you to go to the hospital and get checked over and I know you don't want to, but it will help me to deal with him properly, so go to the hospital and I'll send Amadeus over there to meet you, unless you would prefer a female officer?'

'Amadeus is fine, but do me a favour, don't call Alana, I'll let her know what's happening and Sonya is with her anyway.'

'Okay, I'll call you later.'

I phoned Sonya and briefly explained what had happened and then spoke to Alana, who began to cry despite insisting that she wasn't. Sonya agreed to stay with her until I got home.

Amadeus was waiting at the hospital when I arrived. 'Fancy meeting you here.' I said attempting a smile.

'You look like shit.'

'You're too kind. Right can we get this over with please because I'm tired and hungry and I want to get home to my daughter so she can see for herself that I'm okay.'

He led me through to a private room where a nurse was waiting. Half an hour of being poked, prodded and photographed and ten minutes of a doctor arguing with me about keeping me in for observation overnight and I was finally free to leave on the understanding that I didn't drive for at least the next twenty-four hours.

I slumped into the passenger seat of Amadeus' car, my back aching and my head still throbbing despite the two large pink high strength ibuprofen I had been fed during my consultation.

'Did you ever think that going into this man's house might not have been a wise idea?' Amadeus asked after a few moments of silence.

'Yeah, about thirty seconds after he closed the front door behind me. But what was I supposed to do?'

'Leave would've seemed like a reasonable response.'

'Is that what you do if you think a situation might get a bit lairy, just leave.'

'It's different for me?'

'Oh God please don't say because you're a professional.'

He laughed, 'I wouldn't dream of it, but I have a tracker in my car. The boss knows where I am at all times and more often than not there are two of us.'

Amadeus was right, I was annoyed with myself. I'd known something wasn't right as soon as he'd answered the door, it had been like talking to a different person. I should've made sure that George knew I was there, I should've been able to find my phone in half the time it had taken me. These were not mistakes I would make again.

The car stopped outside my house. 'Would you like me to come in with you?'

'No, you're alright. Best if I go in by myself otherwise Alana will think it's worse than it is.'

'The doctor said you shouldn't be alone this evening; I'd be happy to sleep in your spare room if you wanted some extra support.'

'Thanks but it's okay, I'll ask Sonya to stay.'

'Okay then.'

I pulled on the door handle opening it a crack. 'Thanks for the lift.'

'No problem, and Rowan do me a favour and try and not do any more damage to yourself, I'm just getting used to having you about.'

'I'll do my best.' I replied.

Amadeus stayed until I had shut and locked the front door behind me.

'Mum, are you okay?' Alana sped out of the kitchen towards me. 'Jesus Christ, you look awful. Who did this to you?'

I wrapped my arms around her in a huge hug. 'I'm okay. It looks worse than it is.'

'You have four paper stitches in your cheek and a fat lip,' she said releasing me from the hug and surveying my face.

'It's fine, tomorrow when the swelling goes down, you'll hardly be able to notice.'

'I was really worried about you.'

'I know, I'm sorry but honestly I'm okay and George has already arrested the person who did it so there's nothing to worry about now.'

'How would you feel if it was me that had come home looking like that and then told you not to worry,' she said

'I know it's shit when things like this happen, but we've always known that there would be times when I would come home looking like I'd been in a street fight. Jack did and we accepted that was part of his job.'

'Jack's dead though isn't he so I'm not sure you're helping your cause.' She folded her arms.

'I get that you were worried and I'm sorry that this scared you. I'll be more careful in the future, but this is the nature of my job. Sometimes I have to deal with nasty arseholes.'

She sighed. 'I hope the other person is at least as bruised as you are.'

'More or less.' Alana and I had been having a version of this conversation for the last three years. In the beginning I had offered to quit and find a normal job, but that wasn't what she wanted either.

'Are you hungry? Sonya and I had some of Gran's casserole, but we left enough for you too.'

'Thanks, you better not have eaten all the cake.'

It was late when Alana eventually relented and went to bed with Sonya's full assurance that she would wake her if I wasn't well in the night.

'Thank you for staying.' I said whilst watching Sonya make the camomile tea.

'You're welcome.' She handed me a mug.

'I hope you're not going to lecture me as well.'

'No, I think you've had enough of that for one day. I know it's late but the reason I came round originally was to tell you about the post-mortem on Simon Cummings, do you want to talk about it now or should we leave it for the morning?'

'Now would be good, what have you found out?'

'In addition to the marks on his neck which suggested that he was trying to free himself I also found a substance on his face and some fibres in his hair line, near his ears. I sent them away for analysis and it turns out it was duck-tape.'

'Someone had put tape over his mouth to stop him from shouting out?'

'That would be my guess. So, when the lab came back with that I went ahead and checked his wrists and ankles. Came back with the same thing on the wrists, nothing on the ankles, but when we checked his jeans, we found the same traces.'

'Is there any way of knowing how long he was bound up for?'

'The markings on his face and wrists were almost invisible making it unlikely that it was for any length of time, it's possible it was only for the purpose of transporting him to the barn.'

'Interesting.'

'That's not all, I had the tox screen come back this afternoon and there were significant traces of ketamine in his system.'

'The horse tranquilliser?

'Technically it's classed as an anaesthetic, legitimately used by vets, often for horses yes, but it's been used as a date rape drug as well.'

'Was Simon sexually assaulted?' I asked.

'No sign of that, in this case I would imagine his assailant used it to make him more manageable and less likely to fight back.'

Chapter Thirty-One

For the first time in weeks I woke up feeling rested. As soon as I moved though aches and pains flooded through me. I walked across to the full-length mirror and lifted my t-shirt to display my back, now purple and yellow with bruising from where it had collided with the floor. Despite what I had told Alana yesterday, my face did not look that much better than the previous evening, but at least the swelling around my eye had gone down. I poked at the wound with my finger, wincing slightly. It didn't look like it was too deep a cut, but I'd be lucky to get away without a scar.

I could hear Alana and Sonya chatting downstairs and the temptation to go back to bed was very real. Instead I took an uncomfortable shower, the water battering down on my bruises reminding me that no matter what I did today it would hurt.

'You look terrible,' Sonya said as I entered the kitchen.

'Thanks.'

'So much for it looking better today,' Alana mumbled.

'It does, look I can talk without my lip hurting.'

Alana glared at me.

'I know it looks pretty bad, but I've had worse,' I said before pouring myself a mug of coffee from the pre-made pot and sticking a couple of slices of bread in the toaster.

'Is that supposed to make me feel better?' Alana asked.

I walked past her kissing her on the top of her head before sitting at the table next to her. 'not at all. It sucks, but I'll be okay.'

Alana did not look impressed, 'what are you doing today?'

'I've got a couple of people I could do with catching up with, but other than that I promise I'll rest.'

'Don't forget you can't drive until tomorrow, doctor's orders,' Sonya added.

'I'm sure I'll be fine.'

'You don't know that. I can give you a lift into town and drop Alana at school as well on my way into work.' Sonya said.

'Fine.' I conceded.

I'd intended driving across to the gallery to talk to Nate and see if I could find out why Harmony had thought there was a chance that he was her father. I would've much preferred the option of dropping in on him unannounced, instead I would need to settle for a phone call or asking him to meet me and given the way we'd left things I wasn't looking forward to that conversation.

I was just about finished my second mug of coffee when there was a knock at the door.

'You look like shit,' Amadeus said when I opened the door.

'Don't sugar coat it will you. What can I do for you or were you just popping round to make sure I'd made it through the night?'

'I'm here to take you to DCI Johnston.'

'What does he want?'

'To talk to you about what happened yesterday, I'd imagine.'

'I could've come to him you know.'

'I'm guessing he didn't trust you not to get behind the wheel.'

I groaned. 'I would've got a lift with Sonya.'

'I'm sure you would.'

He followed me back through to the kitchen. 'Morning ladies, how's the patient been behaving?'

215

'What do you think?' Alana said rolling her eyes.

'I suspected as much,' he smiled.

Sonya left with Alana a couple of minutes later. I ate another piece of toast as Amadeus drank his coffee. 'We've had to let Martin Clarke out on bail, I didn't want to say in front of your daughter. He's not to make contact with you or come anywhere near you, so you've nothing to worry about.'

I attempted to raise my eyebrows but had to settle for a strange lopsided attempt that I hoped conveyed I wasn't scared of Martin Clarke.

'Not that you'd be worrying though, I'm sure. And we've got a witness, one of the neighbours said they saw him chase after you down the drive screaming obscenities, they also said that they had heard a lot of noise that sounded like a fight. Liz took her statement this morning.'

'Should I be expecting a lecture this morning?'

'Not for me to say, but the air was blue after you called yesterday,' he smiled.

I'd been thinking about feigning illness to get out of listening to George complain.

Amadeus looked at his watch, 'you ready to go?'

'Yep, wouldn't want to keep George waiting.' I laughed.

I sat back in the leather passenger seat in his car strangely content being chauffeured by him. 'Did you always want to join the police?'

'Not really, but my mother was a woman you didn't cross, and the options were; finish school and go to university, join the military or join the police. I'd had my fill of classroom learning and I had no desire to be going to war so that only left the police.'

'You must like it though, you've stayed long enough.'

'It's a good job, mostly I've worked with good people, and I like to think that I've made a difference.'

'Your mum must be proud of you.'

'So, so,' he chuckled. I'm one of five and I have a sister who's a lawyer, two brothers who took after our father and are in the Navy and a sister who's a nurse and they've all blessed her with at least one grandchild and married someone she approved of.'

'Doesn't she approve of your partner?'

'I don't have one, according to her I'm a lost cause.' He gave me a rueful smile. 'perhaps she's right.'

'You'll find someone when the time is right,' I said, instantly regretting it.

'Are you offering?' he laughed. 'I'm not that bothered, I have a good life and I can't complain.'

'Why did George want me to come in this morning? I gave my statement to you yesterday.' I asked desperately trying to change the subject.

'I think he also has some information on the post-mortem results on Simon Cummings you might be interested in.'

He pulled into the police station car park and then signed me into the building. As we walked up the stairs towards George's office, I remembered the first time I'd been here. For a moment a flood of memories filled my brain, reminding me that if Jimmy had got his way, I would have lost Alana and Jack within weeks of each other. Then I remembered the look on his face as he died, I had no regrets and the reputation it had given me had come in handy more than once.

This was also the first time I had seen George's new office, the old one had been barely more than a cupboard, but now he was a DCI it was much more spacious and even had a large window letting in plenty of natural light.

Amadeus wrapped his knuckle on the door, George looked up and waved me in. 'Try not to piss him off too much, will you, the rest of us have to work with him today.' Amadeus whispered and I tried not to laugh.

'Jesus Rowan…' George said.

'I know I look terrible, blah, blah, etc.' I said sitting down carefully in the chair on the opposite side of the desk.

'Does is it hurt?'

'A bit, not enough to stop me though.'

'If I'd have thought that he would have become aggressive I would never have agreed to you going to see him on your own.'

I frowned. 'You and I both know I would have gone anyway. What did he say when you brought him in?'

'Entitled little arsehole, honestly he was so blasé. When we arrived, he was icing his wounds and telling us he wanted to press charges against you. Wasn't quite so cocky when I cuffed him. Don't get your hopes up though, he has a squeaky-clean record, not even a speeding ticket to his name. With a good lawyer he'll probably get community service.'

'He seemed to be quite upset that you'd paid him a visit at work.'

'That's strange because he was fine with me when I was there.'

'You should take Liz with you next time you talk to him,' I said.

'You think he's got a problem with women?'

'I don't know, he was absolutely fine with me the first time I went to visit. I think it's interesting that he couldn't control his temper'

'He's not supposed to go anywhere near you, so if you see him please, and I can't stress this enough, don't try and deal with him yourself, just call me.'

'I'm assuming you didn't demand an audience with me to talk about Martin Clarke?'

'You've spoken to Sonya, no doubt?'

I nodded. 'She told me about the tape and the Ketamine.'

'Whoever killed Simon was meticulous and planned and that makes me believe that there's a lot more to his death than an unsettled disagreement.'

'What are you thinking?'

'Too soon to tell, but if Patrick O'Brian contacts you would you ask him if he would agree to meet with me.'

'You think Simon's death is linked to Tabitha Adams' murder,' I said.

'I'm not jumping to any conclusions.'

'Drugging him suggests that whoever killed him didn't want him to be able to fight back, you think that means that's because they weren't able to over-power him?'

'Or they were worried about being heard,' George said. 'What are your plans for the rest of the day?'

'I'm going to try to speak to Nate Wallace to see if I can find out why Harmony thought he might be her father.'

'Have you seen much of him since the incident at his gallery?'

'Nope,' I stood up to leave.

'Before you go, I think you need to know that when we were looking into Simon Cummings' background, we came across a link to a previous case.' George said. 'He was arrested in 1989 for possession and another lad was with him at the time of the arrest. It was Gordon Monteith.'

If he had lived, I would have eventually known Gordon as my uncle. Uncovering who had murdered him had led me to the people responsible for murdering Jack. 'I didn't see that when I looked into him.'

'No, you wouldn't have, he was only 13 at the time and it was just a caution.'

'Have you spoken to Harry Aitkens?' The former headteacher had been the brains behind a criminal gang that had dominated the local drugs and burglary scene for more than thirty years.

'Not yet, I'm going to take DS Hargreaves to visit him at Saughton to see if he's willing to shed any light on our dead man.'

'I doubt he'll be willing to help.'

'Maybe not but there's no harm in asking?'

'I'd like to go with you.'

'Not a chance.'

'Why not, you know he always got cocky around me.'

'There is no way in hell I'm going to be involved in you sitting in front of that man, especially with your face looking like that, it would give him way too much pleasure.'

'Fine, you can tell me all about it when you get back.'

'I'll let you know if he had anything of value to add.'

'Before I go, what about Patrick O'Brian, have you found any connection between him and Aitkens?' I asked, mentally crossing my fingers that there was no link.

'No, nothing that we could find.'

I couldn't say why I felt relieved, perhaps it was because I wanted to believe that he was innocent of Tabitha's murder and the friendship, as unlikely as it was, between him and Harmony was real.

Chapter Thirty-Two

There was a black BMW with heavily tinted windows parked in a side street when I arrived at Sunshine Café, it caught my attention because I was sure I had seen the same car outside Harmony's building a few days ago, the same day that Ellie had seen Patrick. Of course, it could be a coincidence, but I made a mental note of the registration number anyway.

Inside the café I sat at my usual table, took a deep breath and called Nate.

'Hi Rowan, it's so good to hear from you, I wasn't expecting you to call,' he said.

'I need to talk to you about the case.' I replied quickly, hoping to prevent him getting the wrong impression.

'Yeah, of course. I'm not in the gallery today but we can meet somewhere else.'

'I was hoping you'd be able to come through to Cuddieford.'

'That would be nice,' he said.

'I would come to you, it's just that I'm not able to drive for twenty-four hours.' I didn't want him to think that an invite to my home town was anything more than necessity.

'Why, what happened?'

'I banged my head, it's a precaution.'

'Are you okay?'

'I'm fine, when do you think you can be here by?'

'umm, give me forty-five minutes, where should we meet?'

'Sunshine Café, it's a little book shop café place, I'll send you the details.'

Billy made his way through the tables with a mug of camomile tea. His smile turned to a look of concern as he saw my face. He put the mug on the table and sat down opposite me.

'Hey Billy, how's things?'

'What happened to you?'

'I'm fine,'

'You not got mirrors in your house? What happened, who did this to you?'

I was, as always touched by the level of protectiveness Billy showed towards me, 'occupational hazard, that's all.'

'And the person responsible what's happening to them?'

'Arrested, bailed and has a restraining order to stay away from me.'

'Umph, bloody good a piece of paper will do for someone who behaves like this.'

'It's okay, I'm not in any danger, I promise I'll be careful from now on. Anyway change of subject please, how are you?'

'Good, yeah well mostly. Actually, there is something that's bothering me a bit.'

'Is Star alright?'

'She's fine, it's not…aw I don't know if you'll think I'm being paranoid.'

'What is it Billy?'

'I'm worried that someone's watching the place?'

I sat forward leaning over the table to hold his hand in mine, Billy had risked everything and turned his back on his whole family to start a new life and the fear that might come back to bite him was something he dealt with pretty well.

'It's just there's a black car parked outside in the alley way. It's been there every day for the last three days. They're watching the café, I'm sure of it.'

'The BMW, with the blacked-out windows?'

He nodded, 'you saw it?'

'Yeah, I noticed it. Why do you think someone would be watching you?'

'I don't know, I'm completely legit these days, most of the folk from my past are either in jail or trying to move on, not the sort who'd want to make waves, but still, it bothers me, you know?'

'I don't think you've got anything to worry about Billy, I really don't think this has got anything to do with your past, honestly.'

'You're probably right,' he said, his shoulders relaxed, he sat back in his chair. 'hold on, do you know who it is?' he asked, sitting back upright again.

'I saw it a couple of days ago and I think they might know that I come here a lot.'

'I thought you said you weren't in any danger?'

'I'm not, I think it's a scare tactic.'

'Still, you need to be careful.'

'We'll be fine.' I tapped him on the hand, 'haven't you got customers to serve?' I smiled.

'Yeah, alright. But if you need me…'

'I know,' I replied.

After Billy had left the table I text the registration number to George, not that I expected anything to come back. They were probably false plates. I was on my second mug of camomile tea when Nate arrived. He looked good, black t-shirt, jeans and leather jacket and for a moment I remembered how I'd felt the first time we'd met. I shook it off when the smile on his face fell to an expression of horror when he saw my bruises.

'It's nice to see you again,' he said, 'I wish it was under different circumstances though. I take it you're no closer to finding Harmony?'

I could see his eyes darting over my face, he must have been desperate to mention my injuries, and I appreciated the effort of not doing so.

'We've gathered quite a lot of information, but nothing that can tell us where she is.'

'It's been such a long time now. I'm beginning to wonder if she's dead.' He looked at his hands and fiddled with a loose bit of skin next to his thumb nail.

I wanted to tell him that I had seen proof of life, that Harmony was alive. Instead, I said. 'It doesn't help to think like that. I'm sure we're going to find her alive.'

'I hope you're right,' he paused. 'What happened to your face?'

I appreciated the fact that he'd tried to make it sound like a passing enquiry but his facial expression betrayed him.'

'Someone hit it.'

'Oh my god,' the words were out of his mouth before he had a chance to consider their impact.

'It's really not that big of a deal.'

He opened his mouth to speak but thought better of it. We sat in silence for a couple of awkward moments before he said. 'I genuinely didn't mean to offend you the other day…'

I held up my hand to cut him off, this conversation hadn't been fun over the phone, and I was in no hurry to have a repeat performance. 'let's just drop it shall we.' I said trying to sound neutral.

'I will I promise, but I wanted to tell you, it wasn't that I didn't think you were capable. I know you are, it's just you're not like anyone else I've ever met, and with everything else that was going on I said something stupid, and I regret it, I really do. And it's hard to accept that someone you care about deliberately does something that puts them in harm's way. And I don't know if after this case is over, we might be able to put this behind us and be friends or not, but I wanted you to know that I realise that I was being a dickhead.'

'I appreciate you saying that, let's just leave it there, okay.' I wanted to say that if Alana could deal with it then there was no reason why he shouldn't be able to. But that would have taken this conversation in an entirely different direction, and I may never find out the information I need.

He smiled, 'Okay how can I help you?'

'Is there a reason that Harmony thought that you might be her biological father?'

His jaw dropped, and he looked at me in silence for a couple of moments before closing his mouth. 'What? Why would you ask that? What the hell, I don't understand.'

'When Harmony came to visit you at the gallery, did you cut yourself?'

'Yeah, the glass I was drinking from broke. Can we slow down a bit, why would she think that?'

'That's what I was hoping you could tell me, because after that visit she took your blood on a napkin to a forensics lab in Dundee and had them run a paternity test against her DNA.'

'But why?' He asked.

'Don't you want to know the result?'

'I don't need you to tell me, I know it will have been negative on the grounds that I never had that kind of relationship with Tabitha.'

'Then what would make Harmony think it was worth checking out then?'

'I don't know. Honestly, I'm racking my brain trying to think what would even have made her think that. Um, I told her that I was very close with Tabitha, that we had a lot in common and that living with her family saved me. I don't know, it was much the same as the conversation we had when you came to ask about her.'

I thought back, perhaps it was hearing someone talk about her mother with that level of fondness that had made Harmony make that stretch. 'You can't think of anything that would give the impression that you and Tabitha were more than friends.'

'I loved Tabitha for sure, but not like that. She was my sister as far as I was concerned and a good friend, but nothing else. I swear.'

'Okay.' I said, it felt like he was telling the truth, that, and the fact he wasn't Harmony's father meant there was no evidence to suggest that his relationship with Tabitha had been anything other than the one he described. 'Do you think there's a chance that Tabitha was having an affair when she got pregnant with Harmony?'

'It was such a long time ago and honestly I think if she'd have been having an affair then she would have left Alistair, especially after she got pregnant. She might have realised later that marrying him was a mistake but when Harmony was conceived, they were in love.'

'Did she have any other friends that she was close to that she might have confided in?'

'Not that I remember, there were artists coming and going at her mum's place, it's possible that she might've kept in touch with someone from those days, but if she did, she didn't include me.'

'Thanks for coming through, sorry to drag you away from your day off.'

'It was good to hear from you, call anytime, I'm always happy to help.' He stood up and put his jacket back on, then he paused. 'Did you actually think I'd had a relationship with Tabitha?' He pushed the chair in and leant both his hands on it.

'I don't know, I hardly know you and frankly in this job it's generally best not to make assumptions.'

'Fair enough,' Nate said, although he was giving me wounded puppy eyes. 'By the way, I almost forgot. I had a request to buy one of Tabitha's original paintings yesterday. I'm not sure if that's important? You sometimes get collectors who get interested if they discover an artist's name is going to be back in the news, for whatever reason. I think they think the value will increase and sometimes it does.'

I took a deep breath, 'it is important, did they leave a name?'

'They said they were enquiring on behalf of Harold Aitkens.'

Chapter Thirty-Three

Nate stayed for a few minutes attempting to chat to me about art and the gallery. Under other circumstances perhaps I would've been interested, but right now all I could think of was phoning George and telling him about Harry Aitkens' proposed art purchase. Eventually Nate made his excuses, kissing me on the cheek before leaving.

Billy brought me a refill of my tea and I could tell he wanted to ask about my relationship with Nate and I was more than relieved when he didn't. I would have liked to have been at Saughton this morning to see what Aitkens had to say for himself, but as George had refused to let me go with him I would need to be satisfied with hearing a retelling of the conversation.

I called George twice, no answer and on the third occasion left a voice message to tell him I had some information for him, hoping that if nothing else, nosiness would force him to call me back. I stayed another hour at Sunshine Café and when I hadn't had a return call, I took a taxi back home.

I would never have admitted it to anyone but the bruises I had sustained at the hands of Martin Clarke were painful and I was weary. When the taxi dropped me off, I was glad to be back home, to take off my jacket and my shoes and lie down on the sofa.

I don't remember closing my eyes, but I must have because I was woken by Alana returning home from school.

'How did you get home?'

'Taxi.' I yawned.

'Have you slept all afternoon?'

'It would appear that way, is there enough of gran's casserole left to do us for tonight's dinner?'

'Probably, I'll go and heat it up, will I?' She didn't wait for my response before walking out of the living room.

I checked my phone, a missed call from George, no voice mail but a single text.

> I hope you're at home resting. Can't catch up today so unless your information is the whereabouts of Harmony or something as equally earth shattering, I'll meet you at the motorway café I like tomorrow 10am. G

I replied with a very quick 'ok' before following my nose to the kitchen where Alana was busy stirring the pot of casserole.

The next morning the swelling on my face had reduced some more but the yellowing of the bruising made it look like it was spread over a larger part of my face. Even if I was the make-up wearing kind there was no amount of foundation that would cover this up. Still, I was grateful for not being in as much pain today and I was glad that I could at least drive myself places.

I arrived first, no surprise there. Despite George being considerably more organised than me in many ways, his time keeping was atrocious. He would blame the job, we would both laugh, and I imagined we'd have this conversation on repeat for the rest of our working days. It wasn't the nicest looking café with its plastic seats and tables giving it a soulless feel, I was much more at home in Sunshine Café, George maintained that he chose the place because of their quality bacon and egg rolls but I strongly suspected that even though there was no need for cloak and dagger on this case he was still uncomfortable about being seen with me too regularly.

George was only ten minutes late and it wasn't long after that we were tucking into our food. 'How was it yesterday?' I asked.

'Okay.'

'How's Harry finding prison?'

'He looks older, but he was still the same smug, pompous bastard he's always been.' He wiped his mouth with the paper napkin before drinking his coffee. 'Then he asked about you and Alana.'

'Did he tell you anything useful?' I knew Harry would have enjoyed the attention of the visit yesterday.

'Eventually. He admitted that he knew Simon, but claimed not to remember the murder of Tabitha Adams. He said Simon was a good worker, but that he was young and greedy. Apparently, he caught him trying to skim off the top. He was inflating prices to his clients and keeping the extra for himself. He got found out and was 'taught a lesson' which I took to mean he was given a kicking by Jimmy and co.'

'Breaking into the house wasn't on his orders then?'

'He says not. Also, there is nothing that connects Patrick to him at all and I doubt he would sanction anything that involved someone he couldn't control.'

'So, no further forward?'

'Not really, what was it that you wanted to tell me about?'

I told him about Nate's enquiry.

'I suspect that Harold Aitkens has nothing to do with any of this, you wouldn't have to Google very hard to find the connection between him and you and it's quite clear that someone is trying to scare you off this case and they probably think dropping his name into the proceedings is a good way of doing that.'

I wanted to believe George. It was unlikely that Harry was involved, but he'd also orchestrated hundreds of burglaries, and managed the whole area's drug distribution whilst being a respected maths teacher and then head teacher. I'd learnt the hard way not to underestimate him. I wasn't prepared to write this off as quickly as George.

'I'll contact your friend Nate today and get the telephone number of the person that made the enquiry, then we'll trace who actually made the call.'

'Okay, it'll probably just be a burner phone though I would imagine.'

'Listen, there is one other thing I need to tell you and before I do, please don't lose it okay.'

I frowned, 'I can't make any promises, what is it?'

'Harold Aitken has just hired Mathew Radley to handle an appeal...'

'What?' I interrupted him. 'There's surely no way that a judge would consider an appeal, there's evidence of him talking about killing Gordon Monteith and…'

George interrupted, 'woah, breathe for a minute, remember the part where I told you not to freak out. It's not an appeal to say he's innocent, there's no danger that would be going anywhere, this is because he feels that his sentence is too harsh. I imagine he's going to play the frail old man card and see if he can either be moved to somewhere a bit nicer or have his sentenced reduced so that there's a chance he can get out before he dies.'

'Any chance he'll be successful?'

'Who knows, but I'd like to think not. This...,' he waved his hands at me, 'is why I couldn't let you come yesterday. I mean I get it, it's totally understandable, he gets under your skin with everything he put you through, but you need to remember that's what he wants.'

'Matthew Radley wasn't his lawyer when he went to trial, why change now?'

'I asked him that, and he said that he came highly recommended.'

'You need to find out where Martin Clarke plays golf.'

'You think, it's him that recommend the lawyer to Aitken?'

'It's just a hunch, that's all. I'd ask him myself, but under the circumstances,' I pointed at my face, 'probably not the best idea.'

'No, leave him to me.'

My phone buzzed. I didn't recognise the number, but I answered anyway.

At first all I could her was a woman crying, my heart raced as I tried to figure out if it could be Harmony.

'I'm sorry to bother you, this is Fiona, I'm...' there was another loud sob.

'Alistair Lockland's PA,' I finished her sentence for her, 'are you okay?'

'It's Alistair, he's just collapsed at work. I phoned an ambulance and they're taking him to the hospital.'

'What do you mean he collapsed? Has he had a heart attack?'

'No, at least I don't think so. I think someone is trying to kill him.' Her voice was shrill.

'Have you phoned the police?'

'No, I don't want to speak to them, I only want to talk to you.'

'Alright, where are you now?'

'I'm still in the office, they wouldn't let me go in the ambulance with him because I'm not family.'

'Okay meet me in the library café in,' I paused to look at my watch. 'forty minutes?'

'Please don't tell anyone.'

'I won't.' I said looking awkwardly across the table at a very confused George.

I hung up. 'I've got to go. Alistair Lockland has just been taken into hospital.'

'They're not going to let you in to see him,' George said.

'I'm not going to see him, that was his PA, Fiona and she was very insistent that I don't involve the police, so you're going to have to trust me to handle this by myself.'

'Alright, phone me when you've finished your meeting with her. I'm going to get Liz to head up to the hospital and see what she can find out.'

'If you do that Fiona is going to know that I told you.'

'We'll be subtle, I promise.'

I sighed, 'I don't suppose I can stop you,' I said as I got up to leave.

As I drove back towards town, the possibility that Fiona was being used as a distraction to stop me visiting Alistair did occur to me, but if she hadn't phoned, I wouldn't know he was in the hospital. She had been more upset than I imagine most people are if their boss is taken ill, which served as further evidence that she was fonder of him than she was prepared to admit.

Fiona was already sat at a table, her hands clasped around a steaming mug. I could see her bloodshot eyes from across the room and her face looked pale, despite her make up. I waved to let her know I'd seen her before getting myself a coffee and settling down opposite her.

'Thank you for coming,' she said

'That's okay, are you alright?'

'I'm sorry for crying so much on the phone, it was the shock you know,' a half smile fleeting across her face.

'What happened?'

'I was working, and Alistair was in his office as usual and then I heard a crash and I looked up and I could see him on the floor, so I rushed in. His face had gone a weird colour and he was clutching his stomach. He was in so much pain he could barely talk. I phoned for an ambulance right away.'

'What had he been doing before he collapsed?'

'He'd been on a business call.'

'What about earlier in the day? Anything unusual happen or how about something that wasn't scheduled in?'

She blushed, 'We were meant to be having lunch together at the Long Mill Hotel. I know what you're thinking, but it wasn't like that.'

'What is it like?'

'I like him, and I know it's wrong, but if he wasn't with Karen or,' she paused and took a sip of her coffee. 'Or if he'd have been willing then I would have.'

'Had an affair?' I asked.

'Yes, he's nice and funny and he makes me feel special.'

'But he doesn't feel the same way about you?'

'The thing is I think he does, and I suppose I should be impressed that he doesn't want to cheat. Have you met his wife?'

I nodded.

'Then you'll understand what I mean. I hear them on the phone sometimes arguing and it's nearly always because she's bought something ridiculous.'

'If he's not happy and he'd like to be with you, why do you think he doesn't leave Karen?'

'I asked him once and he said it was complicated, but he wouldn't say any more than that.'

'You said that you were meant to be having lunch with him?'

'Yeah, and then *she* appears around half an hour before hand, says that the hotel called the house number to confirm the booking and she was just so thrilled that Alistair had planned a nice romantic lunch for them. He could hardly say that he was meant to be going with me, so he went along with it. The thing is I was the one who made the reservation and the only telephone number I gave was my desk phone, so there's no way the restaurant called the house.'

'And how was he when he came back?'

'Distracted, barely said two words to me and went through into his office and shut the door. About half an hour later he buzzed through and asked if I could get him a coffee. I took it through to him and he was full of apologies about lunch.' She looked at me and chewed her bottom lip. 'Then he told me that as of next week I would be the PA to the finance director. I told him that I didn't understand, and he said it was because he cared for me so deeply and that he didn't know how else to keep me safe.'

'Safe from what?'

'That's what I asked and all he would say is that he was the one that had to pay for the mistakes of the past and that he wished things were different. Then he held my hand and said if I knew what he'd done I would want to be as far away from him as possible. After that he clammed up and the next time I saw him was in the office when he collapsed.'

'Did he say anything while you were waiting on the ambulance to arrive?'

'No, he just held my hand. He was in so much pain, he looked really scared. Do you think he's going to be alright?'

'I'm sure he'll be fine. His daughter is missing, the investigation into his first wife's murder is being brought up again, it's probably stress, maybe he has an ulcer or something,' I said hoping that she would be comforted, then finally I asked the question that had been bugging me since she phoned. 'Fiona, why did you call me?'

'Because after your first visit Alistair said if anything happened to him, I was to call you.' She frowned. 'I assumed he had some sort of arrangement with you.'

Chapter Thirty-Four

After some gentle persuasion Fiona had agreed to let me have a look around Alistair's office when everyone had gone home for the evening. The large space felt eerie now that it was empty. Through one of the glass walls there was a clear view of most of the seating area, the other separated him from Fiona but they would never have been out of one another's sight.

'Has his office always been like this?' I asked wondering if this modern set up had been in place twenty-five years ago when he began his affair with Karen.

'No, it was changed about ten years ago. Before that Alistair's office was in the corner of the room and he was completely closed off, not that it would have made much difference because the office floor was divided into pods and there were a row of offices along the other side of the floor where all the managers worked.'

'Hmm, does he like being on view to everyone like this?'

'I think he likes to be able to see what's going on and he has black out blinds if he's having a meeting and wants privacy.'

I opened his laptop, and the company screen saver came to life, the box in the middle demanding his password before I could proceed. 'Do you know it?' She leaned across me obscuring my vision and tapped at the keys quickly.

'What are you looking for?' She asked.

'I'm not sure yet, let's start with his calendar.'

She clicked a button and the screen filled with dates. 'Do you see every appointment he makes?' I asked.

'The only ones I can't see are the ones he sets to private. He hardly ever does that but there has been a couple recently. I did ask him about them, but he said it was something personal he was dealing with and not to worry.'

As I scrolled through the dates and meetings marked with little more than times and initials Fiona gave me a running commentary of each engagement. Then one caught my eye. MC 4pm. 'Who's MC?' I asked.

'Um, I don't know. That one is marked private so it wouldn't have come up on my diary. He left early that day, said he had some errands to run.'

It was the same date that Martin Clarke had attacked me and that can't have been a coincidence. 'Do you know Alistair's ex-son in law?'

'Is that who you think MC is?'

'Do you think that's possible? Did they keep in touch?'

'For a little while after Harmony left, I think Alistair was hoping they'd get back together.'

'Was he annoyed with her for leaving Martin?'

Fiona narrowed her eyes, 'I'm not sure he was annoyed, more frustrated. He was agitated for ages afterwards, especially as she wasn't returning his calls, and no one would even tell him where she was living.'

'To your knowledge did she ever get in contact with him?'

'Not as far as I'm aware. I felt sad for him, but I'm not naïve, I know that family relationships are complicated, and things can't have been easy for her growing up without her mum around. He tried writing to her, but the letters came back not known at this address.'

'I'm sorry I thought you said a moment ago that he didn't know where she was living.'

'He didn't until Martin turned up and said he'd found out.'

'Do you know how Martin knew?'

'Alistair said that Harmony worked with a friend of Martin's and he'd done him a favour by taking it from her HR file.'

'You don't know this friend's name at all do you?' I asked although I would bet money on it being Stephen.

She shook her head, 'no, sorry.'

'Would you say Alistair and Martin were close before the separation?'

'I think Martin thought they were, he used to work here and then not long before the wedding he got a job with another firm. I think Alistair was relieved because Martin used to wander in here like he was second in command, and it drove everyone crazy.'

'Does Alistair play golf?'

'When he has to, if he's trying to win over a client, that kind of thing but he prefers tennis. Why do you ask?'

'Just curious.'

I clicked on different folders on his laptop while Fiona gave me an overview of all the projects he was working on, but there was nothing there that looked at all suspicious. His desk drawers were unlocked and contained very little other than stationery and a very nice Montblanc pen set that looked like it rarely left its box.

'Thanks for staying back and helping me,' I said standing up from the desk and walking towards the office door.

'That's okay, I'm sorry it was a bit of a waste of your time.'

'Not at all.' I said, although I had been hoping for more of a clue as to why he'd requested she contact me if anything happened to him, but there had been no handy envelope with my name on it taped to the underside of his desk, so I had to assume that he believed me capable of doing my job well and finding out the truth of what happened to him.

'Do you still have the coffee mug he drank from today?'

'No, someone from the police came to pick it up this afternoon, they took the coffee machine and the pods as well, but it can't have been what made him ill.'

'How can you be so sure?'

'Because he hated that pod coffee, he called it 'poncey expensive dishwater' I keep a jar of Gold Blend in my desk. I tried to tell them when they were taking it away, but I don't think the man was listening to me. Also, I drank the same coffee and I'm fine.'

'Who else knows about the coffee switch?'

'Just me I think, it was our inside joke. Karen wanted to get the machine, she said it's what people expect these days. Before that we had a vending machine where we all got our coffee. Karen said that was fine for the 'worker bees' but when entertaining clients you have to do better. I don't like her, but I think she was right about this.'

'Where do you get the hot water for your Gold Blend?'

'You can set the machine to give hot water only and I use that.'

'I'll need to take the coffee with me.' I took an evidence bag out and held it open whilst she placed the half empty jar inside.

I called George from my car before heading home.

'Any news on Alistair?'

'We won't know until we get the results of some more tests, probably tomorrow morning. We're looking into the restaurant, and we took the coffee machine from his office, we'll see if that turns up anything.'

'Would help if you'd taken the right coffee.' I replied.

'We took the whole machine and all the pods.' George said.

'But Alistair didn't drink that coffee, he preferred Gold Blend. Fiona told me and she said she tried to tell whoever you sent over as well.'

'Fucking hell. If you want something doing right. I'll get someone to pick it up tomorrow.'

'No need, I've got it,' I heard him tut in the background, but I continued speaking. 'Also, I think that he had a meeting with Martin a few days ago, the same day that he attacked me, it would be interesting to know what that was about.'

'Okay I'll look into it. Where are you just now?' He asked.

'I'm in the car park outside Alistair's office. You want me to swing by the station and hand in the coffee?'

'Yeah, Liz should be there, can you give it to her. I'll call her now to give her the heads up that you're on your way.'

DC Liz Collins was not my biggest fan, if our previous interactions were anything to go by. She was waiting at the reception desk when I arrived. I wasn't surprised that she had no intention of buzzing me through and taking me up to the office. Instead, we were in an interview room where she was silently filling in the first of the three forms apparently required to accept the jar of coffee from me.

'Read this, then sign and date here please,' she said.

'Have I done something specific to piss you off or do you just not like me being involved in the case?' I asked.

Her pen froze a centimetre from the page, and she took a moment before she looked up to face me. 'I'm surprised anyone has the time of day for you around here,' she replied before going back to the form.

I leant back in the chair, 'is that because I managed to find Sally Mitchell when they'd all failed?' I asked, even though I knew it wasn't that.

Liz snorted, but didn't look up.

'Okay, so this about all of your lot who turned out to be on the payroll for Jimmy Murray and Harry Aitkens. I would have thought that you'd be pleased to see the back of people like that.'

She slammed her pen on the desk. 'Do you have any idea how much work you caused? How many appeals were put in after that? Criminals who got out earlier than they should've because the wrong officer arrested them?'

'I'm so fucking sorry that I expected the people responsible for murdering my dad to be held accountable.' I replied.

'I thought he was your uncle.' She frowned.

'Well turns out that he was my father, a fact that had to be hidden to keep Jimmy and co from murdering a baby. So, you'll excuse me if I'm not losing any sleep over the trouble it caused the force.'

'Yeah, well, you're a civilian so you shouldn't be involved in anything. There's a pool going around that you're sleeping with the boss and that's why you get an all-access pass,' she smirked.

I stood up, lifting the jar of coffee off the desk. 'Fuck you, Liz. I don't know how you made detective because you're absolutely shite at detecting.'

She put her hand out to try and take the jar from me. 'You can't take that.'

'Watch me.'

'But the boss will expect it to be sent away tonight.'

'Well have fun telling him why it's not then.' I took the short walk to the door, pausing with my hand on the doorknob and then opened the door. I was pleased to be outside in the cool evening air. I walked briskly to my car throwing the jar of coffee and my handbag on the passenger seat before locking myself inside. I could feel my hands shaking. I hit the steering wheel twice hard with my palms before giving into the tears that were part anger, part grief.

My phone rang, I'd intended to ignore it but it was Alana. 'Hey.' I said trying to ensure that she couldn't tell I was upset.

'Hey, where are you? I was starting to get worried.'

'Sorry sweetheart, I had to drop something off at the police station, but I'm on my way now.'

I dried my face and blew my nose, then opened the window fully so that I could blast myself with cold air as I drove home.

I put the coffee into the safe in my office as soon as I was home, Alana was in one of her more talkative moods and I was happy to listen to her chat about the books that she was reading and her excitement of going to university.

I checked my phone before heading to bed, two missed calls from George and a text that said, 'what happened at the station?'. I considered replying but decided that I didn't want to relive the conversation right now. I would catch up with him tomorrow.

Chapter Thirty-Five

I had ignored two further calls from George before I headed into the shower and one more as I buttered my toast. Part of me knew I was being petty but I'd let my interaction with DC Liz Collins last night get under my skin. It had brought emotions simmering to the top that I thought I had under check. It shouldn't have come as a shock when George was hammering on my front door ten minutes later. Luckily Alana had already left for school and wasn't around to hear us.

I opened the door. 'What do you want?'

'Come on Rowan, I thought we were past this.' George replied.

'Me too.'

'What happened at the station yesterday?'

'Why don't you ask Detective Constable Collins?'

He sighed, 'you really want to have this conversation on your doorstep?'

'Can't say it bothers me.'

'Don't be like this. I thought we were friends.'

'Me too, but apparently your colleagues think there's more to it than that.'

'I wouldn't have thought you'd have been bothered by some stupid rumour.'

He was right of course, I didn't care if people thought that we were sleeping together, if that had been all Liz had said I would have laughed in her face and carried on with my evening. 'You want a coffee?' I asked.

'You're letting me in now, are you?'

'Up to you, you can stay there if you like,' I said as I turned away from the door and headed towards the kitchen.

George took a large gulp of his coffee then looked into the mug as though he wished it was something stronger. 'Are you honestly telling me that you threw a fit because you found out about a rumour?'

'It's a pool actually. And I didn't 'throw a fit',' I replied.

'Liz said that she was filling in the forms and you weren't happy that she'd taken you into an interview room and that you took the evidence away in a huff.'

'And you thought that sounded plausible?'

'No, I didn't. And I know it's a pool, I've got 50 quid on us not sleeping together. I'm hoping to use my winnings to take Mel out for a nice meal.'

I couldn't help but smile.

'I was worried when you didn't answer my calls, it's not like you so I knew something else must have happened.'

'According to your DC, I'm persona non grata at the station because I had the audacity to prove that some of her colleagues were bent.'

His mug was almost at his mouth, he paused before putting it back down without taking a drink. 'It's complicated, obviously no-one likes to find out that their colleagues were on the take, and it had some knock-on effects, but I don't believe they blame you for that.'

'Look I get it. It takes a lot of work to take a case to trial and this revelation meant that some people had grounds for appeal, but you know what, Jack was murdered and Alana could've been too, I have absolutely zero regrets. And honestly if that's how everyone at the station feels then that's their problem not mine and I don't plan to change anything I'm doing, but if she ever speaks to me like that again I will knock her off her feet.'

'I'll have a word.'

'Just keep her away from me.' I said placing our mugs in the sink before heading to the office to collect the jar of coffee. I handed it to George.

'Thanks, what are your plans for the day?'

There was part of me that wanted to tell him to mind his own business and that I regretted involving the police in what had been my investigation. Yesterday I had been taken back to those dark memories where I felt that George was anything but a friend, that he was out to tar Jack's name and had very little interest in catching those responsible for his death. A lot changed during that investigation and over the last couple of years I'd come to trust George at least, even if my feelings towards the police overall were still complicated.

I'd been surprised by how raw my emotions still were and sitting in my car yesterday crying had reminded me that I'd not set aside time to properly grieve, preferring instead to bottle up my feelings to be dealt with another day.

The last couple of years had taught me other things, like having friends was actually quite nice and that the relationship George and I had forged was valuable in a lot of ways. 'I'm going to go and see Stephen Kennedy, Fiona said that someone Harmony worked with had given Martin her new address and he's the only person I can think of.'

'What about Ellie?'

'I doubt it, she was Harmony's friend…' I trailed off; he was right that I needed to think about where my opinion of Stephen came from. It had been Ellie that had told me he was a horrible boss that didn't care about Harmony, that his career had benefitted from the breakup of her marriage. 'You're right it's worth looking into both of them.'

'Did that hurt, admitting I was right' George laughed

I stuck my tongue out and we both laughed, then just like that, the anger that had been sat like a tight knot in my gut dissipated and things felt normal again.

'You'll let me know if you find out why Alistair was meeting with Martin?'

George nodded.

'And if there's any update on Alistair.'

'Of course. You never did tell me why his PA phoned you though.'

'Her boss' orders apparently. If you could sort me out a visit with him that would be great.'

'Interesting, have to see what the doctors are saying about his condition first.'

After George left I made myself another mug of coffee and ate a bag of mini eggs, they'd been in the shops since New Year, but it always felt wrong eating them before March. I made some notes as I sucked on a mini egg, feeling the sugar-coating crack and release the sweet milk chocolate. I had two columns; the first marked up 'Stephen' and the second 'Ellie'.

George had got me thinking, Ellie has seemed so genuinely concerned for Harmony that I hadn't given her proper consideration as a potential suspect. I didn't like thinking that I could have been so wholly taken in by someone, but better late than never.

Stephen had spoked about Harmony in the past tense throughout his TV interview, but he had professed to being her friend on more than one occasion. I'd written it off as all for television at the time, but there was a chance that they had been friends. Ellie had been keen to paint Stephen as the villain and her the concerned best friend and it was more than possible that she had exaggerated how bad Stephen was or that she had projected her feelings about him on to the relationship he had with Harmony.

Ellie did get some credit for trying to get someone to look into Harmony's disappearance, but if she was involved then this would be one way of helping her look innocent. She had tried to insert herself into the investigation more than once and they do say that guilty people do that to try and stay one step ahead of what's going on. But then she had a spare key to Harmony's flat and I could only imagine that Harmony was very selective about giving that out.

I finished the last mini egg and grabbed my jacket, the only way to get a feel for what sort of person Stephen was, was to go and see him.

I'd expected to be made to wait before he made time for me. The downside to turning up announced is often that as retaliation the person makes it as awkward for me as possible. I was pleasantly surprised that, despite being caught completely off guard, he asked his PA to clear his appointments for the next little while and took me through to his office.

'Rowan,' he said. 'you're the lady that's investigating what's happened to Harmony?'

His suit was shiny, his hair gelled back, he had all the appearance of someone who might try to sell you a used Ford Focus at any given opportunity, which was at odds with the way he spoke and different again to the way he'd presented himself on the news.

'Yes, I'm a private detective working in consultation with the police.' I sat down in the chair he directed me to, not one on the opposite side of his desk as anticipated. In the corner of his office there were two yellow leather armchairs separated by a small coffee table. He took the other.

'Would you like a coffee?' He asked.

I thought of the two strong coffee's I'd already had this morning and decided that adding a third was not a good idea. 'No, I'm okay thank you.'

'How can I help you? I assume you have questions about Harmony.'

'I do…'

'I'm surprised that you've taken so long getting around to me.' He interrupted.

I ignored his last comment. 'Do you golf, Stephen?'

He frowned, 'I'm sorry? I don't understand what this has to do with anything.'

'That's okay, you don't need to understand, it's important for me to know if you play golf?'

'I do, my handicap is two,' he beamed until he noticed the blank look on my face. 'which means I'm pretty good, I have a membership at the Cuddieford club.'

'Do you know Harry Aitkens?'

He stiffened in his chair, 'Unfortunately yes, I think the majority of us were very shocked when we found out what he was involved in. But I assure you I only knew him from the golf course to say hello to etc. What's he got to do with this?'

'When you were interviewed on the news the other day you said that you and Harmony were friends, but I've heard that she could barely tolerate you.'

'I think that's unfair. We were friends at one time before…' he looked out of the window.

'Before what?'

'Before I got promoted over her.'

'Didn't you use the break-up of her marriage to your advantage there?'

'I'm not particularly proud of how I behaved, if it makes it any better Harmony was tough and I'm sure she would have capitalised on the situation if the roles were reversed.'

I narrowed my eyes and looked at him, wondering if that were true or if it was just something he liked to tell himself.

'You ever play golf with Harmony's ex-husband Martin?'

He shrugged, 'I'm guessing you know that I do otherwise you wouldn't be asking.'

'How well do you know him?'

'Initially I met him through Harmony, but we had a crossover of interests and friends and we really hit it off.'

'Did that not make for a strained working relationship with Harmony?'

'I kept it from her for a while, but one day she confronted me about it. She was angry because I had mentioned to Martin something that had happened at work that she'd been involved with.'

'Why do you think she was so angry?'

'Because she felt I'd been indiscrete, the firm were getting an award for a project that she had been involved with and I told him about it and I invited him to come along, but I swear it wasn't to piss her off or anything, it just didn't occur to me that it would have upset her.'

'Really?'

'Okay maybe I did realise, but it was too late by then, I'd already invited him, what was I supposed to do?'

'Couldn't you have told him you'd made a mistake and the event was only for employees of the companies involved?'

He frowned 'I mean, I suppose I could've done that.'

'Did you even give Harmony the heads up that he would be there?'

'I guess I hoped that he wouldn't turn up or that she wouldn't care.'

I suppressed the eyeroll I desperately wanted to do; at the moment he wasn't doing himself any favours in encouraging me to think that he was anything other than the selfish wanker Ellie had made him out to be.

'Do you have access to Harmony's HR file?'

'Yes, but I'd need a warrant to be happy handing it over.'

'Understandable, you take the privacy of your employees' information seriously?'

'Of course.'

'Then how come you decided to give Martin Harmony's new address.'

He opened his mouth and closed it a couple of times. 'I didn't' he said with no conviction.

I raised my eyebrows but said nothing.

'It was stupid of me, I regretted it as soon I did it.'

'What I don't understand Stephen, is this, what is it that Martin Clarke has over you that would make you do something like that?'

'I don't know what you mean?'

'I can just about understand you being so focused on climbing the career ladder that you were prepared to use a difficult time in Harmony's life against her, I've had the misfortune to come across people like that before. And inviting the ex along when her team were getting an award, you know try to pull the carpet out from under her, because I'm assuming you were jealous of her being in the limelight, not you. But giving out her personal information to an ex-husband that she has tried to cut all ties with, well that could lose you your precious job, so what would make you want to take that risk?'

'He's a mate, I was doing him a favour, it was wrong I know but I thought he just wanted to send her some flowers or something. Are you saying you think that Martin has something to do with her disappearance?'

'I don't know, we're keeping all lines of investigation open just now. But to be honest Stephen, I don't buy it, so I'm going to ask you again, what is it that Martin Clarke has on you that would make you take that risk?'

His shoulders slumped. 'He caught me in a compromising position with the MD's daughter, she's seventeen,' he said hurriedly. 'It was consensual of course, but I can't imagine she would have been all that happy about it.' He looked at me, I said nothing. 'I don't know how he found out, but he told me he knew I'd got her pregnant and then paid for her to have an abortion privately. It's not something I could let come out so I owed him, he said if I told him Harmony's address then we could call it quits.'

'Wow you're a quality fella aren't you.'

'It looks bad, but...'

'But what Stephen, did you even check she wanted to have an abortion or was that what you wanted?'

'Well, she was seventeen, so it wasn't like she was going to want to ruin her life with a baby is it.'

I imagined getting up from my seat and battering his head repeatedly into a wall, but as enjoyable as that would be I satisfied myself with the fantasy. 'In short then, no. You thought mostly about how the situation would affect you and you had absolutely no regard for how that young woman felt or the potential danger you might have put Harmony in. I mean did you not take a moment to think that when a woman leaves her husband and goes to great lengths to make sure they don't know where they are that there might be a good reason for that?'

'You think I'm scum,' he said, and I didn't correct him. 'I can't believe Martin would do anything to hurt anyone, let alone Harmony. He was a gentle guy.'

'You see the bruises on my face?'

'I didn't like to bring them up, assumed it was an occupational hazard.'

It was, strangely, one of the most sensible responses I'd had. 'Your gentle friend who wouldn't hurt anyone did this to me.'

The shock on his face was the first genuine expression I'd seen on it.

'No, I don't believe it.'

I shrugged, 'why don't you ask him, see what he has to say for himself?' I stood up to leave. 'One last thing, why did you dislike Ellie so much?'

'She wasn't a good fit for the firm, she was too out there.'

'Was that the only reason?'

'Yes. She was actually good at her job, but she quit a few days ago.'

'Why was that?'

'I dunno, she wasn't too happy that I put someone in Harmony's office to take over whilst she's away.'

'I heard you fired Harmony for not turning up to work?'

His cheeks flushed pink, 'that was before I knew that she was properly missing, obviously I reinstated her, and she can have her job back if you guys find her.'

'You think we might not find her?'

'The odds aren't great after all this time, are they?'

'Interesting. I noticed you spoke about her in the past tense when you were on the news as well, like you think she's already dead.'

'No I didn't,' he frowned, 'If I did then it wasn't deliberate. I don't know anything, I swear to you.'

'The police will probably want to interview you as well.' I said before leaving his office.

He stood up almost tripping over the small coffee table, 'You've got to believe me, I wouldn't do anything to hurt anyone.'

Chapter Thirty-Six

I agreed with Ellie's assessment of Stephen's character, if anything my opinion of him was worse after meeting with him. But that didn't mean that Ellie was as squeaky clean as I'd assumed, which was going to make this next meeting uncomfortable. She'd been excited when I'd called and asked to meet her in the Sunshine Café for a catch up. I tried to sound cold and detached, but she hadn't noticed.

I arrived early hoping to have a few moments to myself or a nice catch up with Star but I'd barely sat down when I saw Ellie's yellow duffel coat appear through the door. She waved vigorously at me. And before I knew it she was sitting opposite me talking ten to the dozen leaving me genuinely concerned that I wouldn't get a word in edge ways.

'It was lovely to hear from you,' she said. 'I was hoping you had news of Harmony, but still nice to speak to you, I'm dying to know what's going on with the investigation.'

We were interrupted by one of the waitresses coming over. 'Your usual Rowan?' She asked.

'That would be lovely. Star and Billy not in today?'

'Billy's picking his sister and her fella up from the airport and Star's out the back trying to do a bit of batch baking.'

I had forgotten that Chantelle and Mohammed were due over, and I was sure that I'd accepted an invite to a dinner party to meet them. I hoped that Star would know that I would need reminding of the specifics.

Ellie ordered a hot chocolate and a piece of carrot cake. 'What's been happening? I heard on the news that one of the men convicted of killing Harmony's mum was found dead, do you think it has anything to do with Harmony disappearance?'

'The police are still looking into that,' I replied.

She waved her hand as though she was swotting my response away, 'of course that's the official statement but you're consulting with them so you must know what's really going on.'

'I'm not allowed to talk about it,' I said hoping that would put an end to the conversation.

She tilted her head to one side and looked poised for another objection when our order arrived. I was pleased to have the distraction.

'There's something I need to ask you,' I said before she had the opportunity to say anything else. 'And it's a bit awkward.'

She put her mug back on the table, 'you can ask me anything at all, if it might help you bring Harmony back safe and sound, I'll help in any way I can.' She was calm now, her face serious, it was a relief to find that she was able to set her normal over the top bubbly self aside to talk seriously.

'Thank you,' I paused thinking about how I could phrase my next questions without causing too much offence. 'Someone gave Harmony's new address to Martin and all I know is that it was someone that she worked with. I have to ask, was it you?' Even though Stephen had admitted to it I wanted to ask the question to see what her reaction was like, it might give me an insight into whether she was capable of betraying her friend like that.

'God no!' Ellie's response was immediate and felt real. 'If you excuse the expression, I wouldn't piss on him if he was on fire.'

I suppressed the urge to smile, 'Before you started working for Harmony had you ever had any dealings with Martin?'

'Nope, not before, not now, not ever. I haven't ever met him.'

'You didn't meet him at the award ceremony he gate crashed?'

'No, I heard about that. If you ask me that had something to do with Stephen, but I wasn't there. It clashed with the opening night of A Midsummers Night Dream. I was playing Helena, we ran for three weeks, it was great fun but exhausting.'

'Was there a big audience on opening night?'

She smiled. 'Are you trying to check if I had an alibi? There was the full cast, the make-up and costume people, musicians, directors, designers and so on and then a sold-out audience of five hundred people.'

'Has Martin ever come to the office looking for Harmony?'

'No, he phoned her a couple of times, as far as I know she hung up on him.'

'Did she ever mention him trying to contact her at home or sending her flowers or anything?'

'She was so obsessive about him not knowing where she was living that I think if she thought he had her address then she would've moved again. How long had he known where she was?'

'I'm not sure, a couple of months maybe.'

'Could it have been him that was sending her all the stuff to do with her mum do you think?'

I sat quietly for a couple of moments before answering. 'I doubt it, I don't see how he would have had access to the photograph you gave me or any of her artwork.'

'Maybe he was working with someone else?'

'Perhaps.'

'It could've been that Simon bloke, the one they found dead. He could've been helping Martin to freak Harmony out by sending her all that stuff.'

'Why though?'

She shrugged, 'maybe he hoped if she was scared that she would come to him for protection?'

'That doesn't seem very likely.'

'That's true, she really hated him. She used to say hell would have to freeze over before she willingly had contact with him again.'

'What?' I'd only been half listening, my brain trying to figure out if there was anything that connected Martin with Simon in anyway.

'Harmony hated Martin, he'd made her miserable. He even made the divorce difficult.'

I stood up, 'I'm sorry Ellie but I need to go, there's something I need to look into.'

'Oh okay, do you need any help?'

'No, I'm good just now. Sorry for treating you like a suspect though.' I was satisfied that Ellie was exactly the concerned friend that she had claimed to be.

'That's okay. It would've been exciting under different circumstances.'

I smiled, 'glad it wasn't too bad. I'll phone you soon.'

I weaved through the tables and out the jangling door, I glanced back through the large glass window towards Ellie who'd moved my uneaten slice of carrot cake in front of her and was tucking in. I hadn't paid before I left, but I was sure that Star would let me off just this once.

What She Didn't See

I considered going back to my car and driving the distance to the police station, but overall, it was probably quicker to walk from here.

Chapter Thirty-Seven

I recognised the desk sergeant, though not well enough to know his name. He smiled and said hello, I figured he was having the same problem as me.

'Hi, I need to speak to DCI George Johnston, can you tell him it's Rowan.'

'You've just missed him, he headed out about half an hour ago.'

I should've thought to phone him, 'What about Ama…I mean DI McAvoy?'

'He was with the DCI.'

I sighed, 'Do you know if any of the team are left in the building.' I was crossing my fingers that DS Hargreaves would be around, he was a man of few words and a very dry sense of humour, but we got along fine.

'DC Collins is in.'

'It's fine I'll phone George, thanks anyway.' I'd be buggered if I was going to speak to her again, let alone share my thoughts.

George's phone went straight to answer phone as did Amadeus'. I left them both a grumpy message asking them to call me as soon as possible. I'd reached the crossing and was waiting for the lights to change when I heard someone shouting my name. I recognised the voice and pretended I hadn't heard, whilst willing the lights to change.

'Rowan,' the voice too close for me to ignore.

I turned round to see an out of breath DC Liz Collins. 'What?'

'The sergeant said you were looking to speak to someone.'

'I was looking for George.' I turned away.

'If it's important you should tell me.'

'It can wait.'

'You didn't come over to the station unannounced for something you thought could wait,' she said.

The lights finally changed, and I started to cross the road, Liz followed. 'I'm sorry about yesterday,' she said.

On the other side of the road I stopped, 'are you?'

'I spoke to the boss this morning and he filled me in on the background, I was out of line and I'm sorry.'

'I don't believe you. I think George spoke to you after I told him what really happened yesterday, and you realised that pissing me off was a bad move for you and now you want to sweep it under the carpet like nothing happened. Well, I'm not interested, I suggest you stay out of my way, and I'll stay out of yours.'

'This is ridiculous, if you have information that is pertinent to an ongoing investigation you need to give it to me.'

'Or what?'

She folded her arms, 'I could arrest you.'

I tried but fail to stifle a laugh, 'on what grounds?'

'Interfering in a police investigation, perverting the course of justice.'

I held my arms out towards her, my wrists side by side. 'Go on then, I dare you.'

Her mouth fell open and she stared at me, 'I said I could, I didn't say I was going to.'

'Go away Liz and leave me alone. You've made your feelings on me abundantly clear.'

'What am I supposed to tell the boss when he gets back.'

I shrugged, 'that you suck at apologies, that public relations is not your forte. I'm sure you'll think of something.' I turned and walked away taking the longest strides I could without making myself look silly.

I was almost back at my car when my phone rang. I answered it without looking thinking it was bound to be George or Amadeus.

'Hi,' Nate's voice sounded startled. 'I wasn't sure you would pick up my call.'

'What can I do for you?'

'Are you okay, have you got the all clear from the concussion?'

'Yes, all back to normal, just a bit achy.'

'Good.'

My patience was beginning to wear thin wondering if there was actually any point to this conversation.

'I was hoping you could come and see me, there's something I think you'll want to see.'

'What is it?'

'I got a weird picture in the post. I think it's of Tabitha.' There was a pause. 'It looks like it's of her murder.'

I looked at my watch, it was still early, 'where are you, the gallery?'

'No, I'm at my flat.'

'Send me the address and I'll be there shortly.'

I'd expected he would live near to the gallery so was surprised when his address pinged up on my screen to find that he lived on the outskirts of Dunfermline. It was a twenty-minute drive. I was annoyed to find myself checking my appearance in my interior mirror before getting out the car.

He buzzed me into the building and was stood in his doorway when I reached the second floor. He smiled and I felt that tell-tale flutter in my gut again.

'You look nice.' He said as he showed me through to the living room. There were large canvasses on the cream walls, it felt a little bit like sitting on a sofa in an exhibition.

'Hardly.' I replied knowing that the bruises on my face were anything but attractive, even to me.

'Take the compliment,' he laughed. 'Thanks for coming. I wasn't even sure you would answer the phone.'

In truth if I'd paid any attention to the caller ID I wouldn't have, but I wasn't going to tell him that. 'Sure, why wouldn't I?'

He didn't say anything, I was glad that he wasn't attempting to rehash old ground.

'How was the picture delivered?' I asked trying to steer the conversation to the reason he called. If I could get the picture and leave then maybe this interaction could take place without any awkwardness.

'Royal Mail, in one of those do not bend type envelopes. Do you want something to drink?'

'Water will be fine.'

I waited, perched on the edge of the sofa till Nate returned with glasses of water for us both, a brown envelope tucked under his arm. He leant across me to put the envelope down, he smelt nice. Why did he always have to smell so good? He handed me the envelope before sitting down next to me.

I opened it and slid the A4 piece of paper out gently, turning it over to see the artwork. It was of a young woman, lying in a pool of blood, auburn hair soaking into the dark red liquid, her piercing green eyes staring out from the page.

'What do you think?' He said.

I looked at the envelope, the postmark was local but that didn't mean anything necessarily. 'You were right to tell me about this. It might be nothing, but it feels like too much of a coincidence for that.' I pushed it back into the envelope, trying to touch it as little as possible. 'thanks.' I said turning to kiss him on the cheek at the same time he moved his head.

Our lips touched. I closed my eyes and for a moment I enjoyed feeling the passion fizz around my body, not wanting it to stop. Our kissing intensified, lust very much on the verge of taking over.

I pulled away sharply. 'We can't do this. I can't do this.'

'I'm sorry, I thought you wanted…' he trailed off.

'I did, I do. I don't know Nate, I like you,' despite everything I thought. 'but this can't happen now.'

'I like you too.' He replied.

'I need to go.' I grabbed the envelope and my bag and headed for the door, thankfully he didn't follow or try to persuade me to stay. I shouldn't have come to his home. I should've told him to phone George, and he would've sent round DC Liz Collins who wouldn't be affected by the smell of Nate's aftershave or the twinkle in his eyes when he smiled. She would have just sat in front of him robotically completing a trio of forms before emotionlessly accepting the picture as evidence.

Chapter Thirty-Eight

Sonya was in the police mortuary when I called her. At first, she had been concerned that something was properly wrong because she said I sounded frantic. She had laughed when I had given her the highlights of what had happened and then suggested that I come by for a quick chat.

'You know you're a fully grown woman and it's okay for you to like someone and want to have sex, right?'

'I know but not with someone who is a person of interest in an investigation.'

'It's probably not ideal but would it have been the end of the world if you'd just gone with it and enjoyed yourself.'

'Maybe you're right. It's just he makes me feel…' I paused whilst I tried to think of how to explain it adequately. 'out of control.'

'Sounds like good old-fashioned lust to me.' Sonya smiled.

'I don't like it, but at the same time I really want to.'

'What's the worst that can happen?'

'I have sex with a murderer, or a kidnapper. I get pregnant, I fall in love.'

'Fair point, the first option is less than ideal, but is falling in love so awful?'

'I'm not exactly surrounded by success stories when it comes to love am I.'

'What about Maureen and Eddie?'

'Yeah, but their lives haven't exactly been easy.'

'That had nothing to do with them loving each other though. Stop being such a cynic and allow yourself a little happiness perhaps.'

I stuck my tongue out at her. 'You want to see the picture then? You can help me compare it to the crime scene photographs.'

'In a minute, but first I thought you'd be interested to know the forensics team did manage to get some prints off the sketch book that was sent to Harmony. We're lucky that Tabitha Adams liked pastels so much, it's hard to pick up a pastel drawing without getting some on your fingers, even a long time after the picture was done,' Sonya said.

'And did you get a match?'

'There were a lot of prints, Harmony obviously and then your friend Ellie, but the ones I think you'll be most interested in are Simon Cummings.'

'Bloody hell, so he was the one sending all the stuff about her mum's death to her then.'

'Looks that way. Shall we have a look at this new drawing then.' Sonya brought up the images on her computer screen and we compared them to the picture that had been sent to Nate. 'The body is lying in the right place, but Tabitha's eyes are closed in all of these pictures. Also, the blood pool is uncompromised in this picture and in the crime scene photographs you can see where Harmony walked through the blood and sat down next to her mum.'

Each time I thought about Harmony as a small child sitting in her mother's blood willing her to wake up my heart felt broken.

What She Didn't See

'It's like the photo that was sent to Harmony,' I said. 'The one that must have been taken by whoever shot her.'

'It's hard to believe that they didn't know she was in the room.' Sonya said.

'She shouldn't have been there, no-one would have even looked for her.'

'Small mercies I guess, I can't imagine they would've let her live if they knew there was a witness.'

'I don't know, there's a big difference between killing an adult and a small child.'

'Not for everyone there's not.'

'True.' I sighed. 'Can I leave this here with you,' I said motioning at the picture. 'In case there's any fingerprints or anything on it?'

'Sure. What are you going to do now?'

'I need to find George; something came up when I was speaking to Ellie this morning that I need to run by him.'

'He was on the way to the hospital to see Alistair Lockland, his test results came back, he was poisoned.'

'Poisoned, how?'

'Lycorine, commonly found in the bulbs of daffodils.'

I frowned, 'how do you accidentally eat a daffodil bulb.'

'Don't ask me, I'm guessing it was made to look like something else or maybe dried and added to food.'

'When did he ingest it?'

'I'm not sure, I'm guessing George will know more when he's finished at the hospital.'

I was annoyed that George hadn't phoned to let me know there was an update with Alistair, I wondered if Liz had known where he was when she was harassing me earlier. 'Okay, thanks. I'd better go and get on.'

I phoned George as I walked back to my car and was relieved when he answered on the second ring.

'Did Liz tell you I was looking for you?' He asked before I had a chance to say anything.

'No, why?'

'I heard you were in the station earlier looking for me, so I assumed she would have mentioned it.'

'No,' I considered saying that she was too busy threatening to arrest me but decided against it. 'Why did you want to speak to me?'

'It's Alistair Lockland.' He paused.

My heartbeat quickened, 'is he dead?'

'No, but someone tried to kill him, he'd been poisoned.'

'Sonya said, something to do with daffodils.'

'News gets around fast.' He said, I detected an undertone of irritation that his thunder had been stolen.

'How is he?'

'Stable, according to the doctor. The thing is Rowan he won't talk to me or anyone in my team. He's asking for you.'

'Me?'

'Yes, any chance you can come over to the hospital now?'

'Sure.' I had been surprised when Fiona had contacted me after Alistair collapsed and the revelation that this had been at his instruction was even stranger. Now he'd requested that I speak to him at the hospital. I'd been over my meetings with him in my mind, nothing had stood out in my memory that would have suggested we had made a special connection or indicated that he trusted me and yet he must've felt differently.

'Are you listening to me?' George was asking, I realised that I had drifted off.

'Sorry no, my mind was elsewhere.'

'I was asking if you wanted me to send Amadeus to pick you up?'

'No, I'm in town, I'll drive over now.'

I picked up my pace eager to get to the hospital and find out what it was that Alistair Lockland was only prepared to say to me. As I turned into the car park, I reached into my handbag to grab my keys accidentally opening my phone and dialling Sonya. I was just about to hang up when someone behind me made a sound.

I turned around, 'what are you doing here?' I said as Martin Clarke walked around me coming to a stop between me and my car door.

'You pleased with yourself?' He asked.

I looked around, but we were the only two people in the almost full car park. 'What do you want?' I asked.

'I hate women like you,' he said. 'Don't know your place, meddling in things that have nothing to do with you. Making out that you're some kind of 'police consultant', you make me laugh.' He had used air quotes around police consultant.

'I am working with the police to try and find Harmony.'

He snorted a laugh. 'Not according to the detective that came round to see me, she was very nice actually. Quite sympathetic, agreed that you had no business coming into my home and questioning me like that.'

It had been DC Liz Collins that had been to interview him after he had attacked me, and I was sure that she would have been happy to cast aspersions on my ability and involvement in the case, even to a suspect.

'Why did you lie to me.' I asked hoping that catching him off guard was the best way to get away from him.

'About what?'

'The first time I came to see you. You said that Harmony had come to visit you, said that she told you she was scared that someone was going to try and hurt her and that she was worried about you. You even told me that she was sorry for the way everything ended between you both.'

'That wasn't a lie,' he said.

'Yes, it was, Harmony hated you. She wouldn't have gone to see you voluntarily like that, but what I can't decide is if you made the whole thing up or if she was at the house for some other reason that you don't want anyone to know.'

'I think it's time you came with me,' he said.

I took a step backwards away from him, away from my car, trying to think where I could go to if I was to turn and run right now and if I would be able to outrun him.

'Stop,' he shouted. 'Stop moving.'

I stood still, 'Why, what are you going to do Martin?' I said hoping that it was loud enough that Sonya could hear me. 'Just walk away.'

'No,' he reached inside his jacket and pulled out a taser.

I barely had enough time to register what he was holding before the rods sprung forward latching themselves to my abdomen, the pain searing through my whole body, causing me to drop to my knees. Even after it stopped, I could still feel the pain coursing through me. I stumbled, trying to get on my feet, the sound of his laughter ringing in my ears.

'It's time you stop thinking you're the one in charge of this situation,'

He was standing over me now, I didn't want to look at him, I was focused on getting up and running, which was why I noticed too late that he was holding a short metal bar in his right hand. A short metal bar that was about to smack into the side of my head.

Chapter Thirty-Nine

There was no way of knowing how long I had been out for. When I finally reopened my eyes, my vision was blurred and I struggled to focus on anything. I let my eyelids fall shut again for just a moment.

'Are you okay,' it was a woman's voice, not one I recognised.

I forced my eyes open and tried to manoeuvre myself into a sitting position, an action that was made considerably more difficult by the fact my hands were tied together at my back.

'Hey, are you okay,' the voice said again.

'Where am I?' I asked looking round to find the origin of the question. The auburn red hair caught my attention, just like her mother's. 'Harmony?'

She looked shocked, 'yes, how do you know me?'

I tried a small smile, my head throbbing. 'My name is Rowan McFarlane, your friend Ellie hired me to find you.'

'I'm sorry you got mixed up in all of this,' she said.

'How long have I been here?' I asked thinking about Alana and how worried she would be, wondering if Sonya had heard any of the conversation from inside my handbag. I shivered.

'I don't know, it's hard to keep track of time.' I heard a rasp in her throat, I wasn't sure if she was struggling to keep back tears or if the cold damp building was making her sick. 'Not too long though, a couple of hours maybe.'

A couple of hours, Alana would be finishing school, heading home, wondering what we'd be having for dinner. I wanted to cry with frustration and anger. George would be wondering where I was too, looking at his watch and wondering why I hadn't shown up at the hospital.

'Where are we?' I asked, shivering again, I looked down at my bare legs. That bastard had taken all my clothes but my vest top and pants.

'Martin's dad has a storage unit out near Freuchie, I think that's where we are. It's really rural and hardly anyone comes here anymore.'

I shuffled across the uneven concrete floor towards Harmony. 'Are you okay?' I asked.

She didn't respond, how could she be okay, her ex-husband had kidnapped her and was keeping her captive in a dark damp building. 'How's he treating you?'

'He brings food sometimes and there's a porta potti in the other corner now.'

'I don't understand, why did he do this?' I asked. 'What's this got to do with your mum's murder?'

'My mum?' She asked. 'Why would this have something to do with her?'

'You received the sketch books and the messages about her death,' I said. 'I think we all assumed it was related.' My head was throbbing, and my mouth was so dry I was struggling to concentrate.

'We?' She asked.

'Me, Ellie, the police.'

'The police? Is that why he took the photo of me with the paper?'

273

'I think he was hoping that it would stop everyone from looking for you, if they knew you were alive, but obviously it doesn't work like that.'

'He was angry and shouting about some nosey bitch, I'm guessing that was you he was referring to.'

I'd been called much worse, if it wasn't for the circumstances I would have laughed at the insult. 'Probably, what I don't understand is why he kidnapped you.'

'Do you know why we split up?'

I told her that I had heard about the infertility appointments and the aftermath of that, and that Ellie had told me how unhappy she had been in her marriage.

'Martin doesn't like to lose, he wants everyone to see him as this gentle, mild mannered man, but really he's an absolute control freak. It's not all his fault I suppose. I should never have agreed to marry him, I didn't love him.'

'Then why did you?'

'Dad and Karen introduced us, and they kept going on about what a lovely couple we made and how he was ideal husband material. I'd got to the stage that I didn't want to fight it anymore, going against what they wanted had never got me very far in the past.'

'You married him to please people you didn't like?' I asked.

'I know it sounds mad when you say it out loud, but I thought how bad could it be. I would be married, and they would be off my back and Martin seemed okay, we had a decent amount in common. But it wasn't as straightforward as that, I think Martin was only really interested in me because he thought it would advance his career and then when he realised it wouldn't he was really angry with my dad but he knew he couldn't take it out on him, so he took it out on me instead. After he got his new job, I thought he would settle down, but nothing was ever enough for him, he needed the bigger, flashier house, the newest car in the street. I went along with it all and it probably would never have changed if it hadn't been for him saying he wanted a family.'

'But you'd always told him you didn't want children?'

'I thought he understood, it was one of the very few things I told him he'd need to be okay with if we got married, he said he didn't care, he would be happy if it was the two of us forever.'

'Then he just changed his mind?'

'That's what I thought initially, but honestly I don't think he ever took me seriously about it. I tried telling him no and he wasn't interested in hearing my opinions, we had huge fights and then I came up with the idea that I'd make him believe that I couldn't get pregnant.'

'You must've realised that would only work for so long though.'

'I don't know what I thought and then he had us go to the doctors and I knew the truth would come out and suddenly I saw a way out, a reason to leave. He could save face and tell everyone what an awful person I was, and I could get out of a marriage I never wanted.'

'Hadn't you thought of leaving him before then?'

'Of course, lots of times, it's hard to explain. The way I was brought up after mum died, it turned me into someone who complies to keep the other person happy to stop arguments. But having children was the one thing I couldn't do that with.'

'I can imagine how he reacted when he found out you were still on the pill.'

'I remember standing in our kitchen listening to him rant and scream at me about how much I'd embarrassed him and how awful it was for him to be put in this position. Not once did he ever ask me why I did it, he didn't care why, he only cared about the impact it had on him. He stormed out of the house and by the time he came back I was gone.'

'Where did you go?'

'Ellie's, she let me sleep on her sofa, it was the first time in the longest time that I felt that someone was there for me no matter what.'

'How did Martin take you leaving?'

'Badly. I tried to cut all ties with him, did everything through the lawyers, but he still managed to find out where I lived.'

'Stephen told him,' I said.

She shook her head, 'I knew he was a nasty little snake, but I really didn't think he would stoop that low.'

'Did he come to the flat?'

'No, he sent me letters, pleading with me to come back, telling me that the neighbours were asking questions and he didn't know what to tell them.'

'I didn't see them when I was at the flat?'

'I took them to work and shredded them. I thought he'd got over it and started to move on, Stephen even told me that he was going on a double date with Martin.'

'If Martin was moving on with his life how did you end up here?'

'Have you met Patrick O'Brian?'

'Yeah, he was a big fan of yours.'

'He's a nice guy and I know that sounds twisted, seeing as he went to jail for killing my mum, but he says he didn't do it and I believe him. The reason I agreed to meet with him in the first place is because I wanted to talk to him about what happened that night. Anyway, Patrick has a strong Irish accent, and I knew that wasn't the person whose voice I had heard that night.'

'What does Patrick have to do with Martin?'

'I'm getting to that bit. I was having coffee with Patrick. We thought we'd picked somewhere completely out of the way, but I look over and through the window I can see Martin. No idea what he was doing there, if it was coincidence or if he'd been following me. He started calling me at work calling me a slut and telling me I downgraded from him, nasty stuff. I just hung up on him mostly.'

'He was jealous.'

'Crazy jealous. About a week later I'm walking along the road, and he pulls up beside me in his car and tells me to get in the car, I tell him to get stuffed. He got out of the car and forced me in. He took me back to the house and told me he just wanted to have dinner with me. I'm thinking about all the ways I can get out, but I agree to dinner in the hopes that it will calm him down. He pours us both a glass of red wine and he tries to kiss me, telling me how much he wants me back and if I come back everything will be different. I just wanted to scream and run, but it's not exactly near where I live, and I wouldn't get far on foot.'

'What did you do?'

'I let him think he was winning me round so he would let his guard down. He had already downed a glass of wine, I poured mine in the plant pot near the table. Eventually he starts to get really drunk and I was able get away.'

'Why didn't you tell anyone?'

'I thought about calling this policeman I met when mum died, he'd always checked in on me, but I waited too long to decide.'

Amadeus would have been relieved to know that she trusted him, even if she hadn't reached out to him.

The sound of wood scraping across concrete and then a crack of light breaking through the darkness took my attention. Martin moved the torch around the barn locating us together. I looked passed him to the cold evening outside. It was dark, I hoped Alana would have called George immediately and that a search team would be out tracking me. Although realistically we'd been looking for Harmony all this time and no one had considered that Martin was involved.

'I see you ladies have been getting acquainted. Has she been telling you some sob story about what a terrible husband I was?'

'We weren't talking about you.' I replied, I wasn't about to give him the opportunity to inflate his ego anymore.

'I'm sure you'd like a husband wouldn't you Rowan, someone to come home to every night, someone to make you feel special.'

'I do have someone I go home to. I have a daughter.'

'Not quite the same though, is it?' He laughed.

'A daughter who will have phoned DCI George Johnston the moment I didn't come home tonight.'

'Well good luck with that, your mate doesn't seem to be much of a detective, he's been busy focussing all of his attention on Harmony's dim and distant past.

It had been me that had pushed that angle, who had tried to persuade George that Tabitha Adams' death was connected to Harmony's disappearance, and I had it all wrong. I hated to admit it, but he was right, unless Sonya had been able to make anything out from our final conversation then George wouldn't be focusing his attentions on Martin.

'You're underestimating him.'

'Well, you had better hope you're right otherwise your precious daughter is going to have something in common with Harmony, she'll spend the rest of her life without her mummy.'

He bent down next to me and pulled out a small penknife. I flinched, he laughed, enjoying having the upper hand. He cut the cable ties binding my hands and feet. 'No need for those now, you're not going anywhere after all.'

I said nothing, for now that was true, but I had no intentions of waiting here doing nothing whilst he decided what my fate would be.

He dropped a bag on the ground a short distance away. 'Bon Appetit,' he laughed and then he was gone. The barn doors scraped on the ground, and I heard the clink of a chain.

Chapter Forty

Part of me would rather have starved than eaten anything Martin Clarke had put in front of me, but I didn't let my pig headedness get in the way of common sense. It was likely that I was going to have to get myself out of this situation and that would be much harder to do on an empty stomach. Begrudgingly I ate the pre-packed ham sandwich, trying to ignore the fact it was two days past its use by date. Harmony ate without hesitation.

We ate in silence, me trying to focus on how the hell I was going to get us out of here, trying desperately not to think about how frantic Alana would be right now. I knew she would be having flash backs to the day we were told Jack's body had been found. I'd foolishly promised her then that if I followed in his footsteps and became a Private Detective, I wouldn't get myself murdered. It's not often I doubt my career choice, but tonight I couldn't stop myself imagining how much simpler life would be if I'd just taken a normal 9-5 office job.

When Martin had left it sounded like he'd chained and padlocked the door, so it was unlikely that we'd be able to force it open that way. I refused to give up, there had to be an alternative.

'Is that the only way in and out?' I asked Harmony, pointing vaguely in the direction that Martin had left.

'I think so, I see daylight come in from the holes in the roof, but I doubt you could escape that way if that's what you're thinking.'

'Why not?'

'It's one of those wrinkly tin roofs, it lets through rain in quite a few places so that would suggest that it's pretty rusty. Even if you could reach it, I don't think it would hold either of our weight long enough. Anyway, what are you going to do, jump off a barn roof.'

'Have you thought about escaping?' I asked, hoping that it had at least crossed her mind.

'The first few days, it was all I could think about.' She paused. 'But the more time passed the more hopeless it seemed and, in the end, I decided to forget about it and hope that eventually someone would figure out where I was before it was too late.'

'You think he's planning on killing you?'

'Worse, he wants me to agree to be his wife again and make me have his baby.'

'Why keep you here then.'

'He's trying to break my spirit.'

I felt for her, nearly her whole life she had been surrounded by people with little interest in what she wanted, determined to make her comply with their wishes and mould herself to fit in with them.

'Will it work?'

'Perhaps once it would have, but now I'd rather die.'

I walked towards the doors; my eyes had become accustomed enough to the dark that I could just about make out where I was going. That didn't stop me catching my feet on the uneven floor and almost tripping a couple of times. I felt my way along the large wooden doors and couldn't think of any way that we could open them from inside.

I made my way back to where Harmony had sat silently watching me, knowing that I wasn't going to discover a way out.

'I told you it was pointless,' she said as I sat beside her.

'Had to try though,' I replied. 'How often does he come here?' I asked wondering how long it would be before the padlock would be undone and the opportunity of escape was possible again.

'He comes most days.'

I would have to wait until tomorrow then. The thought of Alana going to bed tonight not knowing where I was or if she'd ever see me again was enough to make tears prick the corners of my eyes. I comforted myself with the knowledge that right now Alana would be in the care of Maureen or Sonya and either would fuss around her and make sure she was safe.

'What about the packages of your mum's things and that photograph, where did they come from?'

'I got a message from some charity that works with ex-offenders, helps them to make amends for their actions. They told me that Simon Cummings wanted to speak to me.'

'What did you think when you got the message?'

'At first, I thought meeting the people who killed mum was a stupid idea, how would that help me, it felt like it was all about them. Like saying sorry would clear their conscience. I was going to reply with a thanks, but no thanks when I got another email and this time it was a bit pushy, telling me it was in my best interests to meet Simon.'

'That's weird.'

'I emailed back and told them I wasn't interested and that was when I started getting the things about mum.'

'You think it was Simon who was sending them to you?'

'I wondered that when I got the messages suggesting they weren't the ones that killed mum, suggesting there was someone else out there, it was a bit warped I thought. I assumed that it must have been this Simon bloke and that he must've kept some of the things he took in the break in.'

'What about Patrick?'

'Well, I thought if Simon had kept some of the stuff from the break in then maybe there was other stuff, I knew that not all of her jewellery had been found when they were arrested, and she had this necklace that was so special that I wondered if there was any chance that either of them had it.'

'Why not meet up with Simon and ask him?'

'He made me feel uncomfortable and I definitely didn't want to meet him face to face, so I looked for Patrick instead. And I'm glad I found him. I got the necklace back but also speaking to him did give me some closure.'

'He told me that he wasn't involved in your mum's death,' I said.

'He told me the same thing and I believe him. Maybe I should hear Simon's side of the story if we get out of here.'

I had forgotten that she had been locked away from the world and wouldn't have heard about his murder. She seemed a little deflated when I explained that he was dead.

'Tell me about your mum.' I said. Harmony's disappearance hadn't anything to do with her mother's murder, but that didn't change the fact that there was something very strange about the circumstances of her death. And why would Simon have started to send those packages now after all this time, if there wasn't more to it that meets the eye.

'What do you want to know?'

'Everything, anything you can remember.'

'Before she died, we would spend hours in her studio, I think it was a like a little self-contained annex that had been built on as an extension or something before we lived there. She must've claimed it for her studio. In my memory it's where I always think of her. I would sit at my little easel and paint or draw whilst she worked on something.'

'How did your dad feel about her having her own studio?'

'I don't know, I thought we had a happy family life, I don't remember them arguing, but I was very small. He was away at work a lot and it was me and mum at home most evenings. She used to say if he wasn't careful, she'd feed his dinner to the dog and I used to giggle and say we didn't have a dog. She would say lucky for him and wrap a plate and put it in the fridge.'

'What about your grandparents, what were they like?'

'My dad's parents were old, even then, and not in that I was a child and everyone seemed old way, they were grey haired and walked with sticks. And they liked everything just so. Didn't have much time for a rowdy little girl. But mum's parents, they were nice, a bit weird in their own way. They were the opposite, no rules, no boundaries. They didn't think school was important. You can get an education from the world around you, sort of thing.'

'Why did you think Nate might be your dad?' I interrupted

'Do you know if the results came back?'

'He's not.'

'Good.'

'Why good?'

'Have you met him?'

I grunted that I had.

'I know you'll think it's weird because he was mum's friend and they practically grew up together, but he wasn't in my life after mum died so it wasn't like he's actually my uncle…' she trailed.

I stretched my neck from one side to the other until it made a satisfying cracking sound and some of the tension was released. 'You like him,' I said.

'I don't know, he's handsome and he has a really nice manner, I felt like we had a connection. It might just have been because he knew mum before, when she was growing up and could tell me things about her. But yes, I liked him and then I had this awful thought, what if he was really my father. I knew I needed to know just to be sure.'

I felt a small twinge in my gut, it could have been the out of date sandwiches, but I suspected that it was jealousy. Ridiculous, as we were both sitting in a building god knows where with little chance of being found. Being part of a love triangle was hardly a priority right now.

'Did anything happen between you?' I said.

'Why?' She asked

'Just curious,' I lied.

'You like him as well, don't you?'

'He's nice, we kissed once.' Technically it had been twice and the second time it had been a lot more than nice.

Harmony laughed and it took me by surprise.

'Are you ok?' I asked.

'I'm fine. I'm just thinking about how stupid it all is.'

She was right, it felt ridiculous to be having this sort of conversation in the almost pitch darkness, locked in a barn miles away from everyone that I loved.

'The night your mum died…'

'Did I see anything?' She interrupted, finishing my sentence. 'No, and honestly I have racked my brains and been to therapy, but I hid in the cupboard and when I came out…when I came out, it was too late.'

'I'm sorry.'

'Everyone always asks me, they can't understand how it's possible that I could have been right there and saw nothing.'

'What do you remember about that evening?'

'I'd been in a mood because I was supposed to be staying with my grandparents, the ones on my dad's side and I hadn't wanted to go. They picked me up from school, but I'd only been there a little while when my grandad said he wasn't feeling well, and they decided that it was best for me to go home. Mum came to get me, we had pancakes and ice-cream for dinner and then we went into the studio. It was past my bedtime, but she said if I was good I could stay up.' She stretched back and lent her head back against the stone wall. 'Anyway, it must've been quite late because I was getting sleepy and then mum went all quiet and put her finger to her lips for me to be silent. I remember hearing this weird sound, like someone tapping. I still hear it in my dreams sometimes. Mum went to the door and when she came back, she looked scared, she lifted me off my chair and told me to get into the cupboard and to close my eyes and not to come out no matter what until she came for me.'

'You think whatever or whoever she saw in the hallway scared her?'

'Scared or panicked, I don't know. I was seven.'

'What happened when you were in the cupboard?'

'I did what I was told, I closed my eyes. I remember hearing the gun shot and my mum gasping and then the sound of footsteps, big heavy footsteps running along the hall, stopping at the studio door.'

'Just one set of footsteps?' I was thinking about Patrick saying that he hadn't gone towards the gunshot, he just legged it after Simon ran off.

'Yes, that I was sure about. Then a noise that sounded like someone spitting, and a chair must've got knocked over. And then it was silent. I was really scared, and I wanted to get out, I wanted to know what had happened and to see my mum. I almost did, but then I heard a man's voice. I didn't recognise it.'

'Who was he talking to?'

'I think he was on the phone, there was one on the table just outside the studio so that mum didn't have to dash away mid-painting if anyone called.'

'What was he saying?'

'I couldn't really hear him properly, it was a bit muffled. Then I heard him run off. I waited a couple of minutes and then I opened the door a tiny bit and I could see her on the ground.' Harmony was crying, I could feel her body vibrating with grief. 'I knew something was wrong, she was just lying there staring at the ceiling, blood coming out of her. I think I understood on some level that she was dead, but I sat next to her and begged her to wake up. And then honestly the next few days were a blur. I just wanted to wake up and discover that it had just been a terrible nightmare.'

'I'm so sorry, it must've been awful. How was it when you went back home after?'

'Horrid and not just because mum was dead, dad seemed different, cold. He hadn't ever been an affectionate parent, but he would still comfort me if I was hurt, but now he could barely bring himself to look at me.'

'I think your grandparents wanted you to go and live with them.'

'I wish he'd let me go. I came home one day after being at theirs for the weekend and almost everything of mum's was gone. Her studio had been stripped bare, the family photos were gone. I found all her clothes in bin bags waiting to be collected for charity and most of her other stuff had been thrown away. Even my bedroom had been gone through. I had to hide things to keep them safe.'

'Did you ask your dad about it?'

'He said it was for the best and we shouldn't dwell on the past or some bullshit like that. Then a week later decorators were in, and that bitch Karen was strutting around the house like it had always been hers. She erased every trace of my mum from the place.'

'You and Karen never got along?' I asked.

'It's hard to get along with someone who behaves like her. I wasn't allowed to talk about my mum, not even at Christmas or birthdays and she didn't much like me seeing my grandparents either.'

It was hard to know what to say to her, I'd experienced rejection from Isobel, the woman I'd spent most of my life believing was my mother, but it was hardly comparable to finding your mother shot dead and have someone take her place so quickly.

'Growing up in that sort of environment must have been tough.'

'I got numb to it, I stopped expecting affection from anyone, but it was difficult and then when I was a bit older, I realised that the boys were paying me attention,' she paused. 'I'm not proud of my behaviour but I started sleeping around, just so I could have those moments of feeling good, knowing that even if it was just for one thing I was wanted.'

'That's when you got pregnant?'

'How do you know about that?'

'Your gran told me.'

'I was only fifteen and you can imagine the judgement I got for that.'

'I don't need to imagine. I got pregnant with my daughter when I was fifteen, Alana was born just after my sixteenth birthday.' As I said her name I felt my gut churn.

'At least you got your baby after all of that.'

I didn't reply, there was nothing meaningful I could say.

'Karen was glad I think, she told me it was my own fault and that dirty little whores don't get to be mummies. Honestly, I wanted to die, because the only thing that had been keeping me going all this time was the thought of my baby and escaping. Afterwards they sent me to an all-girls boarding school, I kept myself to myself, buckled down, worked hard, got good exam results and went to uni.'

'You're an amazing artist yourself, I saw the mural on the wall in your apartment.'

'I had a crazy idea that I could persuade dad to let me go to art school, seeing as I had done everything they had wanted of me. But he was adamant that I do something more sensible, so I went into marketing.'

'Ellie said you're an amazing boss and really good at what you do.'

'It's weird you know, until I met Ellie I didn't have any friends. I stayed away from people at uni, they had tried to make friends with me in the beginning and a couple of guys even tried to date me. People get the message eventually when you say no often enough. I couldn't have friends, I didn't want to risk letting people into my life only for them to end up hurting me.'

'But Ellie was different?' I asked.

'You've met her.' Harmony smiled.

'Yeah, she's pretty special.'

'You're right she is. She came in for interview with pink hair and this bright yellow coat and at first I thought good god, but then she started talking, there was something so engaging about her that I realised I felt relaxed just listening to the sound of her voice. I knew I needed her in my life, so I offered her the job on the spot. Stephen went mental of course, but it was too late and as it turned out she was a brilliant PA.'

'I met Stephen, wasn't a fan.'

'He actually used to be okay when we first joined the company, but the more senior he became the more of an arsehole he was,' she yawned, 'we should try to get some sleep.'

There were two blankets folded up beside Harmony. I was grateful to have something to wrap around my bare arms, but it was far from warm. The cold from the concrete felt like it had seeped into my body and taken up residence in my bones, I wasn't sure I would ever feel properly warm again.

I was surprised how easily Harmony drifted off, forgetting that this had been her normal for a while now. I sat propped up against the wall, my eyelids heavy, but every time they were on the brink of closing an image of Jack's beaten dead body lying on Sonya's metal table sprung into my mind forcing me back to full consciousness.

Chapter Forty-One

I must've slept a little because I was aware of a bead of sunlight coming in from the holes in the roof and dazzling me awake. I looked across at Harmony, her red hair fallen across her face, her body relaxed in a peaceful sleep. She might've been able to get used to the accommodation, but I had no intention of spending another evening locked inside a freezing barn. I had no idea how I would manage it but by the time the sun went down this evening we would be free.

In the daylight I could see properly that Harmony had been right when she had said that we'd never be able to escape across the roof, it was peppered with rust-coloured holes. The barn looked like it had probably once been used for storing farm equipment. I guessed that it hadn't been used for anything much for quite some time though.

I'd been hopeful that I might have found something lying around that I could use as a weapon but no such luck. The only thing I had found was some old fibre glass insulation that had fallen out of the gaps between the roof and the wall, a rusty nail and an empty bird's nest. I was using the nail to try to lever a piece of rock out of the wall when Harmony woke up. She found my suggestion that we find a way to make a run for it unrealistic to the point where she suggested that I might as well save my energy.

She's had a difficult life, I didn't want to think too harshly of her for not wanting to fight, but I couldn't give in, I had Alana to think of. I tried not to imagine what range of emotions she would be going through this morning, instead I thought about Sally Mitchell. She had been held captive for twelve years before I found her and in all that time she had never given up. She had only been a child when Alexander Evans had taken her. If she could keep hope, then so could I.

After what seemed like hours, but in reality was more like thirty minutes, I gave up trying to dislodge a stone from the wall. If only he hadn't taken my jacket then I would have had my sharpened tweezers in my pocket. Luckily Martin Clarke was not a big man and with any luck I would be able to overpower him long enough to make a run for it.

Harmony tried to make conversation with me asking about my life and my family, after a while we fell into silence. She seemed content to sit at the edge of the barn trying to take in as much of the natural light as possible, whilst I felt poised like a coiled spring, taking in every slight noise in anticipation of hearing the key in the padlock, the rattle of the chain and the sound of wood on concrete as the doors opened.

My stomach growled, I tried not to think of all the food I would eat once I was safely back inside my own home. Hours passed but it was still daylight when finally, I heard the sound I'd been longing to hear.

'This is it,' I whispered to Harmony. 'Follow my lead and I promise we'll escape.' She didn't look convinced, I just had to hope that she would run with me when the time came.

'Afternoon ladies,' he smiled smugly as he entered the space.

I sprung up charging at him thrusting all my weight against him, knocking him off balance and causing him to collide with the stone wall.

'What the fuck,' he shouted.

I yelled at Harmony to run and was pleased to see that she didn't hesitate before sprinting out into the afternoon sunshine.

Martin was regaining his balance and if I allowed him to do that he wouldn't let me get the upper hand again. As he staggered to his feet, I kicked him in the back of his knee forcing his leg to collapse under him. He toppled sideways, his head cracking off a protruding piece of stone before collapsing unconscious on the concrete. I pulled myself to my feet and looked at his face, noticing a small trickle of blood leaking from his temple. I didn't stop to see if he was alive, instead I half ran, half stumbled, to the door. My fingers felt numb from twenty-four hours of coldness and pushing the wooden doors shut was more of a challenge than it should have been. I worked as quickly as I could to wrap the chain around the handles before sealing the padlock.

The pathway was broken concrete, overgrown and sprinkled with gravel and smaller stones, every time the sole of my foot connected with it pain seared up my legs, but now was not the time to stop. I turned the corner taking me on to a forest track, the earthy path was much softer making it easier for me to pick up speed.

In the distance I caught a glimpse of Harmony's hair. I ran towards her rounding the corner in time to see Stephen grappling with her trying to force her in the side door of a white van.

There was more fire in her eyes now than I had seen before as she fought him, sinking her teeth into his arm. He pulled it back in shock and pain, I lurched at him.

'Why didn't you just leave it alone,' he shouted in my face as I knocked him off Harmony. He flipped me around slamming my back into the side of the van. 'If you had only walked away, we were only interested in Harmony. You didn't have to get yourself hurt.'

His grip on my shoulders loosened slightly as he was distracted by Harmony veering towards him, a small rock in her hand. She flung it in the direction of his head. He dodged laughing. 'Honestly is that the best you've got.'

I launched my forehead towards the bridge of his nose, connecting with less force than I would've liked but enough to stun him.

'Run Harmony, please just go.' I yelled at her. She stood for a moment like a deer in headlights not sure what the right thing to do was. 'Please.' I shouted.

Stephen moved to stop her, and I took hold of his collar pulling him back, I was relieved to see her turn and run. Realising that he couldn't control us both he let Harmony run turning his attention to me. Stephen was larger than he had seemed in his office in a shiny suit, he was strong too. He slapped me hard across the face before putting his hands around my throat.

I scraped at his fingers hoping that at the very least his DNA would be behind my fingernails. He was talking but I couldn't hear him over the sound of my own blood thumping against my eardrums. All I could think was I couldn't die, not like this, not the same way Jack died. I promised Alana that I wouldn't be murdered, I intended to keep my word.

Suddenly as my brain tried in vain to come up with an escape plan, I felt him release his grip. I crumpled to the floor, gasping for air, confused.

'I couldn't leave you, not after everything you've done to save me,' Harmony said.

It took me a couple of moments to realise that she was holding a baseball bat sized tree branch. Stephen groaned; she must have hit him hard enough to knock him out, but he was coming round. I looked inside the van hoping to find some cable ties, but all I could see were a couple of frayed pieces of rope that I hoped would keep him restrained.

'I need you to stop him from getting up,' I said.

Harmony dropped her knees onto his back, and he let out a pained gasp, he tried to wriggle free but with Harmony's help we held him still, pushing his face into the dirt.

'Thank you for coming back for me,' I said as we'd finished tying Stephen's hands and feet together.

'I couldn't just run away, no one has ever done anything to help me before, lucky I came back when I did.'

My hand went involuntarily to my throat, the skin felt a little bruised and it hurt when I swallowed, but we were free, making it a small price to pay.

'Keep an eye on him whilst I search the van,' it was getting late, and we needed to get away from here. I opened the first of the black bags that had been stacked in the corner and discovered a balaclava, a few large rocks, bits of broken bricks and a practice version of the note that had been attached to the brick that had smashed Ellie's window. I imagined that Stephen had been acting on Martin's orders when he put the frighteners on Nate and Ellie.

The second bag contained a soft cashmere jumper and a pair of dark blue jeans, both far too fancy to be from my wardrobe.

'These yours?' I asked.

She nodded, I threw them out to her, and she quickly slipped the jumper over her head. I was grateful when I discovered that not only did the other bag contain my clothes but my handbag. I searched around for my phone. It had been turned off; I said a silent prayer to whichever gods were listening that it would have some charge left.

6% battery and 1 bar of signal but in both cases it was enough.

Chapter Forty-Two

George and his team arrived in a blaze of blue lights and screeching tyres, he and Amadeus rushed towards us.

George looked at me, 'Thank fuck you're alright.'

For once I didn't have any smart arse retort, instead I rested my head on his shoulder and let him embrace me in the sort of hug you give your kid when they've run off and you've spent what feels like hours frantically searching for them, part relief, part frustration and annoyance. Out of the corner of my eye I could see Amadeus checking on Harmony, the two men insisting that we both needed to go to hospital. Harmony got into the ambulance without protest.

'I should go with her,' George said, 'but I'll see you there ok.'

I tried to tell him that I didn't need the hospital let alone to be taken there in an ambulance but it was clear that he had left Amadeus with strict instructions to put me in one whether I liked it or not.

'I just want to go home and rest.'

Amadeus was not taken in by my protestations, in the end the only thing I negotiated was that I would see Alana before I did anything else and Amadeus had agreed. Even so I was surprised to see her waiting for me as I was wheeled into the building in a wheelchair.

'Mum' she said before flinging her arms around me, her tears soaking into my shoulder through the blanket the paramedics had wrapped me in. 'I thought you were dead.'

'Nah not me,' I tried a smile.

'What the hell happened?' I could see her eyes darting all over me looking for injuries.

'I was just in the wrong place at the wrong time, don't worry this is just a precaution.' I pointed at Amadeus.

She looked at him, 'thank you so much for looking after her,' she said before surprising him with a hug.

'I'm going to get checked over just now, but hopefully I'll get the all clear to come home soon.'

I saw Sonya move up behind Alana, 'Good to see you,' she said before turning to Alana. 'How about we let your mum get looked over by the doctor and we go home and get her some things just in case she needs to stay in.'

'That would be great,' I said. There was no way I was going to spend a night in hospital, but I recognised that Sonya was trying to keep Alana occupied and for that I was incredibly grateful.

Alana agreed reluctantly after making Amadeus promise not to leave my side until she returned.

Stephen had had his hands around my throat long enough to make me start to pass out but not so long that he'd done any real damage, just some bruising that I was reliably informed would be gone in a couple of weeks and a sore throat. A diet of soup and smoothies was the doctor's best suggestion, whilst avoiding anything too hot or too cold. I sat with my feet in a Dettol bath to clean out the various cuts and grazes I'd inflicted on them while making my escape.

I stood patiently and let the police photographer detail my injuries while one of the forensic team collected DNA evidence from under my fingernails and after what seemed like hours I was allowed to shower. I would've rather been at home standing in the shower in my en-suite but right now I was glad to be able to wash off the last forty-eight hours.

Alana and Sonya were waiting with fresh clothes and shoes and finally I felt like my old self again. Alana sat on the edge of the bed. 'You look like crap,' she said.

I smiled, 'thanks.'

'We were really worried about you.'

'I know and I am so, so sorry.'

'If this had been next year and I was away at uni then no-one would have known you were missing.' I could see that she was fighting back the tears.

'You think that you're getting to move away from home and not have me call you every single day to check on you.'

She gave me a half smile, 'I'm not the one who needs checking on.'

The doctor came back into the room and told me that he would prefer if I stayed overnight for observation, but after much resistance from me and many promises from everyone else that I would be looked after, and that I definitely was going home to rest, he could see that he was outnumbered and let me leave.

Arriving home, I was surprised to find my house filled with the smell of lentil soup, for a split second that is before Maureen came rushing out of the kitchen to greet us.

'Oh my goodness, what have you managed to get yourself involved in now. Look at you,' she said, barely drawing breath. She continued, 'when Alana phoned and said the doctor was putting you on a liquid diet, well I said to Eddie I need to get over there and get cooking because she'll not have the energy and Alana has her studies and school.'

'Thank you.'

'Right let's get you into the living room and I'll put the soup in a mug to make it easier to eat.'

I allowed myself to be steered onto the sofa and fussed over for far longer than I would normally have tolerated.

'I'd better be going; I'll pop by and check on you later.' Amadeus said.

Eventually everyone left, as grateful as I was for all the support and particularly Maureen's cooking I was equally grateful to have the peace and stillness of my own home. Alana sat snuggled into me on one side and I found myself almost dosing off.

'I thought you were dead.' Alana said quietly.

'I know. I'm sorry.' Sorry wasn't good enough, I knew that. It didn't convey how deeply guilty I felt and how much I'd let her down.

'Sometimes your job is scary,' she said.

'Yes, it is.'

'I'm glad you're home safe.'

'Me too.'

At some point over the next week we would have the conversation about me changing job and maybe this time Alana would say that was what she wanted, and I would agree to do it, but I would cross that bridge when I came to it.

Chapter Forty-Three

It was late when Alana finally went up to bed, she could hardly even hold her head up fully she was so tired. I should've been equally exhausted but for some reason my mind was too active to want to rest.

A text pinged through on my phone from Amadeus asking me if I was still awake. I replied that I was. A few minutes later there was a gentle knock at the door. I took him through to the living room hoping that the sound of our voices wouldn't disturb Alana.

'Thank you for everything,' I said kissing him on the cheek, then in a moment of confidence I moved my head round slightly and gently kissed him on the lips. For a brief moment it felt like we were both holding our breath before we kissed each other passionately. I straddled over him pulling my top off, desire blocking out the physical pain of the last couple of weeks.

Afterwards we sat next to each other naked on the sofa and I felt like a teenager again. He pulled me into a cuddle. 'I wasn't, I mean I didn't come here expecting this,' he said quietly kissing me on the top of the head.

'I know, but I'm glad.' I replied.

If I had imagined this moment, I'm sure I would have thought it would have been more awkward, instead I had my head resting against his chest, calmed by the rhythmic sound of his breathing. The clock bonged telling us that it was 2am.

'I'd better be going,' he said.

It would have been nice to have taken him to bed, and woken up beside him in the morning, but that was not something I wanted Alana to wake up to.

I walked him to the door, 'I'll see you tomorrow,' he said before bending forward and kissing me goodbye.

When my alarm clock sounded at 7am I could have gladly thrown it across the room for interrupting my happy blissful sleep. There was a moment before I opened my eyes where I wasn't sure if the events of the previous evening had merely been the product of an erotic dream.

Downstairs Alana was already making porridge for breakfast. 'Did you sleep okay?' She asked.

'Not bad, you.'

'Do you want me to stay home from school today to be with you?'

'No, I'm okay honestly and besides I still need to work, there are some questions I need to ask George.'

'Are you sure you're up to that?'

'Yes, I'll be fine.'

George appeared as if magically summoned when Alana opened the door to go to school.

I poured him a coffee. 'How's Harmony this morning?'

'I haven't checked in with her yet, I wanted to come here first.'

'Thanks for getting to us so quickly.'

'Thanks for going to the hospital, even if you didn't stay the night.'

'You want to tell me what happened your end in the last 48 hours so I can fill in all the gaps.'

'Sonya phoned me to say that she'd got a call from you, and she could hear raised voices, she was worried about you, so I got a trace put on your phone, then I came round to see Alana

'I'm so grateful to everyone for taking care of her.'

'It's okay, she'd very bossy though, demanded to know what we were doing to get you back. Martin turned off your phone but it was already on the A92 past Glenrothes by then and we had units out searching for you.'

The image of Martin Clarke lying on the barn floor, blood trickling down the side of his face came into my mind. 'How is Martin, did I…'

'In hospital, concussion and he had to have a couple of stitches where he fell and hit his head.'

'Did they keep Harmony in overnight?'

'Yes, because she was less stubborn than you and in a bit of a worse way too. Malnourished and dehydrated they'll be keeping her in for a few days, I think. Your mate Nate was with her last night.'

At the mention of last night Amadeus crossed my mind and I blushed.

'You a bit soft on this bloke?' George asked in a way I'm sure he thought didn't convey his disapproval.

'Not anymore.'

'Good, not sure you were compatible. Alistair Lockland is going home tomorrow, I know he would still like to talk to you.

I had forgotten all about him, the events of the last couple of days made me think that there was very little he could tell me that would be of interest. Martin and Stephen were in custody and Harmony was safe and finally free to live her life however she wanted. I had been wrong, her mother's death had nothing to do with why she had been taken, instead that had been a cruel red herring most likely at the hands of Simon, wanting to make her suffer for not agreeing to let him unburden his conscience to her.

'Sure, I'll head over this afternoon.'

'You want me to send someone over to take you, if you're not up to driving.'

'I'm good thanks, by the way did anyone let Ellie know about Harmony?'

'Yes, I thought you'd string me up if I didn't call her myself,' he laughed.

After George left I text Ellie to ask her if she wanted to meet for a catch up and de-brief this morning at the Sunshine Café. One hour later I was sitting at my usual table waiting to see her bright yellow coat come striding through the door. In between times Star and Billy had both come over to fuss over me and make sure that my cup of camomile tea was never empty. At this rate I would miss Ellie's arrival because I would be in the loo.

'Sorry I'm late,' she said as she sat opposite me. 'I was at the florist trying to arrange flowers to be sent to Harmony at the hospital, honestly you'd have thought a bunch of wildflowers was the most complicated request they'd ever had, anyway I'm here now. How are you?'

'I'm alright.'

'When DCI Johnston phoned and said you'd found Harmony and you were both at the hospital I couldn't believe it, he wouldn't give me any details at all though. I went straight over but I wasn't allowed to see either of you and I hope you don't mind but when I was finally allowed, I went to see Harmony first and then by the time I'd finished chatting to her and went to find you they said you'd left already. I thought for sure they would have kept you in overnight.'

'They wanted to, but I wanted to go home and be with Alana.'

'Oh of course, poor Alana, she must've been out of her mind with worry.'

'She was.'

'I can't believe it was Martin. I mean we knew he wasn't a very nice man, but even I didn't think he was capable of kidnapping and with Stephen helping him,' she shook her head in disgust.

'How is Harmony?' I asked. I intended to pop in and see her this afternoon after I'd spoken to her dad.

'She's okay, she's genuinely one of the strongest people I've ever known.'

'That's good, she's lucky to have a friend like you.'

Ellie shrugged, 'friends are important.'

I looked across to where Star and Billy were deep in conversation at the counter and took a deep breath in. If the last couple of years had taught me anything it was that friends were essential. 'Indeed they are.'

'So, what happens now, with our case I mean.'

'I have a few things to tidy up and I'll pass anything important over to the police and they'll take it from there. I'll write up a full report for you and send it across with the final bill.'

Ellie looked disappointed. 'Of course, I'm so glad that Harmony is home safe, but I will miss our meetings and helping you out with the occasional thing.'

'Maybe you should retrain as a private detective.' I smiled.

'Think I might stick to acting, but if you ever need a spare pair of hands for anything, or even someone to help you sort out your paperwork, you know how to find me.'

Chapter Forty-Four

I'd let Ellie embrace me in a hug when she left and felt a pang of sadness as I'd watched her brightly coloured self walk out the door and down the street. I text Amadeus, telling him that I was on the way to the hospital to see Alistair and then Harmony. I deleted and re-wrote it half a dozen times and then hummed and hawed about adding the single 'x' but in the end I'd pressed send.

George had said there was no way of knowing how the poison had got into Alistair's system, but they were sure it had been done deliberately, although they had drawn a complete blank on who or why. Alistair had been as George had put it 'a bloody pain in the arse'. He had been reluctant to speak to the police at all and when I went missing, he clammed up completely.

I was thankful that he was alone in the room when I arrived. I pushed open the door and he flinched, relaxing when he realised it was me. He was much thinner than the last time I saw him, his skin was a yellowy grey with an almost waxy look.

I pulled the plastic chair from the side of the room and put it down next to the bed. He shuffled himself into a more upright position. 'Thank you for coming, Rowan.'

'You're welcome, I'm still a little bit baffled as to why you wanted to see me.'

'You know Nell Mitchell, I think.'

I frowned. Nell was Sally's mum but nothing in any of my notes would have given me a clue that the two families were in anyway linked. 'yes,' I replied.

'I went to school with Nell Mitchell, we kept in touch over the years, on Facebook and the like, when Sally went missing I offered to put up reward money. Anyway, I know how much you helped her last year and if Nell had put her faith in you then I knew you could be trusted.'

'Small world I guess.'

He nodded, 'I'd like you to record our conversation please.'

I took out my Dictaphone and hit record, announcing the date, time and participants of the conversation, the way I'd always done. The way Jack had done before me.

'I know you asked to speak to me, do you know who tried to kill you?'

'I do, only they weren't trying to kill me, the intention was to make me very sick, it's a warning you see. If they find out I've had this conversation, then the likelihood is they'll finish the job.' He paused. 'Or worse still they'll go after Harmony.'

'Why don't you start at the beginning,' I said.

'Okay,' he took a sip of water from the plastic cup at his bedside, the sides bent inwards with the gentle pressure of his fingertips. 'When I met Tabitha, it was love at first sight, I know it's wrong to compare a woman, a person to an animal but she was untamed, wild and full of life and it was exciting for me. I thought I would never tire of her impulsive ways, she made me believe I could live my life going in any which way the wind blew us as long as we were together. She was a talented artist as well; I mean you've seen her work so you know what I mean.'

He looked at me pensively for confirmation. I nodded, almost afraid to interrupt his flow with words. Talking about his late wife had lit his face up and he'd become animated in a way I didn't think was in him.

'She was phenomenal. I think I was her safe place, her protective port in the storm. We got married and then we had Harmony and things were going well, our house was full of light and laughter.' He looked down at his hands now and I could see the joy fading out of his face.

'What went wrong?' I asked.

'I was a fool. I took her to a function at the business and she was her usual self, talking to everyone, laughing. People seemed to like her, everyone except my father that it is. He hadn't been keen on our short courtship and wedding, he thought I was rushing into things, that Tabitha wasn't suited to being the wife of a corporate businessman. He didn't like the way she dressed, the way she talked, the way other people looked at her and he told me that if I ever wanted to take over the company, I would have to reign her in, get her to conform. That night we had a huge argument, the only one we'd ever had, she cried, she didn't understand what she had done wrong, and I knew I was being a bastard to her, but all I could think of was my career disappearing in front of me and all because she wanted to be different.'

'Did she comply with your request?' The question nearly stuck in my throat as I thought of Harmony telling me all the times where she didn't fight, instead choosing to give up and conform. I wondered if Tabitha had gone down without challenge.

'Yes and no, she toned it down for functions, choosing to hardly talk at all for fear of embarrassing me and then she stopped coming altogether, told me I would be better going with

Karen, that she fitted in more. But at the same time, she was still going to her artist gatherings and showing her paintings, I was relieved that she did all that under her maiden name. Oh God I can't bear to admit it, but I was embarrassed by her career. She was getting reviewed in national papers and I was embarrassed of her.'

He looked at me, I tried to decide whether he deserved my pity or not, the longer he continued talking the more my gut churned at the expectation that he had been involved in his wife's death.

'Effectively we began living separate lives, we had our own bedrooms and Tabitha spent most of her time in the studio. I tried to encourage Harmony into sensible hobbies, things that would stand her in good stead if she were to take over the company one day. French, Japanese that kind of thing, but Tabitha was fierce, and she encouraged Harmony to draw and paint and my worst fears were being realised that my daughter was also a talented artist. I tried to keep this fact from my parents, and I knew they wouldn't see that as something to be proud of, they might even go as far as to cut her out of their will.' He sighed.

'When did you start having the affair with Karen?'

'She'd been my assistant for about three years, and I knew she was attracted to me, she couldn't have made it more obvious. I tried to let her down gently, getting assigned to someone else or offering her a promotion but she was so resistant. Then I had a conference to go to in Aberdeen and Karen came with me, I had a little bit too much to drink and one thing led to another. I know you'll think this sounds like madness as I've been with her so long, but I don't love her, I never did. I didn't even fancy her. How awful is that.'

He took another sip of water then rested his head back on his pillow and closed his eyes.

'Why marry her then?'

When he opened his eyes there were tears heavy in the corners. 'I'll get to that bit. I was pathetically weak. I enjoyed the unwavering adoration Karen had for me, the lengths she was prepared to go to in order to make me happy. I would sit in the evenings sometimes when I came home late and instead of sitting with me while I ate my dinner, I would find a note on the fridge door telling me the plate was inside and to microwave it, that Tabitha was in the studio, not to be disturbed. I resented her, I resented her art. Even though I knew that I had no right, I was the one having the affair and I was pretty sure she knew. I wasn't exactly discrete, I would put a box of condoms in my suitcase and leave it open somewhere knowing that Tabitha would see it, but there was never any response.'

'What did you expect her to do?' I asked trying and failing to keep my tone neutral.

'I wanted her to beg me to stop, to throw herself at me, kiss me and try to remind me of everything that we used to have. I know why she didn't, she had too much dignity for that and I'd already extinguished a little bit of her fire. She told me once that she wanted a divorce, and I threw a vase across the room and told her if she tried to leave me I would make sure that she would be lucky to see Harmony once a month for a couple of hours. It was unbelievably cruel and unkind; in truth I wouldn't have dreamed of doing it. The way she looked at me after that almost crushed me, every time I caught her eye there was so much hatred and disdain and yet never once did she let Harmony know how she felt. She was a hundred times, if not more, the person I was.'

'How long before she was killed was this?'

'Six months tops.'

'Why didn't you just let her divorce you then you both could have moved on with your lives, you with Karen and her however she wanted.'

'Because I didn't want to marry bloody Karen. I wanted Tabitha, not the bitter, sad women I'd created but the vibrant ball of energy that I fell in love with. I was full of self-loathing and pity. It was all of my own doing, but it wasn't till after she was murdered that I realised that.'

'What made you see what you had done?'

'Karen told me she wanted me to divorce Tabitha, she even suggested that we let her take Harmony, that we could start our own family. Like I say I didn't want to marry her so I told her I couldn't divorce Tabitha, that my father looked at divorce as a personal failure. In short, I told her that divorcing Tabitha would ruin my career. I thought that it would make her back off and stop harassing me. It was the worst mistake I ever made. When I got the call to say Tabitha was dead my whole body went cold with dread, at first I tried to settle my mind that Karen couldn't have anything to do with it, she had been with me all night. But the more I thought about it the more I realised that wasn't true, I had been so preoccupied networking that I couldn't account for her whereabouts for the majority of the evening.'

'Did you ask her about it?'

'Not at first, a couple of days later.'

'What did she say?'

'She said she was only doing what I had asked her to do. She said that I had told her that divorce wasn't an option so the only way we could be together would be if Tabitha was dead. She implied I had asked her to kill my wife.'

'What did you do?'

'I told her she was out of her mind, that I would go to the police. She said that she would tell them that it was me, that I put out a hit on Tabitha. I thought there would be evidence, that the police would realise what she had done, but she'd been clever. She hadn't pulled the trigger herself, instead she'd paid her cousin Simon to do her dirty work for her. They set it up, she would go back to the house and walk down towards the studio, she'd fire the gun and then Simon would run towards it when he got there, he would kill Tabitha using a silencer so no one would ever know there had been two shots fired.'

'What would he have done if Patrick had gone with him?'

'That was a fly in the ointment, the plan had been that Simon would kill Tabitha and Patrick and then put them together making it look like it had been a lovers suicide pact. Obviously, it didn't pan out like that, I don't think Simon expected to end up in jail, but whatever Karen had over him must've been powerful enough to keep him from dropping her in it.'

'Did Karen kill Simon?' I asked.

'He'd been to the house, I heard them shouting. He wanted more money; I knew that she was paying for his lifestyle. I think he was threatening to go public unless she paid him off.'

'Where did that money come from?' I asked.

'Not me, Karen has a trust fund, she's actually extremely wealthy in her own right.'

'Did you know the apartment that Simon Cummings lived in was in your name?'

'No, Karen probably did that because she knew that if the police ever scraped beneath the surface, they would have a link between me and Simon and then it wouldn't be too hard to convince the world that I had wanted Tabby dead.'

'Simon must've had something over Karen that proved her hand in all of this otherwise why would she continue supporting him?'

'He did, that night he'd been smart, which by all accounts might have been the only time in his life. He'd taken a camera with him and taken photos of where the gun was hidden, of...' his voice caught as he tried to speak and instead of words a pained sound came out. He took a deep breath, 'of Tabby's body. But even then, she said that only proved that it was a hit on Tabitha and she could easily make out that it was me that was working with Simon. But you see he had recorded their telephone conversations and there was no getting away from that, no spin she could put on it to make out she was not involved.'

'She could've continued paying him I suppose,' I said.

'At that point I don't think it was about money for her anymore, I think she was afraid that her house of cards was about to come tumbling down, so she murdered him.'

'What about Mathew Radley, where does he fit in to all of this?' I asked.

'That man is a snake, he's Karen's brother-in-law and he handles her trust fund, the family's legal matters and is Karen's personal fixer. I'm guessing that she thought having a lawyer under her thumb might come in handy. On the evening of her sister's wedding Karen drugged her, and then proceeded to have sex with Matthew. She made sure she had plenty of evidence to keep him under control. This happened before I had my...before the affair between us started.'

I wondered how many other people Karen had manipulated and blackmailed, what sort of person would hurt their own sister for personal gain. It was hard to feel sorry for either man though, they'd had choices, perhaps Alistair had truly believed that it was the only way to protect his daughter or maybe he was just afraid of taking the risk.

'She is the most cold and callous woman I've ever known,' he continued. 'After Tabitha died she insisted that she move in, that we throw away everything. Harmony was broken hearted, I tried to reason with Karen, told her that a child needed to be able to grieve and have a connection with her mother. She told me that if she had known Harmony was there that night she would've been dead too, kept reminding me that if I didn't do exactly what she wanted that it wouldn't be hard to rectify that mistake. I know Harmony will never forgive me, but I hope one day she will understand that everything I did was to keep her safe.'

'You think Karen poisoned you?'

'I know she did, she told me the first time she came to visit me in hospital.'

'Why?'

'I lost Harmony a long time ago. When she and Martin separated, she made it clear that she wanted me out of her life. I realised that there wasn't much more Karen could do to me. I told her I wanted a divorce. She went ballistic, said she would find Harmony and make her pay. When you first came to see me to tell me that Harmony was missing, I tried to put on a brave face and make out like I didn't care but all I could think of was that Karen had got to her.'

'I thought you were acting very strangely that day.'

'I went home and told her to tell me where Harmony was, in the end I believed her when she said that she had nothing to do with her disappearance. I thought it might have had something to do with that Simon bloke, I went looking for him, but he swore he had no idea what I was talking about. The longer Harmony was gone the more I believed that she was dead. I didn't care anymore, there was nothing Karen had to control me. She told me she would kill me. Then the day she poisoned me she came to the hospital acting the concerned wife, then when we were by ourselves, she said that she had poisoned my lunch, to remind me that she was in charge. She said she knew where Harmony was and whether I ever saw her alive again was down to what I chose to do next.'

'And you asked Fiona to call me if something happened to you?'

'I understand that must've been quite confusing, it might surprise you to know that it's in my Will. If I were to die of anything other than natural causes my estate is to employ you to find what happened.'

It was strange to think that I was in someone's Will under those terms, but I would've been lying if I had said I hadn't felt incredibly flattered as well.

'Why tell me all this now?'

'I can't go on like this, I can't see that woman's face and not think about all the hurt my years of silence have caused. I don't expect Harmony to be in a forgiving mood, but I would rather die knowing that I had told the truth.'

'Thank you for trusting me with this.'

He nodded, 'would you mind turning it off now,' he said pointing at the Dictaphone. I complied with the request. 'In my jacket pocket you'll find a key, it unlocks a storage container. I didn't throw all of Tabitha's things away, I told Karen I had, but instead I put them all into storage. I wanted to give the key to Harmony myself one day but now I think it would be better if you did it.'

Chapter Forty-Five

I decided to phone George as soon as I walked out of Alister Lockland's hospital room. He blustered about the nerve of the man knowing all this time what had truly happened to his wife and not having the courage to come forward. In part I think he was genuinely horrified at someone keeping a secret like that for so long, but he was also pissed off that Alistair had chosen to confess to me and that once again he was beholden to me for a vital piece of evidence.

I went to visit Harmony later that day when I knew Karen had been arrested. Nate was sat at her bedside and they looked like they were deep in conversation as I pushed open the door. Nate blushed when he saw me.

'You look a lot better than I expected from everything Harmony has told me happened.'

I shrugged, 'just lucky I guess.' I asked him if he would give me a moment alone with Harmony. I wanted her to be able hear her father's story without any input from anyone else.

Nate left, waving awkwardly at us as he closed the door.

'How's it going?' I asked pointing after him.

'Who knows, I think at the moment he doesn't think of me that way, maybe that will change. I'm not sure if I want it too though. Perhaps it would be good for me to spend some time figuring out what I want from my life first though.'

I agreed that after everything she'd been through it would be wise to spend some time deciding what she wanted from life before she involved anyone else in it. I told her everything Alistair had told me earlier. She was very quick to tell me that there was nothing he could do now that would make her feel forgiveness towards him, although I did think that her resolve softened when I gave her the storage unit key and told her that her father had kept everything of her mother's.

'Thank you for looking for me, I'm sorry you got caught up in all my drama.'

'All part of the service,' I smiled.

'Have the police told you what will happen to Martin and Stephen?'

'They've been arrested and charged with kidnapping, assault and attempted murder, hopefully they'll get decent sentences, either way Martin will be somewhere he can't get to you, and you can move on.'

'I don't really know what to do now,' she said.

'I think the point is you can do whatever it is you want. Go back to art school, travel, hell you could even go back to your old job. It's truly up to you now.'

'I've always fancied travelling, I know that was my mum's dream too. Maybe I could take a trip to all the places she wanted to go to, like a homage to her.'

'That sounds lovely.'

We said our goodbyes, I was glad to have found her and that now she knew the truth about her mother's death, I hoped it would help her to lay the past to rest and allow her to look towards the future.

Nate was waiting in the corridor when I left Harmony's room, one foot resting against the wall. 'You going back in?' I asked.

'In a bit, I was hoping to see you though.'

'Oh okay.' I was dreading this chat. I had left him with the impression that once Harmony was found and this case was done and dusted that I would be interesting in dating him. That ship had well and truly sailed for me, whether or not anything further happened with Amadeus it had made me realise what had stirred inside me when I first met Nate had been nothing more than a crush.

He rubbed the palm of his right hand around the back of his neck. 'this is a bit awkward,' he said. 'I know we talked about going out together…'

'Actually, about that,' I interrupted him.

'Before you say anything else, please let me finish. You're an amazing woman, intelligent and beautiful. I think under different circumstances we might have a really nice time together,' he paused.

I couldn't believe it, he was trying to let me down gently, tell me he wasn't interested. I wanted to shout over the top of him that I had changed my mind, but that was just my ego feeling a little bruised. Instead, I let him have his moment.

'It's just your job and I know you're going to be angry with me for saying this. I'm only trying to be truthful though, I couldn't handle it, not knowing if you were okay, if you were going to come home with a black eye or broken ribs, or even if you were going to come home at all,' he looked up making eye contact for the first time in his little speech.

'That's okay, it's better to be upfront with these things.'

'I'm glad you understand. I'm sure you can totally take care of yourself, but I'm looking for a much quieter life than the one you lead.'

'No problem, it was lovely to meet you and I hope you find the right person for you,' I said. I walked down the hospital corridor without looking back, I was sure Nate was a nice guy, but I needed more than nice.

With the wedding in just a couple of days, Star and Billy had decided to close the café to give them an opportunity to get ready, so this afternoon I was meeting Ellie for my final report in the library café. She'd arrived before me and I could see there were already two mugs on the table so I made my way straight to her.

'I hope it's okay that I ordered for both of us?'

I nodded, grateful for the hot chocolate finished off with cream and marshmallows. 'Thanks, this is nice.'

'I got chocolate cake and red velvet. I didn't know which you would prefer.'

'Let's do half of each,' I said taking a knife to them both and putting the two pieces on a plate in front of her. 'How are you doing?'

'Good I think, the last couple of weeks have been crazy and I keep going over it in my head. You both could have died and then I would never have forgiven myself.'

'We weren't going to die, Martin didn't want to kill Harmony, he wanted to control her.'

'He might've killed you though.'

'He could've tried, but I'm harder to kill than people tend to think. What's next for you?'

'I've decided I need a change of scenery, I've got a part in a film that's being shot in the Highlands,' she blushed. 'It's actually a lead part for a change, so I've put my flat on the market and for now I'm going to rent a little cottage near the set and then we'll see where that takes me.'

'Congratulations, that's amazing. Make sure you keep in touch and give me the details when it's coming out.'

'Do you mean that, about keeping in touch I mean?'

'Of course,' and it was true I had grown very fond of Ellie, and I was going to miss the flash of colour and energy she had brought into my life.

'Maybe you could come up for a visit when I'm settled?' She asked.

'I would love that, I must be due a break and a cottage in the highlands sounds perfect.'

Chapter Forty-Six

Thankfully the bruising round my neck and face had faded significantly by the time it came for me to stand next to Star as her maid of honour. Billy and Star had chosen a local village hall to get married in. It had been beautifully hand decorated in pretty bunting for the daytime and twinkly fairy lights for the evening.

Star looked stunning in an off-white dress that looked more like it had been designed as a fairy dress than a wedding dress and Billy had never looked so smart. Robbie has been taken aback when Billy had asked him to be best man, just a few years ago their families had been rivals and now they were friends. Not that the Billy that stood at the far end of the church hall bore any resemblance to the man I first met.

As they read out the vows that they had written I felt a swell of emotions, looking around the guests and thinking about how we'd all come to be in each other's lives reminding me just how much had changed in the last three years. I looked at Amadeus, we hadn't seen each other since that night and I was okay with that, it had been a single perfect moment that both of us had wanted and needed. Perhaps one day I would find someone I wanted more than that with but I wasn't ready.

Between them Maureen, Chantelle, Mohammed, and Star pulled off a reception with enough food to feed three times the amount of guests in attendance. Billy had even made homemade elderflower champagne.

In the previous weeks I'd asked Alana if she wanted me to look for another job. She had told me no, she just wanted me to be more careful. Preparations for her leaving to go to university were in full swing, whilst I was still fight off anxiety every time I thought about her not living at home, each time I glossed it over with a smile and a reminder of how proud of her I was.

George had moved in with Mel and Maureen was interrogating them to see if they were planning on tying the knot as the evening music started up at the reception. 'I want to take things slow, no need to rush anything.' Mel had said and George had told her he was happy to do whatever she wanted, and I was happy for them.

I sat in the corner of the room drinking a bottle of beer watching people dancing in the centre of the room and mingling along the edges and corners. Billy walked across the room towards me.

'What are you doing here, shouldn't you be with your beautiful bride?' I said.

'She's busy chatting to Chantelle, and besides I wanted to come and check on you, sitting all by yourself on the side lines.'

'I'm fine, just enjoying seeing everyone so happy.'

'This is possible because of you, you realise that don't you?'

'What do you mean,' I looked up at him.

'None of this would be possible if you hadn't gone up against Jimmy, we all owe something to your bravery. Now come and have a dance, get involved in the party, you should be at the centre of it all, because all this happiness,' he waved his hand, 'it exists because of you.' He took my hand and led me to dance floor.

Acknowledgements

I would like to thank my husband, Gavin, for his ongoing support, for listening to all my story ideas, for reading my first drafts and for always believing in me.

My daughter Molly who has endless enthusiasm for talking all things books.

Along the way there have been some incredibly important people and groups that have kept my spirits up. My Beta readers, Laura Shepherd my writing buddy and friend for all the chats about books and all your encouragement, Rachel Howells for all our writing sessions and support, Marion Todd for being an excellent sounding board.

Sonya Drysdale and Alana McGrath, I hope your namesakes continue to do you proud, thank you for your belief and support. The Best Seller Experiment, the two Marks and all the other writers so willing to help and uplift one another.

To F&J for being by my side throughout it all.

About The Author

Born in the Kingdom of Fife, Angela spent her teenage years in Penzance before returning to Scotland. She had a varied career from Nursery Nurse to Bank Manager before becoming a full-time writer. Her Rowan McFarlane Detective Mysteries are set in the fictional town of Cuddieford, which lies somewhere between Dunfermline & Kirkcaldy. Angela now lives with her husband in Fife looking out on the River Forth where she can easily see her favourite bridge, the Forth Rail Bridge. When she's not writing she can be found walking the coast or touring the countryside in her campervan.

For more information and to sign up to her newsletter you can visit Angela's website:

www.angelacnurse.com

Printed in Great Britain
by Amazon